Because of Katie

Patty Schramm

Yellow Rose Books
by Regal Crest

ISBN 978-1-61929-380-9

First Edition 2018

9 8 7 6 5 4 3 2 1

Cover design by AcornGraphics

Published by:

Regal Crest Enterprises

Find us on the World Wide Web at
http://www.regalcrest.biz

Published in the United States of America

Acknowledgments

Every book has a crowd of people behind it. Sort of like how it takes a village to raise a child. It takes a small town to put out a book. I want to thank everyone that has helped me out with this one, even in the most remote ways: Jeanine Hoffman, Mary Hettel, Reba Birmingham, Nat Burns, MB Panichi, and my editors Nann Dunne and Verda Foster. Special thanks to Cathy Bryerose for putting this out there for everyone to enjoy.

Dedication

To my mom, Mary Josephine Cecilia Schramm, nee Cronin. She asked me while on a trip to Ireland to write a book with a mean mom. So I did.

Chapter One

KATIE O'BRIAIN'S LEGS burned, and the ache in her muscles shot through her upper body. Pain as sharp as a knife penetrated her temple and beat a rhythm to match her strides. She would do this. She would finish. To hell with the pain.

She focused on the end and shut out the people that lined the streets. The people that ran ahead, behind, and beside her faded away.

She stumbled at the 300-meter mark. Nearly colliding with someone, she righted herself and pushed on.

Her vision blurred.

This isn't going to happen, she thought. Not this time. I will finish. I will finish.

It became her mantra, even as her stride slowed. She rounded a corner and could finally see the orange stripe across the bright-blue mat that covered the street.

One last burst of energy would get her there. Even though energy seemed to have left her a long time ago.

Her legs were numb now, the pain in her temples so intense she wondered if anyone else could hear the drumming in her brain.

She stumbled again and barely managed to straighten in time to cross that blessed line.

Her da was right there, smiling and talking, but she couldn't hear him. She sank into his arms and let him guide her to her chair. He gave her a towel that smelled of rubbing alcohol, which she used to cool herself down.

Slowed breaths, eyes closed, the pain began to subside.

His voice was close to her ear. "Katie, love, I'm so proud of you." He kissed the temple that still throbbed, but Katie only felt relief.

She looked into his pale-green eyes, the same color as hers, and did her best to smile. "I did it. I finished the marathon."

"Ya did, love. We can now put the Dublin City Marathon on your list. Eight hours, fifteen minutes, twenty seconds."

She wanted to roll her eyes, but that would just make the migraine worse. "My last full marathon was five hours faster."

"Your last race doesn't matter." Jamie O'Briain knelt beside her and detached the prosthetic from her left leg. "The only thing that matters is you finished. You did it. And I'm damn proud of ya. *Dadaí* will be just as proud when he finds out." He removed the right prosthetic and sighed. "Katie, love, you didn't use the Vaseline like the physio told you."

"I forgot," she said. Though that wasn't completely true. If she'd stopped to put Vaseline on her stump, her time would have been worse. The red marks might become blisters, but they'd go away. She could use her chair. It didn't matter.

Katie faced Jamie and realized he knew the truth.

"Love, if you don't take care, you won't be runnin' as much as you want to. You know that." He cupped her chin so they were eye to eye. "Tell me what you're thinkin'."

"When I stop, I lose time. It takes too long to adjust the damn things. I'd rather keep running and improve my time."

"You are stubborn. You know that?"

She squinted up at him. His smirk made her smile. "And whose fault is that? Maybe the man who raised me to be like him, hmm?"

Jamie squinted back. "Maybe. How 'bout that man take you home and get you fed? We can talk about the stubborn stuff later."

"You're going to tell Dadaí aren't you?"

Jamie packed her blades away, swung the bag over his shoulder, and rolled her toward the area where Katie would get her completion medal. He sighed. "I should, but I'll let you do the talking. He's your father and he's going to be all fussy over those sores."

"You're my father, too. Why aren't you being fussy?"

Jamie belted a laugh. "Because I'm smart enough to know it won't do any good. You'll just go right back out there and do it again. You stubborn git."

"I'll show him the medal first. Besides, how long can he stay fussed at me? I'm his favorite."

"You're his favorite as long as the other five darlin's aren't in earshot. You know he says that to all you kids."

Katie's smile widened. Her dadaí, Colm, was the kindest man anyone had ever met. And a perfect match for Jamie. She was seven when they met, and Katie remembered every moment of it. The way they gazed at each other, spoke to each other.

Katie had never known her mother, but the moment she met Colm he filled that hole in her life and then some. She couldn't wait to tell him she'd finished the marathon. A full marathon. Forty-two plus kilometers around Dublin.

It was all worth it.

SIOBHAN LANDRY TOOK a sip of her Diet Coke and examined her work so far. The sketch of the man working the bar was rudimentary. She'd tried to capture the classical lines of his square jaw, his ready smile, and the always present twinkle in his sparkling blue eyes. She wasn't so sure she'd been successful, but it was good practice. And the man was so easy to watch. He had a way with people, and that was partly what drew her to this out-of-the-way pub.

Nestled on the edge of the village of Cúnant, Pub O'Briain was part of a 15th-century castle that was still undergoing renovations. According to the information on the paper placemat, the separate building that housed the pub was previously used for various purposes: to house soldiers, as a guest house, as a private home, and now as a pub. It stood at the end of a long, steep driveway that led to the castle.

Not one of the largest castles she'd seen in her short time in Ireland, but it was big enough. At four stories high, settled on a hill, it was imposing from the village; though she'd not been able to get a very good look at it in her first three weeks in Cúnant. Buckets of rain fell from the skies, interspersed with minutes of sunshine, followed by wind and more rain. She'd read that in October, well, most of the year, Ireland was wet. Especially along the coast. But this was crazy.

The rain, along with a strong wind, likely explained the pub's emptiness. Though during the last twenty minutes, people started to trickle in.

Siobhan preferred the busier times, so she could observe and sketch the people that came and went. In slow times, such as now, she worked her way through the menu. She'd pretty much tried everything and made mental notes of what not to try again. She'd even done the touristy thing by ordering a pint of Guinness. The taste was so much better here than in Indiana.

Just the thought of her former home made Siobhan wince. It hadn't been easy to leave her mother, yet at the same time, it was the easiest thing she'd ever done. Weird. She felt guilty that her mother was on her own now, but she was surrounded by her church pals so she shouldn't be too lonely. The guilt was heavy, but the moment Siobhan realized her mother was still friends with her ex-girlfriend... That's when the move got easier. Six weeks later she was beginning to feel at home in Ireland.

Though she regretted giving her mother her new cell phone number. Apparently, Mary Landry had trouble understanding the five-hour time difference. So Siobhan took to turning the damn thing off. She'd rather listen to voice mail she could delete than talk to her mother every day.

"Nothin' comin' to mind?"

Siobhan's attention was drawn to the young waitress who had materialized at her side. She gave her a small smile. "Sadly, no. Just touchups on a previous sketch."

Siobhan considered sketching Tabby next. She was an adorable brunette with a round face and big eyes that shouted innocent and naïve.

Tabby had a grin that covered her entire face, her eyes twinkling. "Well, it's early days. Rain's lettin' up. Could be the perfect man will come through the door, and you'll be wanting to do more than draw him." She winked and moved to another table.

"Only if he's a she," Siobhan muttered. Nonetheless, her gaze fell on the front door just as it opened.

The person entering caught her attention instantly. Not because of the well-worn, heavy raincoat or the orange-and-green shoes.

Beneath the raincoat, soon slung onto a hook near the door, was an athletically built woman with bright-red hair, longish on the right side and shaved nearly bald on the left.

No. That wasn't what caught Siobhan's attention.

She was drawn in by the friendly smile and the mischievous glint in her amazingly green eyes. Siobhan wasn't far from the woman, and those eyes practically glowed as she entered the pub.

Within moments, the old man who was at the pub every day and whom Siobhan had nicknamed "Norm," slid off his stool at the bar and enveloped the woman in his big arms. She laughed at something he said, and the sound gave Siobhan goose bumps. He released her and handed her over to the man behind the bar.

The man's handsome face alight with joy, he also clasped her to him, his hug more intimate and loving than Norm's. As soon as he released her, he met the man behind her, whom Siobhan hadn't noticed, and embraced him as well. Their kiss was passionate and welcoming, and it brought sudden tears to Siobhan's eyes. They were so obviously in love.

The other man cupped the bartender's—she remembered then his name was Colm—face in his hands and kissed him once more before shedding his raincoat and following the woman farther into the pub.

It wasn't a very big place, but it felt crowded as more people poured in, all of them intent on greeting this woman, shaking her hand, and patting her on the back. Colm kept his arm around the man she assumed was his partner as they proudly watched over the crowd and the woman in the middle of it. Siobhan wondered if one or both men were her parents.

A pang of envy hit her; she wished her parents had been so loving toward each other.

Siobhan's attention went back to the woman who gracefully worked her way through the people that surrounded her. Several wore raincoats and must have just arrived, but Siobhan wasn't interested in them. She kept her eyes on the woman as she disappeared through the door to the kitchen.

Siobhan closed her eyes and memorized the woman's features; then she opened her eyes, took out a pencil, and began to sketch.

KATIE MADE IT to the office, closed the door, and collapsed on the settee. It was old and lumpy, but at that moment she simply didn't give a toss. She'd not expected such a crowd when coming to the pub.

Jamie texted Colm they were on the way home, and he must have started up the gay phone tree to get all their friends to welcome her back. They'd only been gone a couple of days, but she should have known he'd do this. It was a bit overwhelming. They were all so proud of her for finishing her first full marathon in five years. She fingered the medal that hung from the ribbon around her neck. It was worth it. Even if the migraine was now full-on.

She closed her eyes as the pain started along the sides of her face, gradually making it behind her eyes and taking over her head. Her stomach was in need of purging, and she fought the urge to vomit.

These fecking migraines pissed her off.

She wanted to run and run every day. It was part of who she was. Jamie insisted on more rest, but if she rested too often she'd never keep herself fit enough to run hours on end.

She didn't hear anyone come in but felt the gentle touch of her da as he took her hand. "How bad is it, love?"

"Bad." Any sound or movement would be disastrous at this point, and they both knew it.

A cool rag was placed on her forehead. "Time to get ya home."

"Can't I sleep here?"

"No, love. Especially not on this tatty old settee. It's dark out now, and the rain stopped. Best we get you home."

"Dark? Did I fall asleep?"

"For a couple of hours. Up with ya now." Jamie slid his arms under her and cuddled Katie close to him as he lifted her from the settee.

Katie had flashbacks to being a little girl and getting carried around as they played together. "Da..."

"Hush. Keep yer eyes closed. Won't be long."

Katie did and leaned her head against his shoulder. The movement was torturous, especially on her stomach, but it didn't last long. Jamie's long strides took them to the castle and into her room quickly and quietly. Her siblings weren't around, so they must have gotten the message to let her rest. She dearly wanted to see them and hoped she'd be able to in the morning.

"This sucks," she muttered.

"It does, indeed." Jamie carefully set her on the bed and helped her undress. He doffed her prosthetics, and she placed her head on the pillow as he covered her with the duvet.

Another cool cloth against her forehead lessened the pain a bit. She heard Jamie settle on the floor beside her bed — as he'd done a dozen times before.

"Let me know when you want your meds," he said.

"Okay." Her stomach didn't feel stable enough for a sip of water, much less the pill that would ease the pain.

She felt his big hand close around hers as she tried to relax and let sleep take her again.

Chapter Two

THREE DAYS LATER, Katie felt like herself again. She let her siblings ooh and ahh over her medal and regaled them with the adventure of running the marathon. But this morning Katie relished being alone. She was a morning person, so six a.m. — when she could run and not see a single soul — wasn't a difficult time to rise.

The cool sea spray felt heavenly as it drifted across her overheated skin. Sweat ran down her face, and her shirt was glued to her body. The temperature wasn't even eight degrees Celsius, yet she felt as though she'd been running in the hot summer sun. Instead she'd been running in the frosty October morning, wearing purple Lycra shorts and shirt, sweating like a stuck pig.

It had to be because she was going farther and faster today. She'd spent too much time lying in bed. She had to work up her strength and endurance if she were to run the London Marathon at the end of April.

Five years ago, she'd completed it in three hours and forty-five minutes. This year she didn't hope for a time that good, only to finish the race. And she couldn't do that if she didn't push herself.

Her thighs screamed at her as she hit the steep incline to the cliff's edge. They burned when she reached the last few meters to the top, where she paused and gazed out at the Celtic Sea.

Dark rain clouds blotted the horizon, but closer to shore the morning sun shone brightly on the water and caused little sparkles along the cresting waves.

Katie stretched her legs to keep them from cramping up, and her gaze wandered. This had always been her favorite spot. She could sit and listen to the sea for hours, lost in thought — or no thought at all. She came here when she needed time to herself. In a family of six kids, that happened a fair few times.

She caught sight of someone sitting on one of the flat rocks she normally perched on when coming to the cliff. She jogged in place and viewed the interloper. Not that she owned the cliffs, but she felt like she did. It was her place, after all.

The woman had long blonde hair, tied in a ponytail that settled in the center of her back. Katie could just see her profile, and that alone made her want to see more. The woman had her face turned toward the sun as if soaking up the warmth. Her pale-blue jumper was too big and hid what Katie imagined was a lovely figure. She sat cross-legged on the rock with something lying in her lap. Katie was tempted to approach her but had to get back home before her dadaí got all fussed about where she was.

As if the man had ESP, her mobile rang. She didn't bother to glance at the phone, just tapped her Bluetooth and said, "I'm on my way home." She started down the hillside slowly, careful to avoid the more slippery spots left from yesterday's rain.

"Katie, love, ya been gone going on an hour. Where on earth have you gotten to?"

She bit her bottom lip. If she told him she'd gone to the cliff, he'd be spitting mad. But it was useless to try to hide things from him. "To the cliff, but I'm almost down the hill and to the path back to the village."

"I should be giving you a good tongue lashing, but I'll wait 'til you get home."

"Dadaí, if I don't get fit I won't finish the London marathon."

She heard his heavy sigh and stifled one of her own. "We'll be talking about that later. Soon as you get to the pub, have a talk with Rory, will ya?"

"What's he gone and done now?"

"Tabby."

"What?"

"He's taken a shine to Tabby, as you know. But now she's crying in between the tables she waiting on. She's had ta take four breaks, and if he don't fix it, I'm gonna fix him."

Colm was rarely angry, but this time he sounded like he meant every word he said.

"I'll attend to it after I take the stew to Mrs. Kerry."

"Thanks, love. Be careful."

"I will." Katie disconnected the call and ran harder and faster than before, hoping to wear out some of her own anger at her git of a brother before she got to the pub and whacked him a good one.

THE RAIN STARTED just as Katie left home. By the time she'd gotten to the pub, after seeing to Mrs. Kerry, she was soaked. She shook off as much water as possible the moment she stepped in.

The place was unusually empty for early afternoon. Katie hung her rain slicker on the coatrack and ran a hand through her short red hair. Currently Jamie was tending bar, which meant Colm was running the kitchen and hopefully had not yet killed her little brother.

She settled onto a stool in the corner of the bar and waited for Jamie to finish his chat with Buster Galway. Buster was older than dirt. His once ginger hair was now completely white, and only a hint of the coloring remained in his scraggy beard. Katie smiled when he waved at her and remembered how she loved to play with his beard as a child. Buster was the closest she'd ever had to a granddad. The sweetheart dug into his pie as Jamie approached.

"'Lo there, love." He leaned across the bar to kiss Katie's cheek. "How's Mrs. Kerry?"

"She's grand. Said to thank you for the stew, but if you could see to sending a pint of ale next time she'd be much obliged."

He threw his head back and let loose a big belly laugh. "Did she now? Well, sure and certain I'll get her one for dinner. But your dadaí isn't gonna — "

"Jamie O'Briain, you will not be sending ale to Mrs. Kerry. Are ya daft?" Colm came out of the kitchen and hit his husband with a dishtowel. "Her liver is shite. You'd be killin' her."

"I'm mad?" Jamie now turned to him. "Colm, love, Mrs. Kerry is a grown woman of ninety years. If she wants ale she should get ale. I don't think the good Lord is gonna take her after just one pint."

Colm crossed himself. "Heh. Fat lot you know." As if just noticing her, Colm turned his attention to Katie. "Don't be letting the mad one here get away with this. Okay?"

Katie put her hands up, palms forward. "Oh no. I'm not gettin' involved here, Dadaí. I love you both."

Colm narrowed his crystal blue eyes at her in a mock glare. "Always takin' his side. Nothing ever changes."

Katie laughed and dodged the tea towel that swung her way. "I think I'll get me jacket and help out for a bit, after I talk to Rory. Safer than gettin' between you two."

Colm swung again, just catching her shoulder as she hopped off the stool and headed for the back room.

She still heard their good-natured sparring as she went through the wooden, double doors and nearly ran over Tabby, their only employee that wasn't part of the O'Briain clan. Katie helped her steady her tray of food just in time to prevent a huge mess.

"Sorry, Tabby. I was in a hurry to get away from me dads."

"No worries." Tabby flashed her a grin that didn't quite reach her eyes. She appeared flustered, and her usually bright-blue eyes were cloudy and grey. She glanced at the tray and quickly excused herself to get the food to her table.

Seems Colm was right. Poor Tabby was rattled.

Katie continued to the kitchen, where Rory was cooking. His back was to her, but his shoulders were slumped forward. No one else was there, so she went to him and nudged his arm, causing him to miss the burger he was about to flip.

"Hey!" He glared at her and grumbled, "Don't be doin' that. I'm working."

"I think you're pouting, but call it what you will."

"Not pouting," he said, though his bottom lip stuck out just a bit. It reminded her of when he was little and didn't get his way. Even at the age of twenty-one he had boyish features that attracted a lot of attention from the young ladies. He had long, beautiful lashes that complemented his soft, doe-brown eyes. She had to reach up to muss his short black hair. He was at least two heads taller than she was.

"What did you say to upset Tabby?"

At the mention of Tabby, Rory's face flushed, and Katie got all the information she needed. "Rory, you're a twat. Whatever you said to that girl, you go and take it back. She looked ready to cry when she went out to serve her table, and Dadaí said she's been crying most of the afternoon."

"I didn't say a thing."

He refused to meet her gaze, and Katie knew damn well he wasn't being truthful. "I'll take over while you go sort this out."

"I'm not—"

"Oh, but you are. I know you better than you think. You fix this and you fix it now." Katie put on a white chef's jacket with her name embroidered on it and grabbed the spatula from him just in time to save the burger. "I hope the customer wants well done."

"It's medium rare," Rory mumbled.

"Lovely." Katie tossed it into the trash and started a new one. "Talk to Tabby."

"You're not my ma, Katie."

"No, but I been acting like your ma for too long now. Time you grew up. Go. Now."

Rory muttered something at the same time Tabby came back. Before she could speak, Rory ushered her to the back door that led to the alleyway.

Katie grinned as she finished cooking up the burger. Colm wandered in then, and after updating him on the latest family drama, Katie fixed the rest of the customer's dish, checked the table number, and headed into the dining area.

SIOBHAN SAW TABBY come rushing out of the kitchen, her shaking hands trying hard not to spill the food she placed on the table not far from where Siobhan sat. The poor girl was clearly upset. At least the people she waited on were empathetic. The older woman gently touched the girl's arm in a calming gesture and spoke quietly to her before the waitress hugged the serving tray to her chest and returned to the kitchen. But not before a pause at the door that had Siobhan wondering if she was going to change her mind and not go in. Tabby took a long, deep breath and pushed through.

A few moments later, Siobhan turned to a fresh page in her sketchbook to work on the drawing from a few days ago. A waitress entered from the kitchen. The woman's gaze locked with hers, and for a moment, Siobhan couldn't speak. It was the woman whose sketch she was working on.

Then the woman blinked, and their contact was lost as she looked down at the tray of food in her hands.

"Uh, hello. Here's your order. Stew and white bread, with a hamburger, yeah?"

"Yes." Siobhan noticed the woman wore a chef's jacket with "Katie" embroidered in green over the left breast. "Thanks, Katie."

"You're welcome. Anything else I can get ya? Another drink?"

"No, thanks."

"Okay." Katie didn't leave.

Siobhan's stomach grumbled, reminding her of just how hungry she was. It was embarrassing as Katie obviously heard it, too. Siobhan expected a comment about how much food she'd ordered, but Katie was quiet. Siobhan found herself caught by those eyes again and forced herself to turn away. Staring was rude. She could almost hear her mother's voice saying the words.

"Did—did you make this?" Wow, that was so lame, Siobhan thought.

Katie nodded then seemed to find her voice. "I did. My brother overcooked the first one. Care to see if it's right now?"

"Sure." Siobhan sliced into the burger. It was just the right combination of pink and grey. Perfect. Like the woman standing to her right. Perfect. Perfect teeth, a smile that was as wide as the Celtic Sea, soft skin that wasn't pale or tan, but somewhere in between. Again, Siobhan was drawn to her eyes. "Looks great."

"Right. Good. Enjoy." Katie took a stumbling step backward and hurriedly disappeared into the kitchen.

Siobhan let out a long, deep sigh, closed her eyes, and tried very hard to calm her hammering heart. It wasn't the first time she'd seen an attractive woman, and she was sure it wouldn't be the last. But had any of them ever elicited such a reaction before? Siobhan didn't think so.

Ultimately, it didn't matter. She seriously doubted Chef Katie was interested.

KATIE FORCED HERSELF into the kitchen on unsteady legs. Her hands shook as she put away the serving tray. Had God ever made such an amazing creature? It was the woman she'd seen earlier in the day. Golden hair like the sun, captivating eyes the color of a summer sky, lips made for kissing... Katie had to take a deep breath. She let it out slowly as Colm called out the next order. She barely heard him, listening again to the woman's soft voice. American. She was sure of that much and adored the accent.

An American in their pub. That had to be a first. Tourists didn't typically find their way to O'Briain's. Cork was the closest city, and there wasn't much about Cúnant to bring outsiders around. She wondered how the lovely lady had found them.

"Mary Katherine Cecilia!"

Colm's use of all three names always brought Katie to attention. She found him staring at her with a bemused grin. "What?"

"What, my ass. You're to be doin' the cooking while Rory is doin' — whatever Rory's doin'. Right?"

"Yes." Katie shook herself and started working on the next order. She felt his gaze on her and knew what was coming.

"So, ya saw her, did ya? The young lady in the back." It wasn't really a question. Her parents could always read her like a book. Sometimes she hated that.

"Yes." She kept her reply succinct hoping he'd stop. He didn't.

"She's a beaut that one. Did ya at least get her name?"

"No."

"Ah, well, I guess I'll need ta do it for ya."

"No!" She nearly dropped the spoon into the stew when she whirled around. **Colm** was laughing at her. "Feckin' spoon," she said. "Needs a longer handle."

"Needs a chef that's payin' more attention to the food than the patrons."

"Ha-ha."

Colm gently took the spoon out of her hand. "Go an see if you can at least get the girl's name. Won't do no good to have you here daydreaming and cussing about the spoons."

"Well you're stuck with my daydreaming until Rory and Tabby get back."

"That's a whole other story."

"Why?" Katie started preparing a salad. "What happened?"

"I sent them home. He's a mess and so is Tabby. Poor girl left in tears."

"What's wrong with him? I taught him better than that."

"You did, but this one's different. I'd say your little brother has fallen hard and don't have a clue what to do next. I want to wring his neck for upsetting Tabby worse than before. Maybe we could both talk to him tonight."

"Sure. We'll try to get him fixed up."

"Until then, if you have a mind ta, how 'bout finishing that salad and getting it out to table five. Reckon they're hungry now."

"Sure thing." Katie did as he asked, her mind now focused on Rory and his foolishness.

By the time Katie was able to check in on her mystery woman, more than an hour had passed. She and **Colm** split the table-waiting duties, since Jamie was busy at the bar, so she hadn't been to her table in a while.

Katie worried the woman might have gone. She made sure there wasn't too big a mess on her jacket and stepped into the dining area. The blonde woman was still seated in the back, her hair pulled into a ponytail. She was bent over a book of some kind and completely lost in thought.

Katie hesitated to go, until **Colm** gave her a none-too-gentle shove in the right direction. Katie stumbled a bit, righting herself by the time she reached the table. She cleared her throat, hoping she wouldn't scare the woman.

The woman looked up and caught Katie with her light-blue eyes. Katie didn't try to hide the goofy grin that filled her face. "Hi. Was your food good?"

She smiled back. "Excellent. Perfect, actually."

"Ah." Katie froze up again. What the hell was wrong with her? "Would you like another drink?"

"No, thanks."

Katie noted that she had her arms over the big book in front of her, hiding whatever she was doing. Maybe part of a picture, but Katie wasn't sure. "So, I was wonderin' how you found us here. We don't get tourists here much. Not sure we've had an American before."

"That obvious is it?" She laughed softly. "I'm not a tourist. I live here."

"What? Ya live here? In Cúnant?"

"Yes to both." She turned her head sideways, her expression one of curiosity. It was cute. "Are you surprised?"

"Yes. Never heard of anyone living here that wasn't born here or had kin here. I'd probably know if you were born here. So you must have kin here."

"Small towns are like that here, too, huh?"

Katie nodded and slid into the booth across from her. "You got me wanting to know more. If that's okay."

"Why not?" She shrugged. "My granddad was born here. Fergus Byrne. His family went to America when he was in his teens."

"Byrne? Lots of Byrnes around here. My best friend is Cassidy Byrne."

"Probably a relation to me, then."

"Is your last name Byrne?"

"No. Landry. Siobhan Landry." She held out her hand.

Katie glimpsed the portrait of a woman on the sketchbook under Siobhan's arms. It was a bit like gazing in a mirror. She could see her own eyes. "I'm Katie O'Briain. My dads own the place." She was reluctant to release Siobhan's delicate hand but didn't want to be rude.

"Oh? Did you say 'dads'?"

"Jamie and Colm. **Colm is helping me with the tables, and Jamie** is tending bar."

"Colm is so very sweet. I've seen him tending bar, and I must have talked to him for a couple of hours the first day I got here. He was fascinated to have an American in the pub."

"That's why he tends bar most of the time. He also likes to gossip, so beware."

Siobhan laughed softly, and the sound made Katie smile. "I'll keep that in mind."

"So, Siobhan. That's a proper Irish name. Not too common in

the states though is it?"

"No. My granddad insisted. It was his mother's name, and I'm proud to have it. My mother hates it." Her eyes dipped down, and Katie was sorry to lose contact with them. "No one can spell it, though. My teachers kept trying to spell it like it sounds. I remember my second grade teacher tried to tell me it was spelled S-H-I-V-A-U-G-H-N. My dad set her straight pretty damn quick."

"Did you argue with her? Or were you the kinda kid that shut up and did what she was told?"

"A little of both. My dad tried to teach me to stand up for myself. I told her how to spell my name. She told me I was wrong and made me stay inside during recess to write it out twenty times. My dad showed her the school records, but she insisted they had it wrong. I was transferred to another class the next day. Never had a problem from my teachers after that."

"I can't imagine a teacher doin' such a thing. And to a little girl. Good thing your da was there to set them straight."

A shadow passed over Siobhan's lovely features, and Katie wondered what she'd said to bring on such sadness. She was instantly cross with herself. As usual, her mouth kept going when it shouldn't have.

"I'm sorry if I said something wrong."

"No. You didn't." Siobhan closed up her sketchbook, put her pencil into a rolled-up pouch, and stood.

Katie did as well, sure and certain she'd said something wrong. "Should I get your check?"

"Please."

Siobhan waited patiently as Katie got the check, then paid her with a twenty euro note. "Let me get the change."

"No. Thank you." Siobhan touched Katie's forearm, and it caused instant gooseflesh.

"Will you be back?" Katie couldn't think of a single thing to say. She didn't want Siobhan to leave. Nor did she want her hand to move away, but it did.

"Probably. I live up the street, and this place has the best stew."

"It does indeed." Katie gripped the euro note like it was a lifeline. "See you next time."

Siobhan smiled and walked out of the pub and into a rain-free evening. And then Katie realized something and rolled her eyes, pissed at herself. "I didn't get her damn number."

Chapter Three

SIOBHAN SAT CROSS-LEGGED on the flattest rock she could find, her sketchbook resting on her knees. Before her was the Celtic Sea. She'd been staring at the sparkling water for so long that her eyes burned, but she wanted to soak it all in. Every shade of blue, every bit that reflected the afternoon sun, all the way to the rough, craggy rocks below. Her butt was numb from the cold wetness of the stone, but she was reluctant to get up.

The sea crashed against the shore, and the sound soothed her. She finally closed her eyes, working to keep the vision in her head. After a few moments, she pulled out her pencil and began to sketch.

She'd first get the initial shape of the seascape, then begin adding watercolors to bring it to life. At least she hoped it would come to life. Siobhan was never certain if her visions translated exactly onto paper. She was never completely satisfied with anything she finished. Granddad told her more than once that she was a talented artist. He loved everything she did. Even those awful Popsicle stick things that kids make in kindergarten. When she was going through his things she found one. The glue had disintegrated, and some of the Popsicle sticks had fallen off, but that didn't seem to matter. There it was, in the top drawer of his desk. To Granddad, Love Siobhan written in block letters underneath what was probably supposed to be a house.

It wasn't the only thing, either. Every birthday card, Father's Day card, Christmas card she'd ever made was stored in a shoebox on the top shelf of his orderly closet. In his den he'd hung a few sketches and paintings she'd done as a kid, and one that got her an A in her high school art class. One painting was done with watercolors and depicted a horse going through a dressage course. It was the only painting Siobhan was proud of. And the only one she'd brought with her.

She left so much back in Indiana. The house Granddad lived in sold within two days of being listed. She felt like a traitor selling it. As if by staying in that two-bedroom, single-story dwelling would keep her close to Granddad. Ultimately, it was the right thing to do. He wanted her to sell it and use the money to travel.

"Go to Cork," he'd said. "I want ya to see the place of me

birth. It's a beautiful land, sweetheart. You'll never tire of painting it."

Siobhan took his gnarled hand in hers and held it gently, afraid to hurt him. He was so fragile, lying in that hospital bed. She'd never seen him look so vulnerable.

"I'll see if I can get some more time off work. Maybe I can go next year."

"No." His watery eyes held hers, and she fought to hold back her tears. "You sell this house. Use the money from it and what I have in the bank and you go. Quit that job. It doesn't suit you and you know it." His smile was warm as he lightly gripped her hand. "You're an artist. You can work anywhere. Go. Be the woman we both know you to be."

She wanted to argue with him. She wasn't as brave as he always said she was. If she were brave, she'd have the guts to tell her mother to let her live her own life. Instead, Siobhan allowed Mary to control her. She always had.

The only time she'd ever stood up to her was when she decided to move in with Granddad. Hospice nurses were already visiting him, but he'd been clear that he wanted to die in his own home. He couldn't do that without someone there all day long. Siobhan was willing to fill in the gap.

Her boss at the museum was more than kind in allowing her to bend her work hours around the availability of the nurses and helpers that came and went. Her job might have been boring, but the people she worked with were amazing in her time of need.

Mary Landry was the only stumbling block. She wouldn't spend more than an hour or so a day with her own father. She tried to get him placed in a nursing home, but he signed a durable power of attorney and named Siobhan as his caregiver. She was also the sole executor of his will. He didn't trust Mary to abide by his final wishes.

Siobhan leaned over him and kissed his scruffy cheek. She made a mental note to ask Diane, the morning caregiver, to give him a shave. "I love you, Granddad."

"Does that mean you'll go?"

Siobhan smiled, enjoying the look of expectation on his weathered face. "Yes. I'll go to Ireland and stay as long as the money holds out. Or I find a job."

"Good girl." He closed his eyes and went to sleep.

It was the last time she spoke to him.

Siobhan tried to shake off her melancholy and get back to the sketch she was doing. People and animals came easy to her, but landscapes were so very different. A landscape's colors were always changing with the time of day, amount of sunlight, type of weather, time of year...and it was this challenge that kept her in Ireland. After traveling around the country for a few weeks, Siobhan settled in Cúnant and applied for a permanent residency permit. She had no intention of going back to Indiana. Regardless of what her mother had to say. If she was frugal, she could live on the money Granddad left her until her art started selling. For the first time in her life, Siobhan felt confident about her ability as an artist.

She took a deep breath of salty air and wondered why it'd taken her so long to get to this point in her life. That answer came easily enough in the form of her mother.

She shook her head, as if to clear her muddled brain, and tried again to focus on the scenery around her.

She nearly fell off her rock when someone called her name. She carefully turned around and saw Katie standing a few feet away, on the footpath that led to the village. Her hair was wet with sweat that dripped down the sides of her lovely face. Her skin was flushed, and her breathing steady, but fast, as she jogged in place. Her smile was genuine, and Siobhan smiled back.

"What are you doing out here?" Siobhan asked. "Aside from the obvious."

Katie laughed and the sound warmed Siobhan. "I run here every day. First time you noticed, though."

"Really?" Siobhan turned completely around, and that's when she realized something else she hadn't noticed. Katie, though clearly athletic with her strong build and muscular arms, was running without legs. Well, she had legs, but they were prosthetic. Metallic actually with oddly curved feet that seemed to bounce as she jogged in place.

"Yes," Katie said, either unaware of Siobhan's staring or simply used to it. "I've been a runner me whole life. And this here path is where I like to run most. Might not be the same time of day, but every day that I can, I'm running here. I love the smell and sounds of the sea."

"Me, too," Siobhan said once she'd found her voice. "Sorry I didn't notice you before."

Katie shrugged. "No worries. Gotta get moving before I cool off too much. Bye." She waved and was off like a shot.

Siobhan had seen Katie a few times now and never suspected she had a prosthetic leg, much less two. As she moved toward the village, she ran as if she were born with the prosthetics. Maybe she'd worn them her whole life.

Siobhan wanted to know more, but again her mother's voice intruded saying it'd be rude to ask questions. It wasn't nice to pry into other people's lives.

She stayed on the rock for a few more hours, but nothing came to her. The sketchbook felt like it weighed a hundred pounds, so she tucked it into her oversized messenger bag. She placed the pencils in their holder, slung the bag over her shoulder, and headed in the opposite direction as Katie. Siobhan got all of three steps before her cell phone rang. Not many people had her number, and her stomach sank when she saw the caller was her mother.

She had to answer it, or the woman would call her until she did.

"Hi, Mom."

"Did I wake you? You sound tired."

"No. I've been up. It's one in the afternoon here. Remember, I'm five hours ahead of you. Why are you up so early?"

"I have an appointment with Doctor Collins. My sciatica is acting up again."

"Sorry to hear that." Siobhan adjusted the phone and her bag and continued walking. "How are things otherwise?"

Mary Landry never shied from gossip, despite her protests that it was rude, and she began her weekly litany as to what was going on in the lives of everyone in town. Mary reckoned that if people shared the information with her it wasn't gossip. Never mind that the people she spoke about weren't the ones offering up the information.

The list always included people Siobhan didn't know or care to know, but she tried to be attentive, speaking the right responses at the right time.

"Oh, and did you know that Terry Jones's daughter doesn't want to be her daughter anymore?"

Siobhan had to think about who Terry Jones was before she replied. "Why doesn't Angie want to be her daughter anymore?"

"Well, she's decided she wants to be called Andre now and that Terry has to refer to her as her son."

Uh-oh. Siobhan readied herself for her mother's coming tirade. "So Angie wants to become a boy?"

"Wants to? She thinks she is a boy. Claims she was born in the wrong body or some such nonsense. I told Terry it was just a phase and the girl would come to her senses. She's only fourteen.

It'll pass. But Terry and her husband are letting her pretend to be a boy. I think it's so wrong and so does Brother Bob. He promised to pray for the Joneses and have a talk with them after church."

Soon as her mother took a breath, Siobhan said, "Don't you think they know their child? I mean, if it's a phase, so what? Let the child do what comes naturally. If Angie wants to be Andre, then let her. She knows her body better than anyone else does. I'm glad her parents are supporting her. Too many kids kill them-selves because their parents don't support them."

"God doesn't make mistakes. These people act like God messed up their child. It's wrong and it's going to hurt Angie when she's older. What if she wants children? She can't have chil-dren if she becomes a man, or whatever."

"Mom, do you realize how weird that sounds? You don't have to give birth to become a parent. There are a lot of kids out there that need parents and lots of people looking for children. It all works out if that's what you want. I don't plan to ever give birth, but I might adopt someday."

She heard the exaggerated sigh and wished she'd never engaged her mother. Sometimes it was easier to let Mary just ramble on, pretend to agree, and hang up before the call got too long. Too late now.

"Siobhan Landry, you have no idea what you're saying. Of course you should have children, but they need a father. You should get married and you'll change your mind. You'll want children when you find the right man."

That man doesn't exist, she wanted to say. Instead, she chose to bring the call to a close before Mary started spouting bible verses, or worse, tried to tell her thirty-year-old child that being a lesbian was just a phase. "Sure. Look, Mom, I'm glad you called, but I need to pop into the store for a minute, and you know how I don't like to be rude and talk on the phone while I'm shopping."

"Of course not, dear. I should shower and get going. I'll call you later in the week. Take care of yourself. And let me know when you're coming home. Brother Bob would love to see you."

Siobhan bit her tongue hard enough to draw blood. Brother Bob probably didn't care if she ever darkened his doorstep again, but Mary Landry was determined they'd make a great couple. Good thing her mother couldn't see the expression on her face. "Sure. I'll check my schedule and let you know. I love you, Mom."

"Goodbye." Her mother disconnected, and Siobhan blissfully tucked the phone into her back pocket.

The call wasn't as painful as most calls from her mother. She was certainly in a better mood than usual. She was too busy complaining about Angie, or Andre, Jones to get after Siobhan about her own sexual preferences. She felt bad for Terry, who would have to hear Mary's yammering on and on about Andre every time she saw her. She wondered if the Joneses would be smart and find a new church. Brother Bob would soon be preaching about the sanctity of the body given to us by God, etc. She doubted they'd be able to last long under his not-so-subtle pressure.

She would, however, say a prayer for Andre in hopes that, if a transition was what he wanted, he'd get the support he needed and not have to wait until his thirties to feel free enough to be himself.

KATIE PAUSED AT the rocky cliff's edge where she'd seen Siobhan earlier. She did a few leg stretches and adjusted the socket on her right leg. It was rubbing against her stump, and while she wanted to run longer, she knew it was time to head home. At least she'd made most of her six-kilometer distance.

She really hoped the blistering would stop before the Clonakilty Waterfront Marathon next month. But the socket on her right leg was causing her problems. She'd have to make an appointment for an adjustment soon. She'd be damned if she would miss the marathon.

She stared out at the sea as dark clouds moved in from the north. More rain. But there was a rugby match on telly tonight, so that meant the pub would be busy. She welcomed it as she needed to take her mind off the pain from the prosthetics.

Katie started a slow jog toward home, and her mind wandered back to Siobhan. She had seen her several times along the coast, in that same spot, a sketchbook on her lap. Often she'd have her eyes closed and her head leaned back as if in deep thought. Katie wanted to approach her several times, but there was something so very private about her that she never could find the right moment. She didn't want to interrupt.

Luck was with her when she spotted Siobhan in the pub the other day. And once again, Katie had managed to see her and not get her feckin' phone number. What the hell was wrong with her? Why did the sight of Siobhan make her brain stop functioning?

Dammit all. The woman was simply breathtaking, and when Katie was near her, all speech just stopped. Like right now as she saw Siobhan come out of the local market. Katie waved when Siobhan looked up. Next thing Katie knew, she was jogging toward Siobhan, who stopped to wait for her.

"Long time no see," Siobhan said, smiling at her.

Katie smiled back. "Small village. Hard to avoid people for long."

"Quite true."

They stood for an awkward moment before Katie got her shite together and asked, "Can I get your number? I'd love to take you to lunch sometime. Maybe just coffee or tea?" God, she sounded like a school girl just now.

"Uh, okay. But I don't have anything to write it down on. How about I come by the pub tonight? I can give it to you then, assuming you'll be working."

"I will. Ireland is playing South Africa tonight. Pub's gonna be a bit full."

"Is that football or rugby?"

"Rugby. Got a fair few months before football starts again."

Siobhan laughed. "I only know that baseball season starts in March and ends in November. Granddad loved baseball."

"Well then, you'll have to tell me about him and baseball. Can't say I know much about it."

"Deal. See you tonight."

Katie watched her leave then jogged home, feeling much lighter on her feet than moments before.

Chapter Four

KATIE STOPPED AT the entrance to their family home, always a bit in awe of the place they lived in. It had a lot of names throughout history, but when they moved in, it was declared Castle O'Briain. The pub sat at the edge of the property, closest to the village. In her own research, Katie found the castle once overlooked the village, but as the village grew in size, it encroached on the edges of the castle grounds. Eventually, the castle was surrounded by shops and homes.

The driveway ran behind the pub and wound its way up a steep hill until it reached the graveled area in front of the main house. It was hard to tell the age of the castle, or that most of the interior had been renovated, but it didn't matter to Katie. She loved the look of it. The main house had three stories and was flanked on the left by a tower, which had yet to be renovated, and on the right by the remnant of a chapel. That was their current project. Her parents wanted to make it into a B&B that would eventually fund the rest of the renovation.

She smiled despite the pain in her right leg as she jogged to the front door by means of the short ramp that Jamie put in last summer. The wide, oak door creaked a bit as she opened it. She stepped into the great hall and took a deep breath. She was incredibly proud of the floor mosaic that was the centerpiece of the hall.

When they first moved in, they found the mosaic mostly destroyed. Colm wanted to put a new floor over it, but Katie located two boxes full of the little squares that made up the coat of arms of the Murphy family, the first to own the castle. Putting the pieces together was a gigantic puzzle, and at fourteen, Katie was keen to do it. It took over two years, but it was her proudest moment when she could show her parents the result of her hard work.

Now the green-and-white shield, with the same colored banners flying around the edges of it, gave life to the hall. Inside the top half of the shield, against the green background, was a golden lion. Katie's favorite part, it had taken the longest to put back together. She'd had to create several new tiles to fill in the missing ones.

Below the lion, on the white of the shield, was an apple tree.

Those apples were a pain, but worth the effort as the red stood out against the green tree.

A helmet balanced above the lion, topped with a red-and-white hat, topped with another lion. Voila, the Murphy coat of arms.

Katie pulled herself out of her reverie and settled into her wheelchair. She doffed her blades and discovered her right stump was bleeding. She put the blades across her lap and wheeled herself to her room and her first-aid kit. She was wrapping her stump when Jamie entered.

"Pushin' yourself too much, love."

"Only way to get fit enough to finish the race, Da." Katie wheeled around to face him.

"Ya don't have to finish it. Just competing is—"

"Isn't enough. I have to finish." She held his gaze, knowing he only did this because he worried about her. But she was nearly as stubborn as he was and wasn't about to back down. Not on something this important. "Where's Rory?" she asked, moving on to the reason she and Jamie were home. He'd sent her a text message that Rory was there, and it was time they talked to him. Jamie decided to do this talk, since Colm had already had one with the boy and made no headway.

Katie really didn't feel like discussing her own issues. Rory was much easier to focus on.

"In the sitting room, but don't be thinking this discussion is over," Jamie said.

She rolled past him close enough he had to back up or risk getting his toes run over. She didn't respond to his comment, knowing it'd be useless.

They found Rory on the sofa in front of the TV, messing about with his mobile phone. She knew full well he heard her and Jamie enter, but he chose to ignore them. Katie wasn't going to take that. She rolled to the sofa and over his toes.

"Hey! What's that for?"

"Ignoring me." She took the phone from him. "We need ta talk."

"I don't want to—"

Jamie settled in the armchair next to the sofa. "Not givin' you a choice here, lad."

Katie stayed in front of Rory. "Ignoring the problem with Tabby isn't gonna make it go away. So, start talking. From the beginning."

Rory leaned his head back and sighed as if this were the

worst day of his young life. "We kissed."

"That doesn't sound like the beginning," Jamie said.

"It is. I mean, we'd been chatting a lot. Then texting each other, even if we were both working. It was fun." He shrugged, still staring at the ceiling. "I walked her home from work, and when we got there, I kissed her. No big deal."

Katie would have run over his toes again if he hadn't suddenly moved them. He was watching her now, and she was very sure he knew how mad she was. "A kiss is always a big deal, ya git. What did you say to her after that?"

"Nothing."

"Nothing?" Katie and Jamie chorused the word. Katie said, "Nothing as in no texts, no chat?"

"I mean, we chat at the pub."

"You kissed the girl then decided not to speak to her. Have ya any clue how much she's hurting right now?" Katie really, really wanted to give him a good whack.

"I guess. Sorta."

"Rory O'Briain, you get your arse off this couch right now and you fecking call Tabby." Katie tossed his phone at him. "You have two choices. You apologize and beg for forgiveness, or you tell her how you really feel about her and hope she gives you a second chance." Rory started to reply, but Katie stopped him. "That's it. Two choices. Go. Call her."

Rory hesitated, his gaze searching hers. After a moment, he stood, kissed her on the cheek, and strode out of the room.

Jamie laughed softly. "Couldn't have said it better meself. Katie, I don't know how you do it."

"Me either. But if I ever have children of me own, and they turn out like Rory, I'm going to blame you."

"Me? How's it my fault if your kid is like Rory?"

"Because Rory is like you, and you'd be the kind of granddad that influences the little ones." She wagged a finger at him. "I'm done being ma for now. Next time, it's your turn."

Jamie got up and caught her before she could wheel out of the sitting room. "Katie, you're the best thing that ever happened to me and Dadaí. Don't know what we'd do without you."

"I'm hearing something behind your words, Da."

"Yeah. Now that Rory's sorted." He squatted in front of her, resting his hands on hers. "You are our first child, and we don't want nothing to happen to you. That includes fussing over how much you're pushing yourself. I know that these marathons mean something to you, but you mean more to us than anything in the world."

"I understand, Da. But you have to let me do this. Please." She turned her hands over so she was holding his. "I can't explain what it means to me. Running feels like all I have left."

"You've got your family, darlin'. We're right here."

"Yeah, but that's not what I mean. I love you all, but I need more. I need — a purpose."

Jamie cupped her cheek with his hand and kissed her forehead. "Then I'll pray you find it. Just tell us what you need. Promise?"

"I promise."

He stood and she wheeled toward her bedroom, hoping he didn't see her sudden tears.

SIOBHAN SETTLED INTO a seat near the front of the pub and opened her sketchbook. At five-thirty in the evening, the pub wouldn't yet be full of customers. That would start around six. Mostly there'd be people crowding around the long, curved bar to watch the game. She'd sketched the bar once, loving the shiny mahogany color. At least twenty people could sit there at one time, and another dozen would be standing around it on the weekends.

The eating area was built around a dance floor that probably could hold ten people if they crowded together. A karaoke machine sat in the corner. Siobhan always left before karaoke began. Drunken singers weren't something she enjoyed.

Her gaze moved to the door just as Katie entered. Now that was something she could enjoy; remembering Katie in her tight, Lycra, running outfit was always nice. It was never a chore to watch an athletic woman in skin-tight clothes.

This evening, Katie wore black jeans and a long-sleeved, green polo. The color suited her and highlighted her eyes. She spoke to her father before heading into the back room. Siobhan had written her cell phone number down and stuck it in her wallet just in case Katie really wanted it. She doubted anything would happen between them, but she could certainly use a friend.

Ireland was a cool place to live, and it felt very much like home to her, but Siobhan was lonely. Without her granddad, she didn't have anyone to talk to. Even though he wouldn't have been able to join her, she missed being able to pick up the phone and call him. She could call her mother, but she never seemed interested in anything Siobhan had to say. She wouldn't say her mother didn't care about her, just that her mother was self-centered. She was always more concerned with herself, but after Siobhan's father died, she seemed to get a lot worse. It didn't help matters when Granddad left everything he had to Siobhan.

Siobhan wondered just how pathetic it was that she had no friends from the US trying to contact her. She'd considered setting up a Facebook account, but who would see it? Other than her mother and her mother's church friends? Most of whom were aghast that Siobhan remained true to the Catholic faith her granddad introduced her to. One of the old ladies, whom Siobhan referred to as the Indiana Contingent of the Religious Right, called Catholics idol worshipers. They believed that only Christians were on the right side of things. None of them bothered to acknowledge that Catholics were also Christians. It was all crazy, and Siobhan didn't understand any of it. It hurt her head to think about it.

She turned her attention back to her sketchbook. The empty page mocked her. She felt like sticking her tongue out at it.

"Fancy seeing you here."

The very female voice drew Siobhan's attention to the woman standing beside her booth. Katie's smile filled her face as she took the seat opposite Siobhan.

"Well, I did say I'd come over."

"So you did." Katie rested her arms on the table.

"Are you working tonight?"

"Nope. Got Tabby and Conor waiting tables, and Da and Danny cooking. I'm free."

"Free? Good. I was worried you might charge me for your time."

Katie laughed. "Well, you're new here. For now it's free." Her smiled never wavered, and Siobhan wondered if Katie was indeed "free."

Siobhan opened her wallet and handed the paper to Katie. "As requested."

Katie studied it for a long time before she pulled out her phone and typed it in. "I'll text you so you have mine." She did and it was Siobhan's turn to smile.

The entire conversation had no subject and neither of them seemed to have much to say, but Siobhan couldn't deny the quiver in her belly or the simple fact that she was enjoying herself.

They sat in companionable silence for a while, eventually

interrupted by a lanky teenager wearing a black T-shirt with the pub's name emblazoned on it in gold lettering. He had a pad of paper and a quirky grin on his dark-skinned face. His curly black hair was tucked under an "O'Briain's Pub" ball cap. He gave Katie a sideways glance then focused his attention on Siobhan.

"Care for a drink?"

"Diet Coke," she replied.

"Water." Katie gave him a little push when he didn't leave right away. As soon as he was gone, she said, "Sorry about that. Conor's seventeen and apparently born without manners."

"It's okay. I don't think I've seen him before."

"He usually works on karaoke nights. He likes to run the computer and equipment. Our dads pay him extra for it, hoping he's saving up for when he goes to university. I think he's saving the money for a motorcycle."

"He's your brother?" Siobhan hoped she didn't sound rude, but there was nothing alike between Katie and Conor. And not just their skin color. Conor had a wide nose where Katie's was slim. His face was more rounded, and his eyes were nearly black. Just before Katie answered, Siobhan realized how stupid her question was.

"We're adopted," Katie said, as if she had to explain it often. "Rory and Danny are twins. Identical. Conor is next, then Casey who's fourteen, and Kyra is twelve. Rory and Danny just turned twenty-one, though you'd never know it from the way they act. Rory and Danny were a special case."

"How so?"

"Da's friends with a woman that works with kids in need. She heard about a set of twins here in Cúnant that needed an emergency home. Our dads had fostered kids before, so they said to bring them over. It was the middle of the night, and wouldn't ya know it, the little shits never left." Katie laughed and Siobhan joined her.

"Your parents sound amazing."

"They can be. They can also be pains in the arse. But I love them both."

"I can see that by the look on your face."

Conor returned with their drinks and placed them on the table. "Are you two hungry? Da's got the stew ready."

"That's why I come here," Siobhan said. Katie nodded and Conor wandered away.

"So, what brings you to Ireland? Not that I'm complaining, but we don't get many Americans settling here."

"I promised my granddad I'd bring him home when he died — toss his ashes into the Celtic Sea. I planned to stay a couple of weeks then go home. But I sort of fell in love with the place. And I needed a new start, so I applied for residency."

"Well, that's good for me then. Now I know yer not gonna up and leave before I have a chance to get to know ya."

Siobhan felt a blush color her cheeks. "You want to get to know me?"

"Of course." Katie took a long drink of her water, but her gaze never left Siobhan's. "Why wouldn't I?"

"I — I don't know. I've never had anyone tell me they wanted to know me."

"Not ever? Not a friend, or, erm, boyfriend?"

"Never a boyfriend. I've had a couple of girlfriends, but they never said that to me. I mean, I guess we got to know each other eventually, but it didn't seem to matter. The relationships were short-lived anyway."

"Their loss." Katie winked at her, and it made Siobhan sport a silly grin. "My gain."

They were interrupted by Conor and two hearty bowls of stew. He put them on the table and left them alone again.

Their conversation turned to commentary on the stew and how good it was. Siobhan enjoyed their easy banter and was almost sad when they finished eating. She dropped her napkin into the empty bowl and silence surrounded them, even as the pub became louder with more and more people coming in.

"The match is due to start soon. Would you care to have a wander with me?"

"A what?"

"A wander. A walk. I could show you parts of the village I bet you've not gotten to yet."

"Sounds great." Siobhan had already stashed her sketchbook in her messenger bag, which she grabbed as she stood up. "I'll just get this paid for first."

"No need." Katie got up as well, and they stood face-to-face for the first time. Siobhan was a bit taller. As they gazed at each other, Siobhan wished she could take Katie's hand and stroll out the door together. Instead, she shoved her hands in her pockets and let Katie lead the way.

It was going to be damn hard to keep her hands to herself.

KATIE KEPT HER hands in the pockets of her jeans as they

strode through the village. She barely knew the woman beside her, but her instincts screamed to just take hold of her hand. That was a first. She'd been with women before; her longest relationship was with Fiona, and that lasted almost six years. Katie didn't have the same pull with Fiona that she had with Siobhan. She wanted to reach over, take her into her arms, and kiss her breathless.

Instead, she realized Siobhan was speaking, and she had no clue what the woman had said.

"It's interesting that the church is right in the middle of the village. I've noticed that in the few places I've managed to see here. Are all the churches Catholic? I know this one is, since I've been to mass a few times."

"You've been to mass here? I don't believe I've seen ya."

"I always sit in the back, and I'm the first to leave," Siobhan said.

Katie thought that merited exploring later. "Well, on our side of the pond, we build the church and the village comes along after. It's built to circle the church since that was always the central part of people's lives."

"Makes sense. In America, we sort of build the church wherever there's space. Some places have more than one."

"Ah. Catholic and Protestant then?"

"Yeah, but Protestant doesn't really cover it. In the town I'm from, we have Methodist, Baptist, Southern Baptist, two Churches of Christ, Jehovah's Witnesses, one Catholic, and one Apostolic. Oh, and the Church of the Nazarene. There are more in the township though."

"More? Bloody hell. How many people live in your town?"

"About 3000 give or take those in the township."

"And they all get on?"

"Mostly," Siobhan said. "I can't recall there ever being any major fights. Though one time the Baptist minister got into major trouble for having an affair with the wife of the minister of the Church of the Nazarene. I'm not sure if the congregation was more upset about the affair itself or that he did it with someone from another church. Anyway, my mom keeps up with all that. I don't really care what they're doing. I'm sure there are good people in our town, but a lot of what I see is plain and simple hypocrisy. Even at St. Agnes, where I go to mass. It's an American thing I guess."

"Oh no. Plenty of that here, too, sad to say. I don't know from the big cities, but when everyone knows everyone else, there's bound to be drama."

"Amen to that."

Katie stopped them at St. Mary's. "Did ya know the knight that built this building started it in 1390?"

"I didn't."

"Well, it's on the plaque by the door. Don't suppose ya read Irish?"

"Not that well. Granddad taught me to speak it, which was awesome because we could say stuff in front of my mom and she didn't have a clue what we were talking about. It was like a secret language when I was a kid."

"I think your granddad sounds like a grand fella. Maybe I can help ya learn to read it better then?"

Siobhan turned to her, and despite only having a faint light from the street lamp, Katie saw something in her eyes that gave her goose flesh.

"I'd like that a lot."

"Perfect." Katie let the silence hang between them for a long moment then took a step closer to Siobhan. They were almost nose to nose. Her heart hammered in her chest like it wanted to get out of its cage. Her hands shook, and she had to shove them back into her pockets.

Despite the low lighting, Katie was sure she saw something pass over Siobhan's features, seconds before Siobhan backed away.

"So, any other interesting spots to show me?"

Katie hid her disappointment as best she could. Another second and she was sure to have kissed the woman in front of her. "You say you live near the pub?"

"Yep. Above Cronin Apothecary. In the yellowest building I've ever seen in my life."

Katie laughed. "Well, we do enjoy a spot of color."

"A spot? It's flanked on the left by a bright red building and on the right by a green one. There are at least six other buildings on the street in different colors. It's like living in a rainbow."

"You don't like rainbows?"

"I love them, just not used to living in one." Siobhan led the way as they started toward the pub. "I don't think I've ever seen a more colorful neighborhood. Where I'm from, most houses are white, blue, or made of brick. On occasion, you'll find a white brick house, but not much else in the way of colors."

"How boring."

"I suppose it is. Maybe that's part of what Granddad missed."

"And the sea air I'd guess." Katie took a deep breath and slowly let it out. "Ya cannot beat the clean air."

"That's true. We lived close to a waste-processing plant. If the wind blew the right direction, or wrong direction depending on your point of view, it was damn stinky."

"I'll make a note not to visit your hometown any time soon."

"Good choice."

They ambled along the quiet street in silence. Katie's desire to hold Siobhan's hand grew so strong that she made fists in her pockets to keep her hands still. The closer they got to the apothecary, the more Katie wanted to find a way to extend their time together. It wasn't quite eight at night, and the pub would still be full to bursting. She didn't want to go there and didn't want to go home and be alone.

Siobhan stopped at a side door to the apothecary, keys dangling from her fingers. "Well, it's been a nice walk. Thanks for the insider tour."

"No problem. I'd be happy to extend it in the daylight if you'd like."

Siobhan paused, and for a moment Katie thought she'd decline her invitation. Instead, she smiled and said, "Cool. I'll have to take you up on that but maybe not for a few days. I'm going to be in my apartment for a while painting, and I'm sure I'll need to get out and about when I'm done."

"How long will you be painting?"

She shrugged. "Depends. I've been known to be inside for a few weeks working. I'm never sure when or if inspiration will hit me. How about if I call you?"

"That works, but you've got to at least come out to eat, right?"

Siobhan edged a little closer to the door, and Katie could tell by her body language she was done chatting. "I stocked up the fridge earlier today, so I should be fine."

"Well, do remember to eat. I'd hate to find out ya starved to death with a paintbrush in your hand."

Siobhan laughed and opened the door to the stairway that led to her apartment. "I'll be fine. Thanks, Katie."

"You're welcome." Katie waited until Siobhan was inside and she heard the door lock before heading home. She bypassed the pub, preferring to be alone while she puzzled over the woman that had quickly gotten her full attention.

Chapter Five

SIOBHAN CLOSED THE door, leaned against it, and sighed. After waiting a few moments to be sure Katie was gone, she stepped outside. She needed to think. She was very sure that Katie almost kissed her. Would have kissed her if Siobhan hadn't stepped away.

What the hell was she thinking? Katie was cute and nice, and it wouldn't have been a bad thing to kiss her...right?

Wrong. It was a very, very bad idea. Siobhan wasn't going there again. The last time she'd kissed a woman she barely knew...it all turned out so awful. She just couldn't allow herself to go there again. Cúnant was a small place, and she'd see Katie everywhere if things turned out badly. Then where would she go? Bad enough she had to hear about Susan nearly every time she spoke to her mother. At least she didn't see her every day.

She had to concentrate on herself first. Ireland was her home, a dream she'd had since her granddad first talked about his homeland. Siobhan was absolutely confident she could create a new life here, become a new person. The old Siobhan wasn't worth much of anything, no matter how much Granddad would disagree. After all, Siobhan's mother told her that often enough.

At some point, when was unclear, her life had stopped being her own. Maybe it was after her dad died. She'd felt responsible for her mother and spent more time with her than at her job or with her girlfriend.

Eventually, she gave up her apartment and moved in with her mother.

Then Grandma got sick, and Siobhan split her time between Mom and Grandma and work. When Grandma died it was rough, and she was lucky to be able to help and comfort Granddad, the single most important person in her life.

Then he was gone and it wasn't long after his funeral that Siobhan had her epiphany. Her mother started in on Siobhan for something—she couldn't even remember what. Maybe it was the awful breakup of her relationship with Susan. Or how she parked her car in the driveway. Or that Granddad left all his money to Siobhan. It didn't matter. It was the moment when Siobhan realized she needed to take control. Her life needed to revolve around her. No one else. Understanding that brought an amazing amount of relief. The anvil that held her down had been tossed away like a pebble.

She couldn't pack fast enough. Couldn't get on the plane soon enough. Couldn't get into her new apartment soon enough. Once her few possessions arrived, Siobhan made the empty rooms feel like a home.

And as she wandered through the quiet village, it became clear to her she was home. What wasn't clear had to do with a certain adorable red-haired woman who, no matter what Siobhan was thinking about, managed to make her presence known.

Damn.

Siobhan pulled her cell phone from the back pocket of her jeans and was about to text Katie when the phone rang. She almost hit the red button when the caller ID showed her mother's number.

With a heavy sigh, she swiped across the screen and answered. Old habits died hard. "Hi, Mom."

"Are you still up? I never know when I'm supposed to call you."

"I'm up and taking a walk at the moment. Like I said, if the evening news is on, it's too late to call. Okay?"

"I'll try to remember." Her mother paused and Siobhan steeled herself for the onslaught she knew was coming. "The mother-daughter dinner is scheduled for December fifteenth. I've already bought the tickets."

Of course. "I'll try to make it."

"Try? Honestly, Siobhan, it's not like you have a real job. Why can't you commit to coming over at least for Christmas? Is it such an inconvenience to see me?"

Siobhan knew better than to answer that honestly. "No. It's just that I do have a lot going on. I'm looking for a place to exhibit some of my work. I've seen a couple of tourist type stores that have paintings from local artists hanging up. I just need to get a few pieces finished so I can approach the store owners."

"You can do that anytime. The dinner is only once a year."

And so is your birthday, Mother's Day, Thanksgiving...Siobhan wanted to smack her head into the tree she was approaching. "If it's that important to you, I'll be there. Okay?"

"Good. And make sure you bring a pack of playing cards that say Ireland on them. You know how Wilma loves collecting them."

"Of course. Look, Mom, it's getting late. I really need to head back home. I'll talk to you later."

"Don't forget."

"I won't."

"I'll remind you," her mother said. "Good bye."

"Bye," Siobhan said to the silent phone. No, "I love you" or "I miss you," just "Good bye." She slid the phone into her back pocket as she came around to her apartment door. She could use a drink right about now but didn't want to risk seeing Katie at the pub. She no longer felt like talking.

Instead, she went to her apartment, took a cold beer from the fridge, and headed for her bedroom. A little TV, a bit of alcohol, and a romance novel would bring the evening to a decent close. She glanced at the book she'd randomly chosen and groaned just a little. While it was her favorite author, she knew there'd be a hot sex scene in the first few chapters and now wondered just how good an idea this was.

"IT'S A BAD idea," Katie said. "Period. And I'm not gonna do it."

"Why not? You told me to." Danny stared at her with eyes identical to Rory's and a grin as wide as the River Lee. "And it worked."

"Because you've known Maria since you were four years old. That's different and you know it." Katie bumped him with her wheel as she moved past him and into the sitting room from the kitchen. He was mad if he thought she was going to give in and kiss Siobhan.

"You're chicken. That's all."

She rolled her eyes but kept her back to him. She didn't want him to know he was right. She'd never hear the end of it. "Danny, I've only known her a few days. Some lesbians might move fast and be living together inside a week, but that's not me and you know it."

"It could be." He came to stand in front of her.

Katie had to crane her neck up to see him. "Not a chance. I've proven what a bad idea that is. You didn't see the expression on her face last night. The last thing she was wanting was a kiss from me."

"Ah, but the look on your face just now says you are sure to be wanting to kiss her. And you don't know what she was thinking. Besides, what's the harm in one little kiss?"

"Ha. Ask your idiot brother. He still hasn't sorted it out with Tabby, though she's working later today."

"No way. I'm stayin' away from that mess."

"But you're jumping into mine?"

"You're reasonable." He squatted in front of her, still sporting a grin. "And I want to see you happy. Seems like Siobhan does that."

"Maybe when I've known her a few months, we'll see. If she even comes around anymore. I coulda scared her off, ya know?"

"Doubt it." Danny kissed her forehead as he stood. "Gonna get me something to eat. I got rugby practice this morning, then I've got to pick up Rory's shift at the pub."

"Why? Where's he gonna be?" Katie was half-afraid to ask, and Danny's face confirmed it.

"He's fixing to surprise Tabby when she's done with her shift. I heard him say something about flowers, but I didn't ask and I don't wanna know." With that, he left the house.

"Flowers? Really?" She continued on to her room to get ready for her run. Today was her long run, and she planned to make the hour-fifteen-minute time. Last week she was off by twenty minutes. That wouldn't do. Her stamina wasn't up to where it needed to be. Nothing was gonna stop her from doing the London Marathon. And she'd finish it, too.

She'd finished every marathon she'd entered, except one. And lucky for her, she couldn't remember everything that happened to stop her. The only thing she knew was that she woke up some days later with a monster headache and no legs.

And no girlfriend. Katie lost her career, her girlfriend, and her legs in one fell swoop. How she managed to live at all was something only God could answer.

Maybe the worst part had been Fiona. Six years together and Katie would have thought Fiona and she could get through anything. But as soon as "anything" sprung up, Fiona ran off. Maybe her dads were right, and Fiona never was the woman for her. But Katie's heart longed for someone to fill that empty space and ease the constant ache.

Was Siobhan that woman? Would she want to be married? Have kids?

"I could ask her," Katie said aloud.

"Ask who what?" Colm stood in her doorway and watched her don the blades to her residual legs.

"Just muttering to meself. Shouldn't you still be in bed?"

"I wanted to speak to ya before you went on your run."

"Uh-oh. Dadaí, if this is about me running—"

"It is and I expect you'll listen. Or pretend to. I know you came home the other day with your stump bleeding where the sockets attach. We've spoken about this before. I know Da was in here chatting with you, but we both know he isn't gonna do the tough talking, so I'm here." He took a deep breath, and she knew she was in for it. "Katie, love, no amount of running for a marathon is worth you hurting yourself. You have to be careful, or you could get an infection, and you know what happened the last time."

Katie didn't fancy remembering it. She rubbed her right leg, which was shorter than her left. After the incident, she still had a bit of leg past her knee. She would have had more if an infection hadn't caused the doctors to take it. The infection wasn't her fault, but they both knew the consequences if one got out of hand.

"I'm fine. Just a bit of rubbing. I need to keep up my running schedule or I won't even make it halfway. I barely finished Dublin."

Colm was well and truly frustrated, and she hated that she caused it. She loved him dearly, but he had to understand. Running was as important as breathing and the only thing left that she could still do. "I can't be missing this one, Dadaí. I just can't."

"Katie, what're you trying to prove?"

"That my life isn't over." She spoke quietly and wasn't sure he'd heard her. It was so bloody frustrating. If she didn't train, she'd never finish. If she didn't at least try, she'd never forgive herself. She felt weak and absolutely hated that. She was strong. She'd always been strong. Until Colm pulled her into his arms.

It shouldn't be so hard, and it was damn unfair. In her dadaí's arms, Katie cried. After a few moments and enough tears to soak Colm's shirt, she pushed herself away and stood. "I love you, Dadaí. But please, let me do this. I need this."

"Sure and certain?"

She nodded, and he hugged her again. Katie said, "And don't be telling Da I cried like a babe with a wet nappy. Okay? He'll just worry."

"You know I can't keep secrets from him, but so long as he doesn't ask..."

"Thanks." Katie wiped her face on the sleeve of her shirt then gave her sweet father a kiss on the cheek. "See you at the pub."

"Okay, love."

She took a deep, settling breath and headed out the door.

THE MORNING AIR was crisp and cool, but Katie didn't feel the chill. Her body responded well to the exertion, but her right leg didn't. Needles of pain kept shooting up it with each step. Only halfway through her run, she wanted to scream. She pushed through the pain and continued down the curvy road that served as her longest running course.

Only locals knew about this road, and she felt pretty safe to be here. Still, she wore a fluorescent yellow vest. Perhaps she should have stayed to the footpath she normally took. The road was getting rockier than she expected, and each uneven step seemed more painful than the last.

A string of curse words flowed out of her mouth when she was forced to stop. She sat along the side of the road and removed the blade from her leg. Blood seeped through the nylon sheath over her stump. The wounds had opened again, which meant she'd have to take a couple of days off from running so they would heal. She didn't need this.

She managed to stand and started the slow, long journey back home.

A car came around the bend a little too close to her, and Katie had to dive into the ditch. Good thing for her it wasn't full of water or nettles. She was very allergic to nettles. She crawled out just as the car stopped a few meters away. She considered giving the driver a good bullocking but stopped when Siobhan got out.

She was dressed in bright-yellow sneakers, tight jeans, light-blue button-down shirt, and had an expression on her pretty face that was at once horror filled and relieved.

Siobhan said, "Oh shit! Katie, I'm so sorry. Are you okay?"

"I'm fine. What happened?"

"I had trouble shifting as I went around the curve. Still not good at using my left hand for that." Siobhan stood in front of her, and Katie inhaled a wonderful scent of coconut oil. Siobhan touched Katie's face. "You've got a cut above your eye. I'm so stupid, and I'm even more sorry. Let's get you to my car, and I'll dig out the first-aid kit."

Katie wiped at her face when she realized something warm was dripping down. It wasn't much blood, but she did welcome the chance to sit. She sat in the passenger seat of the Mini Cooper and waited.

Siobhan was back straightaway. "Let me clean this up first." She did and Katie closed her eyes and enjoyed the feel of Siobhan's gentle touch. "There." She placed a plaster over the cut. "How about I take you home?"

"That'd be grand, thanks. Me leg's hurting a bit."

Siobhan settled behind the steering wheel as Katie put on her seatbelt. "Did you hurt it jumping into that ditch?"

Her face was pale, and all Katie wanted to do was smooth the worry away. "Nah. It was a problem well before that. Sometimes I get a bit of pistoning in the socket of my blade. It's been bothering me a couple of days and got worse today. I need to get it adjusted is all."

"Pistoning?"

"Yeah. Means me stump is moving up and down when I walk. Or run."

"Sounds painful." Siobhan finally started the car again, and they were on their way.

Katie shrugged. "You get used to stuff like that. Sometimes I get phantom pains. Not much to be done."

"Phantom pains are where you feel the limb that isn't there anymore, right?"

"Yep. And it's no fun, let me tell you. I get an itch I literally can't scratch. Or my foot will hurt like the devil, but it's not there."

"That can't be nice." Siobhan's attention was on the road, but now and again Katie caught her looking sideways at her. She seemed nervous.

"It's not, but nothing to be done so no sense crying about it. I'm still here, living and breathing. That's all that matters."

"You've got an incredible outlook, Katie. I admire that."

Katie scoffed. "It's not always positive, so you might want to hold off on the admiration. I've been through me share of depression."

"I can't imagine what you've been through, but you have to admit you're strong for being here now, right? I mean, not everyone would be out running every day. I'd say most people would be happy to be walking. But you're out here pushing yourself. That's a big deal."

"You should speak to me dads," Katie said, watching every move Siobhan made. A bit of hair was loose from her ponytail and caressed the side of her face. Katie itched to touch it.

"Are they unhappy that you're running?"

"They're unhappy that I push meself. Just today Dadaí was all fussed that I was running so much. He seems ta think it's too early to be doing another full marathon. But I've been running in half marathons for a year now, and Dublin was my first full marathon in years. I'm ready to do another."

"He's worried you'll hurt yourself?"

"Or that I'll get sick from the stress, or run the race and not finish, or any number of things. It's hard to tell just what, but there you go. He's a dad. It's his job to worry, or so he says."

"My dad worried about me all the time. He got me a cell phone when I hit sixteen and started going to parties and driving a car. He wanted me to be able to call him anytime, anywhere. Plus, he could call me, though he never did."

"Did you have to call him?"

"One time, yes. I went to stay the night with a girl from school. I think I'd just turned sixteen. As always, the cell phone was tucked in my pocket—it was a flip phone." She laughed softly. "My friend didn't tell me her older brother was having a party. Lots of kids around college age. He taught us how to make a screwdriver, and I ended up drinking some of it. Nastiest thing I've ever had.

"The party ended up with a lot of drunk people, which I could handle, but when the drugs started going around, I called my dad. I faked being sick, and he came and got me. No questions asked. I went to bed feeling the most secure I'd ever felt in my life."

"Aw, he must be a wonderful fella."

"He was," Siobhan said, clearing her throat. "He was killed in a car accident ten years ago by some kid texting and driving. I'll never understand what could possibly be so damn important that you have to have your phone grafted to your hand."

"Me either. I have one and only text the family with it and use it for emergencies. I'd rather talk to someone face-to-face, ya know?"

"I agree. Face-to-face is always the best."

"Just one more reason I like you."

Siobhan pulled into the driveway to Katie's home, parked the car, and gave her a sideways glance. "You have other reasons?"

"I do indeed." Katie opened the door and stepped out. "I'd be happy to tell you each and every one of them if you'd fancy having dinner with me tonight."

"Are you asking me on a date?" A smile quirked at the corner of Siobhan's mouth.

"Call it a date if you want, or just dinner. But I like being around you. So, what do you think?"

"I think I'd love to. Text me the time and place. I'll be there."

"Or I could just call you. Better than texting, ya know?"

Siobhan laughed softly. "It is. Are you sure you're okay? Do you need help getting inside?"

"Nah. My wheelchair's in the foyer if I need it, and I'm pretty sure Danny's still home. He'll help me if I need it."

"I'm really sorry —"

"Don't. It was an accident." Katie tapped the gear stick. "Though maybe you want to get some more practice in."

"I promise."

"Great. See you tonight." Katie forced herself not to limp as she headed to the front door. She waved as Siobhan drove away. When she turned to go inside, Danny was standing there with a stupid grin on his face. She waggled her finger at him. "Not a damn word. Not one damn word."

SHIOBHAN TOSSED ASIDE the fifth shirt she'd pulled from her closet. This one was pale blue and one of her favorites. Would Katie like it? This was a date, right? Or just two friends enjoying a meal? Or both?

Why the hell was she so nervous? Siobhan sighed heavily and flopped onto her bed. She'd said yes before her brain had a moment to figure out what was going on. Of course she wanted to go out with Katie. She was fun, smart, adorable...and way out of Siobhan's league. Right?

What exactly was her league, Siobhan wondered? Whatever it was, she doubted women like Katie were part of it. Seemed the only women that ever chose Siobhan were the ones that wanted something from her. Like to be the girlfriend between girlfriends. The woman that they just kept until someone better came along. And someone always did. But not for Siobhan.

Even Susan, whom she thought she had a decent relationship with, went back to her girlfriend, whom she'd never really broken up with in the first place. But Susan was the first woman that Siobhan's mother thought was acceptable. Though she never acknowledged that Siobhan and Susan were lovers, Mary sort of approved because Susan went to her church.

Two years after Susan ripped Siobhan's heart out and stomped on it, Mary was still happily chatting away with her every Sunday. She claimed it was because Susan sat near her during services, and it would be rude not to talk.

Siobhan knew it was because Mary had a better relationship with Susan than she did with her own daughter. Siobhan could probably thank Susan for the fact that Mary, more or less, accepted that she was gay. That was something at least. Unless it came to Brother Bob, who Mary insisted would fix all Siobhan's problems if she'd just give him a chance.

But none of them were here, in Ireland, invited to dinner with a vivacious, adorable woman named Katie. That's where Siobhan's thoughts needed to be. Not on what was left of her dysfunctional life in Indiana.

And hadn't she just recently decided to build her life here before diving into a relationship? If that's even what was happening. Siobhan admitted to being lonely and needing someone to talk to. But was that all she wanted from Katie?

Truth be told, no. She wanted so much more. Despite her earlier promises to herself, despite the fact that she could be making a huge mistake, Siobhan wanted to risk it all. Maybe they'd just be friends. Maybe they'd be more.

She stared at her reflection in the mirror and sighed. "It's all about me now, right?" she asked herself aloud. "I need to concentrate on what I want. Nothing else."

So to hell with it. She wanted to enjoy an evening with Katie, and if it led to more, so be it. If not, that was okay, too.

She resolutely picked up the pale-blue shirt and slipped it on, buttoning it almost to the top. It fit her form perfectly, giving her a nice, girlie figure. She undid a few buttons, exposing her cleavage just a bit more.

Siobhan took a deep breath, tucked her cell phone into her back pocket, grabbed her keys and wallet, and headed out the door.

The restaurant Katie chose was on the opposite side of the village from the pub. Siobhan wondered if she wanted to be away from the prying eyes of her family. What would that be like? Always having brothers and sisters around, bickering, laughing, loving? Siobhan felt a momentary pang of jealousy. But the thought of Mary Landry giving birth to any more children gave her chills. Dysfunctional wouldn't even come close to that particular family environment.

Siobhan entered a place called, simply, Cronin's Restaurant, and stood near the doorway as her eyes adjusted to the lowered lighting. Unlike restaurants back in Indiana, there was no sign that said "Wait to be Seated" or "Hostess Will Be With You Soon." She liked that about Ireland. Very laid back and relaxed. Never in a hurry.

She surveyed the place. It was oblong shaped, as many buildings here were, and it didn't take her long to find Katie seated at a table for two in the center of the restaurant, along a wall of windows that faced the street. She smiled when Katie waved as she joined her.

"No trouble finding the place?" Katie asked.

"None at all. Though I have to admit it's not the only place with Cronin as the name."

"Yeah. Lots of those Cronins in County Cork. Rather like Jones in Wales. They're everywhere."

"Or Smith in the US." Siobhan settled into her seat and took a moment to steal a glance at her date. Katie's hair looked a deeper red than it had been the other day, and she wondered if Katie had dyed it or if it was the play of the dim lights against it. Either way, it was nice. Even the shaved half fit Katie's personality. Like she was showing that there were two parts to her. One full and fun, the other held close to the vest.

Siobhan's gaze moved to the green-and-white rugby shirt with the top three buttons undone, showing the pale skin at the base of Katie's neck. There nestled a necklace with a pendant that Siobhan couldn't quite make out the shape of. It was partially hidden by a small, silver cross.

When she glanced up again, Katie was watching her in what Siobhan perceived was the same way she'd been watching Katie. It made her laugh.

"What's funny?"

Siobhan shook her head and took a sip of water. "It's just...I don't know. Like we're sitting here checking each other out."

Katie leaned forward a little, her eyes never leaving Siobhan's. "I mean, it's okay to look, right? I do admit that I really like what I see."

Siobhan was absolutely certain her face was beet red. Whether from the sudden heat or embarrassment or both, she wasn't sure. She cleared her throat as she tried to form a reply. "Well, I suppose that's okay. I mean, if you like what you see. I'll admit to the same. I mean that I like what I see. I never thought a woman could look so good in a rugby shirt."

Katie smiled, and the corners of her eyes crinkled. "It's me favorite shirt. Ireland national team shirt, actually. But I'm glad you like it. It's comfy, and I wanted to be comfy tonight." She eased her hand across the table until it covered Siobhan's. "I've never been so damn nervous in me life. Da finally made me wear this because I'd gone through half me clothes."

"I have a hard time believing you're nervous."

"Why's that?"

"You seem so confident. You did ask me, remember? Not like I had the confidence to ask you."

"You could have." Katie gave Siobhan's hand a squeeze. "I'd

have said yes."

"I never would have tried. That's just not me."

"No matter. We're here now." She placed a soft kiss across Siobhan's knuckles and released her hand. Siobhan wanted to reach out to continue the contact but didn't. Instead she folded her hands into her lap as a waiter came for their order.

Siobhan let Katie choose for her, not even sure if her stomach would allow her to eat whatever she ended up with.

When the waiter was gone, Katie asked, "So why did you want me to order for ya? I know you can read a menu. I've seen ya do it."

There was a teasing in her voice, and Siobhan smiled. "I'm nervous."

"Don't be. This is just us having dinner. No expectations. I promise. I just want to get to know you better. Is that okay?"

Siobhan nodded, not trusting her voice. And not able to yet trust Katie, even if her heart told her she could. It'd been so very wrong before. But really, what would it hurt to get to know her better? It seemed they already had a lot in common, including the inability to pick appropriate clothing on the first try.

The waiter supplied her with a pint of Guinness. She held hers up to Katie's and said, "To getting to know each other."

"I'll drink to that." Katie tapped her mug to Siobhan's and took a healthy swig of her beer. "So, how are you finding Cúnant? There enough for you to do here? Are you bored yet?"

"Hardly bored," Siobhan said. "I love being close to the water. I've never so much as had a creek nearby. Our home wasn't in a big city, but it was populated enough that it always felt claustrophobic. I don't think I could ever take living in a city. I think I'm suited for village life."

"Same here. Though sometimes I wish a few of my family members would find another place to live." She rolled her eyes and laughed. "And I'd start by kicking my brother all the way to Dublin if I could."

"Which brother?"

"I have to pick? I can't send them all away?"

Siobhan laughed again. "I don't think your parents would like that much. They seem pretty attached to you all. I've seen them with your twin brothers—Danny and Rory. Wasn't Rory the one with the relationship problems with Tabby?"

"You've a good memory. Yep. It'd definitely be Rory. He's a right pain in my arse. And he's not solved a thing with Tabby either. I've a mind to slap him around until he does, but Da won't let me."

"He looks old enough to be able to figure things out for himself."

"Ha. If only that were true. Well, he is twenty-one, but I'm surprised he can tie his own shoes on most days. He hasn't a clue how to treat a woman, even though he's trying very hard to learn. I just feel sorry that Tabby is the one he chose to learn on. She's never been all that confident about herself, and Rory isn't making things easier.

"The other day he spent the entire morning talking to her on the phone—even though she lives three streets away. I heard some of what he was saying, all sweet and lovey. But soon as she showed up at work, he practically ignored her. I don't get him. It's like he's in love with her one minute, and the next he can't stand to be near her."

"Did she talk to him?"

"She tried, and they got into a fight. He said something about not doing things at work, which I can get, but you can't just ignore the poor girl. She doesn't deserve that sort of treatment. I think Dadaí is considering whether or not to fire Rory."

"Wow. He'd fire his son over the waitress?"

"He would. Rory's the problem, not Tabby." Katie took another swig of her Guinness and put the glass down hard enough to slosh the liquid around. "So he'd be the one I'd kick out. Just for being an arse. You're lucky you don't have siblings."

"I don't know about that. I always wished for them. At least one other kid to keep me company. But I think that's why I was so close to my granddad. He always looked after me when Mom and Dad were at work. He was probably the best playmate I could have had anyway. If I'd had to share I probably would have been jealous."

"Are you the jealous type?"

"Depends." Siobhan grinned at her, noting the teasing in her voice. "I can be very damn jealous."

"Hmm. Something to consider then." Katie leaned back as their dinner was served. Irish stew along with a salad and small loaf of brown bread. She closed her eyes, took a sniff of the scent, and opened her eyes. "My dadaí is an excellent cook, but he can't make stew this heavenly. Only Mr. Cronin can. And it makes Dadaí kinda mad."

"It smells delightful." Siobhan also closed her eyes. She crossed herself with a quick prayer, opened her eyes, and dug in. The taste matched the scene perfectly. "I would love to give my compliments to Mr. Cronin. And to you for ordering it."

"It's the only reason I come here," Katie said around a spoonful of stew. "At least twice a month I'm in here for a quiet meal, alone. You're the first person I've brought here in a long time." Her voice took on a wistful tone, and Siobhan wondered who that other person might have been. Perhaps an ex-girlfriend?

"Then I thank you for bringing me here. I might have to come more often. Just don't tell your parents. I get the impression they like it when I come to the pub."

"Of course they like it. You're a regular now, and they miss you if you're not there. Besides, last night Dadaí couldn't stop yammering on about your drawings. Seems he's a fan."

Siobhan blushed again and wished like hell that didn't happen to her so easily. "I'm looking for a place to sell my paintings. Maybe he'll want to buy one, eventually."

"You can hang them in the pub if you want. Put a note in the corner that tells the price and all. We've done that before. Dadaí would love it, though he might buy them all the way he talks about you."

"I'll think about that. Thanks. I don't have anything ready yet, but I hope to by the end of this month. It's not easy to go from my drawings to a painting I'm ready to show the world. I'm very particular."

"Are you too particular to maybe let me take a peek? I've only ever gotten a glance at your work. I'd love to see it sometime. If that's okay with you."

Siobhan thought about that for a moment. She'd never shown her work to a lot of people, though she understood it was good enough to sell. That didn't mean she had the confidence to sell it. But it was, after all, why she'd quit her job and moved to Ireland. The money Granddad left her was meant to keep her going while she built her career as an artist. She had to sell them at some point.

"I'll let you know. I'm always scared to show off my work."

"Scared? Of what? I won't touch them. I promise."

"Oh, that's not it. I'm just worried you won't like them. My mother always said I wasn't very good and should just stick to my day job. She always complained when I spent an entire weekend in my art room working on a painting instead of spending time with her."

"That's not right. My dads would never have done that. They are always right behind each of us to encourage us in whatever we're doing. All parents should be like that."

"My dad was. Granddad always encouraged me, especially when Mom was getting to be too negative for me to handle. He's the whole reason I'm here. He kept trying to get me to leave Indiana and chase my dreams. I only stayed because I couldn't bear leaving him." She wiped away the tears that came every time she spoke of her granddad. "Cancer sucked the life out of him, but not the love. That crazy old man left me everything he had. So I quit, packed up, and moved here."

"Your mom must have been pissed."

"Worse. She's in denial. Thinks I'm going to come home any minute now. I told her I'd applied for a residency permit, but she's not hearing me." Siobhan sighed. "Not much I can do about that. I'm not going back. Well, maybe for a visit, but that's it. I'm here to stay."

Katie's smile nearly split her face, and Siobhan found herself matching it. Katie said, "I like the sound of that. How about a drink to your granddad? May he rest in peace and thanks for bringing you here."

"To Granddad." Siobhan raised her glass, took a sip, and let the smooth Guinness settle her. She'd never spoken so candidly about her family to anyone. Not even Susan. What was it about Katie that made Siobhan feel so comfortable?

"So, what was the job you quit?"

"I'm an art historian. I was working for a local museum as a curator. It was an okay job, paid the bills and all that. But I wanted to be creating art, not cataloguing it."

"Do you feel better now? Doing your dream job as an artist?"

"Freer certainly. I'll have to let you know if it's better once I try to sell my work. I have an appointment later this week with a shop owner to ask if he'll sell a few of my pieces. We'll see." Siobhan's attention was again drawn to the circular pendant on Katie's necklace. "Can I ask what that pendant is? The one behind your cross?"

Katie fingered it for a few seconds before she answered. "It's St. Michael. Patron saint of police."

"Michael—the archangel. Were you a police officer?"

"Garda, yeah. For ten and a half years." Her eyes clouded over as they took on a distant expression. "I dreamed of being a garda since I was a little girl. Never thought of anything else. But after I lost me legs...I guess I could have done office work. They did offer it to me, but it wouldn't have been the same. I wanted to be a garda, on patrol, protecting people. Helping people. Not chained to a desk doing civilian paperwork."

It was Siobhan's turn to take Katie's hand. "I'm sorry. That can't have been easy for you."

"It wasn't. Still isn't. It's been five years now, and I still can't believe I'm not a garda. I have a few mates that I talk to now and again. Some come into the pub, or I see them in the village. Lots of them I see on Facebook, but it's not the same. They're my friends, but I'm not connected to them anymore." She shook her head and pulled her hand back from Siobhan. "It's hard to explain."

"You don't have to," Siobhan said softly. "I've never felt connected to anyone other than my dad and granddad. I can't understand how you feel, but I do understand loss, and I have an inkling that's pretty close to what you're going through."

"Yeah." Katie pushed her bowl to one side. She hadn't finished it, and Siobhan worried their change in topic had taken Katie's appetite.

"So, you run a lot. Is that just to keep in shape?"

A sparkle returned to Katie's eyes. "I'm a marathon runner. Have been since I was sixteen and ran my first race. I'm training for the London Marathon in April."

"Wow. I can't imagine running from here to the pub, much less a marathon. That's like ten kilometers, right?"

"That's not a marathon. A half marathon is twenty-one kilometers, and I've been doing those for about a year. I did my first full marathon in Dublin recently. Forty-two plus kilometers. I barely made it to the finish line, so I've been running a lot more to get my stamina up."

"You're making me tired just thinking about it. But it sounds exciting and something you're passionate about."

Katie shrugged. "After the garda, it's all I have left. I've always been passionate about running. Even before I started racing. I've dreamed of doing all the major races in Europe and America. But that's a ways off. I want to conquer London first."

"I have a feeling the English have no idea there's going to be an Irish invasion."

Katie laughed, and the sound warmed Siobhan's heart. "Maybe you can come with me. Be part of my team. Da always comes with me, but you'd be welcome to join us."

"Consider me there. But right now, I'd love to know what's for dessert."

Katie choked on her drink, her face turning red as she caught her breath. "Uh, well, I hadn't—I mean I'm not sure—you like ice cream?"

Siobhan laughed. "Who doesn't?"

"Good. They have homemade vanilla that's amazing. Let's get some of that. Okay?"

"As long as you don't choke on it."

Katie was still coughing but smiled anyway. "I'll do me best."

TWO HOURS LATER, Katie accompanied Siobhan back to her flat. It wasn't especially cold out, and for once they had a nice, clear night sky. Katie enjoyed the evening so much she didn't want it to end. A few years ago, she'd have done her best to get Siobhan to invite her to stay the night. Truth be told, she wasn't even sure she'd be able to do it. She hadn't been with anyone since the incident that took her legs. How would Siobhan act if they started to make love? Would she be repulsed by her stumps?

Would Katie even remove her prosthetics?

Would it all be so awkward that they'd lose the moment?

Did Katie want to set herself up for failure?

"Penny for your thoughts." Siobhan's soft voice stopped Katie's ridiculous ruminations.

"Sorry. I was thinking of how much fun I've had tonight."

"Fun? Really?"

Katie stopped her with a touch on her arm. She found herself mesmerized by Siobhan's eyes and the openness she found there. "Of course. You're an amazing woman, Siobhan Landry. Don't let anyone tell you otherwise."

"Thanks. I had a nice time, too." She started walking again. Her hand brushed against Katie's, and in an instant Katie found their fingers wrapped around each other. It was a gentle, intimate touch that sent shivers through her body.

Katie was quiet until they reached Siobhan's door. She didn't release Siobhan's fingers as she took her free hand and cupped the side of Siobhan's face. Their lips met in a tentative kiss, from which they both pulled back a fraction of an inch before coming together again in a full-on proper kiss that left Katie senseless.

When the kiss ended, Katie was at a loss. She didn't want to stop but knew instinctively she had to. But the passion was there in Siobhan's expression. While they weren't going to act on it now, Katie knew Siobhan felt the same way she did.

They gazed at each other for forever before Siobhan leaned forward to give Katie one last kiss. She said, "I need to get to bed.

I want to get up before dawn so I can sketch the sun as it comes over the sea."

"Then I'll let you go. Maybe I'll see you on my morning run."

"I hope so." Siobhan ran a finger along Katie's swollen lips. "I so very much hope so."

"Good night, Siobhan." Katie released her hand and stepped back.

Siobhan opened the door and moved partially into the hallway. "Good night, Katie." Then she closed the door.

Katie leaned against the side of the building and sighed. Her fingers retraced where Siobhan had touched her moments ago, and she closed her eyes to replay the kiss in her mind. No words came to her that could describe how she was feeling, but she knew, deep down, that Siobhan was unlike any woman she'd ever met.

Chapter Six

SIOBHAN STARED AT the blank canvas with a look that could wither a flower. Her palette was ready. The photo she'd taken at the beach yesterday rested on a tiny easel on the window sill. The vibrant blues and greens of the sea's waters lapped over the dirty-tan sand and rocks with a gentle, yet forceful motion. It should be sparking her creativity. She should have a paintbrush in her hand already.

Even her perfect memory of the changing colors of the tide as the sun rose to its full glory wasn't helping her. She wanted to paint. But her brain simply said, "No."

She put her palette away, took off her dad's old shirt that she wore to paint in, and left her studio. She wasn't going to spend an entire day trying to figure out how to put the picture in her head onto the canvas. That either happened or it didn't, and staring at it only gave her a headache.

Besides, the one thing she was for sure able to think about was Katie. They'd had such a wonderful time the other night, and Siobhan could spend hours replaying that first kiss. Katie touched a part of her that no one ever had, not even Susan, and it scared her a little. That's probably why she'd avoided the rocks along the path that Katie took on her run. She was hiding.

But why?

Katie was sweet and kind and considerate. Attributes she couldn't give to her previous girlfriends.

At well past noon, Katie wouldn't be on her run. Siobhan decided to try the pub. Katie spent a lot of time there, and if she wasn't there, her dads would know where she was. Seemed they kept careful track of her, though Siobhan didn't think Katie noticed it.

She looked forward to seeing Katie as she stepped closer to the pub.

As if the fates were laughing at her, Siobhan's phone rang. She knew instinctively who it was. "Good morning, Mom," she said.

"Is it morning there? I thought it would be later."

"It's morning for you." Siobhan glanced at the time on her phone. "And it's pretty damn early. Why do you need to be up at seven? You're never up before nine."

"I have an early dentist appointment. No big deal, but I think he's going to have to give me another filling. That means drilling, and that means pain medication. You know I react badly to that shot they give you, so I asked Susan to take me. She'll be here in about ten minutes."

Siobhan nearly stumbled down the steps as she left her apartment. "Susan's taking you? Why can't you drive?"

"I always feel woozy after they inject that stuff in my gums. So I told her if she'd drive me, we'll make a stop at Bob Evans's for breakfast then maybe go to Walmart to get a few things."

"You aren't supposed to eat so soon after getting a filling, are you?" Siobhan asked, trying to gloss over the fact that her ex was driving her mother around.

"I can eat as long as I don't chew on that side of my mouth. I've done it before."

"Okay. Well, I hope it all goes well then." Siobhan shivered when the wind picked up a bit as she walked to the pub. "I'm heading out for a late lunch right now."

"Oh, Susan just pulled in. Do you want to talk to her?"

"Seriously? No. You know I don't. I'm sorry, Mom. I'll call you tomorrow to see how you're doing." Siobhan hung up, even though Mary was still speaking. She shoved the phone back into her pocket and walked faster. She just wanted to be someplace where the people were nice to her and maybe even appreciated her. She was rounding the corner to the pub when the phone rang again. She didn't bother to see who it was when she answered and said, "I told you I don't want to talk to her."

"Her who?" Katie's voice was a welcome surprise. "Someone bothering you?"

"Just my mom. Sorry. I thought she was calling back. She's got some crazy idea I might want to talk to my ex-girlfriend."

"Would you fancy talking to me instead?"

"Any time."

"Good. I'm at the pub."

Siobhan smiled as she opened the pub doors and spotted Katie leaning on the bar. "So am I."

Katie smiled back, strode up to Siobhan, and kissed her before she was completely inside the building. Katie helped her out of her coat and hung it up. She escorted Siobhan to a table near the back and sat beside her so they both faced the front of the pub.

"That was a nice welcome."

"I was hoping to see you. Been a couple of days." Katie held

Siobhan's hand and rubbed her thumb over Siobhan's fingers. "I was missing you."

"You were?" Siobhan knew she sounded weirdly naïve, but it really did surprise her. "That's so sweet."

Katie shrugged and turned in her chair to face Siobhan. Her lips were soft as they met Siobhan's for another kiss, this one gentle, more intimate. "I meant what I said. I've not seen you the last two days."

"I was trying to paint." Siobhan had to look away from those intense eyes. Katie wasn't bothering to hide her passion, and it made Siobhan want to respond to it. In the back of a pub certainly wasn't the place. Her mind might be on the cautious side, but her body damn sure wasn't.

"What're you working on?"

"A seascape, but no matter what, it just isn't there. I finally gave up today and decided to come here." She glanced at Katie, who had a bemused look on her face. "I was hoping to find you so we could spend some time together."

"Great minds," Katie said and kissed the top of her hand. "Would ya like to eat something first? I can go to the kitchen and get it all made up for you."

"That'd be great. I skipped breakfast."

"That's bad." Katie stood up and lightly smacked Siobhan's hand as if she were a little kid. "That's not allowed in the O'Briain house. Breakfast is the most important meal of the day."

"So I've heard," Siobhan said with a laugh.

"I'll bring you a bit extra out. Have anything in mind?"

"Bread and stew would be awesome."

"Fancy a pint to wash it down?" Katie asked.

"I do. I'd like to wash down more than the food with it, though. Might even need two pints."

"I'll help you sort that through, Siobhan. You won't need the second pint." She released Siobhan's hand and headed for the kitchen.

Siobhan watched her go, enjoying the sway of her hips as she walked. It was hard to believe the legs she used weren't her own.

"Hi there." A young girl, maybe about twelve or so, stood next to the table. Her long red hair was tied in a ponytail, which lay across one shoulder. It obscured the breast pocket of her navy blue jacket, but Siobhan could still recognize the logo of the local secondary school. The girl wore the requisite white, button-down shirt under the jacket and a skirt that matched the navy blue and came down to just above her knees. She looked at Siobhan with a curious expression on her face. Siobhan wondered if they'd met before.

"Hi. I'm Siobhan."

"I know. I'm Kyra."

"Kyra. Nice to meet you." Siobhan held out her hand, and Kyra took it. Her grip was surprisingly strong.

"You're going out with my sister, Katie."

Had Katie mentioned Kyra's name before? Siobhan couldn't recall. "I did. We had a lot of fun, too."

"But you never called her back. Two days now. You have to call her. She likes you a lot, and you need to make sure you tell her if you like her back or not. If you don't, then tell her now."

Whoa. Siobhan wasn't ready for this. What a precocious kid. And a kid that looked like she meant every word she said and maybe rehearsed saying them.

Siobhan started to reply when Katie came over with a pint of Guinness in each hand. She looked from Kyra to Siobhan and back again as if trying to assess the situation. She put the pints down and took her seat next to Siobhan.

"Kyra, why are you here? You should be in school."

"Short day," she said in way of an explanation. Her eyes never left Siobhan's. "I'm waiting for an answer."

Siobhan narrowed her gaze, but the kid didn't back down. "I like her, and I promise not to go so long without Katie knowing why. Fair enough?"

Kyra's expression softened just a little. "Fair enough. For now." She turned on her heels and went through the doors to the kitchen.

Katie let out a nervous laugh. "Well, it seems you've passed Kyra's test. Didn't know she had one, though, or I'd have warned you first."

"She surprised me. I'd say your sister cares a great deal about you and your relationships. She's very protective."

"She's twelve and still trying to decide if she's a little kid or an adult. I don't see her going through puberty for very long. She's gonna go right to adult, that one. Did she bother you?"

"No. I think it's adorable how much she loves her big sister."

Katie's expression showed her indulgence. "I guess so. Now, let's have a drink, and you can tell me all about your mom's issues with your ex."

"You have all day?"

Katie took a swig of her pint and smiled. "I do indeed."

"Susan is the daughter I never was, I guess. Attentive, compliant, always at my mother's beck and call. I can't even begin to understand why, but they're like two peas in a pod."

"Did you and your ma have a falling out?"

"Sort of. A couple of times, actually. She was never close to her father, my granddad Fergus, and resented how close he and I were. She was his only child, so I'm his only grandkid. Mom says he spoiled me and that made her mad."

"Of course he spoiled you," Katie said with a smile. "That's what grandparents are supposed to do. I think it's a law."

Siobhan laughed. "Maybe. I guess she eventually got over that but didn't like that I spent so much time taking care of Grandma when she was sick, then, in turn, taking care of Granddad. She kept telling me I have my own life to live and shouldn't have to be stuck with the responsibility of taking care of my grandparents." Siobhan paused to take a swig of beer. "But who else was going to do it? My dad would have, but he died a few months before Grandma got sick. I never understood how my mother could be so uncaring about her own parents."

"Did something happen between them? Did they not approve of your da or something?"

"Don't know. Mom won't speak of it, and Granddad said it was her story to tell. Far as I understood, they didn't have any problems with my dad. But I don't think I'd have noticed if they did anyway.

"But then, just to make her life more miserable, I told my mom I'm gay. Granddad, bless his soul, told me he already knew and was happy I'd figured it out. Mom—well, she yelled a lot. And loud enough for the neighbors to hear it."

"And you still talk to her?"

"I do. She's my mother. Even if she thinks my being gay is a phase, or that when I find a man I won't want a woman anymore, she's still my mother and I'm all she has in the way of family. Except for Susan."

"Ah, Susan. The ex." Katie reached across the table and took Siobhan's hand in hers. "The blind woman."

"Blind?"

"Oh, yes. Blind because she clearly didn't see what she had in you." Katie pressed a light kiss on the back of Siobhan's hand. "You're a treasure, Siobhan. You've got a heart of gold and it's Susan's loss for sure. Your ma spending time with her is mad."

"I know, right? It's like they're best friends. And Susan is just as gay as I am. She's back with her ex—I was the in-between woman—and happy as can be, from what I've heard from Mom.

She doesn't seem bothered by Susan's sexual preferences. Only mine."

"You're her kid. I'd say it's different with you."

"Maybe. But does she have to be all close to the woman that broke my heart? I mean, I'm over it now. It's been a few years, but it still smarts that she's so damn close to Susan."

"Maybe you need to tell her that."

Siobhan considered that for all of two seconds. "No way. It'd open up a whole new can of worms. Bad enough I have to go there in December for some stupid dinner with Mom's church cronies. I don't think I could stand being there with her all pissed at me."

"You're in a right pickle then." Katie kissed her hand again. "I don't know your ma, but I can see it's bothering you. I understand that you don't want to get her angry, but I still think talking to her is the best idea. You have to get it off your chest."

Siobhan sat back and sighed. Katie was right. She had to stand up to her mother. At some point, she needed to let Mary know that her actions hurt her more than her words ever could. Siobhan didn't want to alienate the only family she had left, but did she really have a choice?

She did and that choice was almost too much to think about. Continue to be a coward, or stand up to Mary. Coward equals easy. Standing up equals hard.

"I can see your brain is working very diligently on this." Katie held both of Siobhan's hands. "Have a think. It's not like you have to choose right now or even today. But I believe you'll have to say something to your ma eventually. And when you do, I'll be right here."

"Right here?" Siobhan asked. "In the pub? By my side? At your house?"

Katie laughed softly. "Wherever you need me to be."

"Right now I need you to be taking me for a wander. Having you by my side will be very nice."

"Consider it done."

THEY HELD HANDS during their stroll through the village. Katie enjoyed pointing out buildings and landmarks to Siobhan. She was genuinely interested, and Katie was proud to show off her home. They stopped near the bakery beside a statue of a famous rugby player. Katie pointed to the plaque, which was in Irish.

"Think you can read that?"

Siobhan let go of her hand and squatted in front of it. The plaque and statue were bronze, and the sunlight shone off the metal enough that Siobhan needed to get closer to read the words. She carefully said them aloud, then translated. "Seamus O'Connor, son of Cúnant, best something to walk the earth. He died in 2013 aged sixty-seven."

"That was pretty close. The 'something' is a scrum-half, and he was magic to watch. Da and me would catch every game on TV and go to the local matches when he had time off. Seamus played for Limerick most of his career and made five caps with the national team."

Siobhan had the look on her face of someone trying to puzzle out how to fly a space ship.

"Sorry. Rugby, if you haven't already figured out, is the most amazing sport in the world. Rather like your football—only our players don't need to wear protection."

Siobhan laughed. "I've heard that before. Not much protection worn in baseball, except for the catcher and the plate ump. We're going to have to watch a game together so you can explain stuff to me. It's the only way I'll ever learn."

"There's one on TV tonight. We'll have dinner at the pub, and I'll be your guide to the greatest sport on earth." Katie took Siobhan's hand and pulled her closer. "Then we'll go to the castle and snog a bit on that really comfy settee."

Despite the laughter, Katie managed to get several, sweet, loving kisses out of Siobhan.

"So, are all rugby players as big as this guy?" She pointed to the statue.

It wasn't exactly life-sized, but it was easy to see how strong Seamus was. His muscle definition was that of someone who could win weight-lifting competitions.

"Most, yeah. They need to be. It's not a gentle sport. I used to play before..." She hesitated, hating to always end up reminding herself, or others, what she could no longer do. "Anyway, my team was made up of women gardai. We played to raise money for charity, but that didn't stop us from being highly competitive. I got a few good knocks in, let me tell ya. Broke my wrist three times. The dads always asked me to take it easy, but how do you do that in a full contact sport?"

"So you ignored them?"

"Of course. To be fair, they've always been looking out for me that way. I never sat still for more than ten minutes as a kid. I climbed anything I thought I could, no matter how high it was, and got into everything I saw. Didn't matter if there was a bull on the other side of the fence, if I wanted to go see what was there, I was off and running. And the dads couldn't keep up with me."

"Sounds like you were a holy terror," Siobhan said.

"Maybe. I don't remember it like that, of course. Just me exploring what was around us. I'm surprised I wasn't always wearing one of those harnesses they sometimes put little kids in to keep them from running off."

"Would you have run off and out of their sight?"

"Always. I've been curious my whole life. When I was about Kyra's age, Da said he thought I'd be an engineer since I was always taking electronic stuff apart. Problem was that I didn't always put it back together in working order. Or any order." She grinned at one particular memory of her da's face when he saw the remains of their new toaster.

"Sounds like you had quite the adventure growing up. Were you always in this village?"

"Outside it. Da built a house on some land he inherited. He rents it to the man that works his sheep in the field next to it. Da owns about twenty acres and figured it should go to good use. I can show you if you'd like. It's about a twenty-minute walk."

"Are you up for it? We've been walking for a few hours now."

Katie wanted to be angry at the question but held her tongue. There was no distance she couldn't walk or run if she felt like doing it. "Why wouldn't I be?" She regretted the question when it left her lips. The expression on Siobhan's face told her how innocent her comment had been.

"I'm sorry. I didn't mean anything by it other than I don't—I mean I thought maybe you'd be tired."

"I'll let you know when that happens, okay?"

"Sure." Siobhan released Katie's hand and took a half step away from her.

"Good." Katie started toward their old house, letting the grumpy feeling grow as they walked. Siobhan was a sweet woman, but what a daft thing to say! Was she up for it? Seriously? Had the woman not seen her walking through the village all afternoon? Had she not seen her running just the other day? Did Katie look suddenly tired? Where the hell had that come from?

They got to the dirt road that would take them to the house, and Katie stopped. It did no good to spend her time brooding, such as she was. She turned to Siobhan, and her heart sank at the obviously hurt expression she was sporting.

"Ever since I got home from the hospital, people have tried to treat me like I'm a little kid or an old, invalid lady. I learned to walk on these damn things and managed to finish a bleedin' marathon, and still people ask me if I have any stamina. Well, I do. I have lots of it. I'm still an athlete. I work out every morning, run my distance, eat well. I'm no different from anyone else apart from the very obvious. Anyone that sees me with pants on thinks I'm a regular person. You did, until you saw me running. I get so tired of people treating me with kid gloves."

"That's not what I meant at all," Siobhan said at a moment when Katie wasn't quite done with her speech. "Is it so bad that people care about you? That they think your health should be above other things? Even things you think you can handle? I can see you're a strong woman, physically, but that doesn't mean I can't be concerned. It was a simple question."

"One that I hear every day of my life, Siobhan. I'm just tired of it."

"I don't doubt that you are, but it's not a question I've ever asked you. How was I to know it was a sensitive subject? Katie, if we're going to continue this relationship, we can't be snipping at each other like this. You have to talk to me. Tell me the things that bother you so I can avoid pushing your buttons. I don't want to do that. I genuinely wanted to know you weren't overtired and pushing yourself. Just let me in, okay?"

Katie took a long, deep breath to center herself. She was, as usual, overreacting. This was not how she planned to start their relationship.

"I'm sorry. Can we start this over? I don't want us fighting already."

"We're not fighting." Siobhan took hold of her hand. "We're discussing. And now that we've stopped walking, should I be guessing that we're here?"

"We are indeed. How 'bout I show you around. If Daniel's home, I'll see if it's okay to visit the sheep."

"You visit sheep?"

"I do. I've even got my favorites, and if they're not too far afield, he'll let us go in to see them. Trust me. It's fun."

"I never thought I'd go visiting sheep. I mean, it's not like you can't see dozens of them around every corner."

"True, but it's different when you can see their faces and how sweet they can be. A little skittish around new people, but it'll be fine. You'll see."

DANIEL O'HEARNE LOOKED older than Siobhan expected. He was a bit taller than her with broad shoulders and thick silver-gray hair. His hands dwarfed hers when he took hold of them for a hearty shake. His fingers were thick and pudgy, much like the rest of him. But his greyish eyes were kind and his gap-toothed smile charming.

"So, ya'd like to have a bit of a look at the sheep, eh?" Daniel's accent was much thicker than Katie's, and it took some getting used to.

Siobhan said, "I've never seen a sheep up close before. I grew up in a small town, but the only farm animals in the area were cows and horses. Never got too close to them either."

"More's the pity," Daniel said. "The flock is in the east pasture. You girls feel free ta visit 'em. I need ta get ta town for some feed."

And with that, he headed for his truck and left them alone. Katie took Siobhan's hand and guided her to a metal gate, which she opened and gestured her to walk through. "They're not far away. Probably just got fed so they'll be content. I think you'll like this."

"Does Daniel raise them for slaughter?"

"Oh no. He's too kind hearted. Just keeps them for the wool. Sells a few now and again to other farmers for breeding, but that's it. He won't sell to a farmer that raises them for meat."

"Awesome. So, let's go pet some sheep."

The herd, as Daniel said, was close by. Katie approached them and was greeted by Nate, Daniel's border collie. He recognized Katie instantly and made soft snuffing noises as he danced around her legs. She rubbed his ears and neck then let him get acquainted with Siobhan.

Katie was genuinely shocked when Nate slathered doggie kisses all over Siobhan's face.

Siobhan giggled and gently pushed him away, while using the sleeve of her jacket to wipe away the slobber. "Friendly guy."

"I've never seen him do that. You must have a way with animals or a scent he really likes."

"Well, I guess I've always been a magnet for animals, but really. He almost French kissed me."

Katie joined in on the giggling. "I'd have made ya brush yer teeth before I kiss you again if he'd done that."

"Oh really?" Siobhan stared at Katie with one hand on her hip. "You don't want to kiss me right now?"

The look on Siobhan's face melted any resolve Katie had. How could she look so damn sexy after wiping dog slobber off her face? Her eyes issued a clear challenge, and Katie wasn't one to back down.

She cupped her hands around Siobhan's face and kissed her for all she was worth. When done, it left them both a little breathless. "You were sayin'?"

"Um, I forget?"

"Was that a question or a statement?"

"Both." Siobhan touched her fingers to Katie's lips and sighed. "I don't believe anyone has ever kissed me like you do, Katie."

"I'll take that as a compliment."

"And you should."

Katie felt her cheeks heating with a blush and turned away. "So, let's go pet some sheep, shall we?"

KATIE WAS LATCHING the gate when Daniel returned. She offered to help him unload his truck, but he declined. He always wanted to do everything on his own.

"So, you're the American I hear folks yammerin' about in town," Daniel said to Siobhan. "Heard you're a Byrne. That true?"

Siobhan gave him a sweet smile. "My grandda said it's true. He was Fergus Byrne."

"D'ya know if his ma was named Aileen?"

"She was. She and her husband, Galvin, moved to the states when my granddad was young."

"I think I'm yer cousin. My ma was a Byrne and had a brother named Galvin. Died in '75 I'm thinking."

"That sounds right. Aileen died in the early '80s. Wow. This is so cool." Siobhan sported a grin from ear to ear. "I always wondered if I had family over here."

"Oh, girlie, ya got plenty to go around. I got four boys of me own and six brothers and sisters. Let me just say we have enough little ones to start our own village," Daniel said with a hearty laugh. "Let me tell the missus about you. She'll be wanting to set up a party."

"Wow. Just...wow. I can hardly believe this is happening."

"Believe it," Katie whispered. To Daniel she said, "We can

have it at the pub so Briana doesn't need to do anything. What do ya think?"

"I think that's a grand idea. I'll talk to her tonight." He pulled out a cell phone. "I assume you have one of these damn things?"

Siobhan exchanged numbers with Daniel. "I can't tell you how much this means to me, Daniel. Granddad would have been so excited to know about you and your family. He really missed Ireland, and it took him years to get me to come over here. I just wish he was still around."

"I'm surely sorry he's not, Siobhan. But we'll have a drink to him at the party." Daniel tucked his phone into the pocket of his jeans. "Now, if you ladies will excuse me, I best be tendin' to the flock. I'll call you tomorrow, Katie, and set things up. Okay?"

"It's a deal." Katie gave him a handshake, and when she stepped back, was surprised to see Daniel wrap Siobhan into a bear of a hug. She'd never seen him do that with his own kids, much less a stranger.

"Welcome home, Siobhan," Daniel said. "It's good to have you here."

"Thanks." She kissed his stubble-filled cheek, and he headed for the field.

Katie took Siobhan's hand to lead her back to town. "That was...weird. First, I don't think I've heard him say so many words unless he was watching football and had a couple of pints first. Second, it's just amazing that he's part of your family here. And he hugged you! That never happens. I don't think I've even seen him kiss his wife."

"Sounds like there's a third thing coming."

Katie laughed. "The third thing is that I need to call Cassie and find out if she's a cousin, too. Before you know it, you'll find out you're related to half the county."

"As long as I'm not related to you — by blood I mean."

Katie squeezed her hand. "Well, tenth cousins would be acceptable I think."

"Okay, but anything closer, and we'll have to call off the whole relationship," Siobhan said with a silly grin.

Katie stopped her long enough to give her a repeat of their heated kiss. "Shame. I rather like kissing you."

"Hmm, me, too. Well, if we are related it'll be our secret. Right?"

"Right, weirdo."

"Weirdo? You calling me a weirdo?" Siobhan said with fake indignation.

"That I am."

"Take it back."

"Nope." Katie bit her lip to keep from smiling. "I call them like I see them. And you, dear Siobhan, are a weirdo."

"Uh, I'm not the one that goes around petting sheep."

"No, you just get French kisses from dogs."

"He did not! I stopped him before he got too enthusiastic."

"Sure. That's your side of the story. Perhaps I should ask Nate."

Siobhan hip-checked her as they grew closer to the village. "You do that. And while you're interrogating a dog, I'll be talking to Daniel to get some dirt on you. After all, he's known you for years. There's got to be something interesting he can tell me."

"You think so?"

"I do."

"Well, good luck with that. Doubt he'll remember much."

"Wonder what his wife knows."

Katie stopped walking then. Briana wasn't much of a gossip, but sure and certain she'd let loose some tales about Katie as a girl. Briana was a good ten years her senior, but they'd spent a lot of time together off and on through the years. Would she think of something embarrassing to tell Siobhan? Hell, was there anything embarrassing to tell? Katie didn't think so. Well, she hoped not.

"Ah-ha. Finally got a reaction out of you. Okay, so whatever I can't get Colm to tell me, I can probably get out of Briana. Noted."

"Wait, what? You've been talking to dadaí? 'Bout what?"

"You. Lots and lots of stuff about you." Siobhan walked on and Katie had to jog a few feet to catch up.

"I had no idea. What does he say?"

"I'm not giving up what I know." Siobhan wound her arm around Katie's waist, and the closeness felt so right that Katie found herself returning the gesture. Siobhan said, "He's a good listener, too. I don't think I've ever had an easier time talking to someone—except for you."

"Good to know," Katie said. They'd reached the pub, and it looked to be filling up. The rugby match would soon be starting. "Still want to learn about rugby?"

"Buy me a pint, and I'll learn anything you want to teach me."

Katie grinned as they walked into the pub, thinking of a lot of stuff she'd like to teach Siobhan—and it involved them both being naked. She shook those thoughts and planted Siobhan at the bar, near the TV. "I'll get that pint, and you'll get to learning about rugby."

Siobhan rubbed her hands together with glee. "Bring it on."

Chapter Seven

KATIE TIMED HER run the next morning so she would be at the top of the hill by sunrise. She hoped to find Siobhan seated on the rock, as she had been before. But once Katie got there, she was disappointed. Siobhan was nowhere to be found.

Katie even jogged to the rock to be sure.

No sign of her. Her good mood fell as she returned to the path and finished her run.

She was coming up the driveway to the castle when her mobile rang.

It was Rory. She almost didn't answer but knew he'd just keep calling if she didn't.

"Hello, Rory. What's going on?"

"Where are you?"

"In the driveway."

He disconnected and was suddenly running to her like he was being chased by the hounds of hell. "You didn't answer your phone."

"I didn't hear it. Don't always get a signal when I run. What's going on with you?"

"I need your help," he said as he walked beside her. Though walked wasn't a good description. More like he paced, taking two or three steps to her every one.

"Rory, you're my brother and I love you, but I can't keep cleaning up your messes. You're gonna have to learn how to deal with women all on your own."

"Women? No, that's not the problem."

Katie stopped and stared at him. "That's always the problem."

"Not this time. Well, maybe a little, but that's for later. This is much, much bigger."

"I'm going to beat you about the head and face if ya don't tell me what the hell you're yammerin' about."

Rory bit his bottom lip, something he did when he wasn't sure what to say. Sometimes he did it right before he lied.

Katie held up her hand. "You best tell me the truth, or you'll be wearing my leg up your arse."

He seemed to consider that then followed her to the front door. He was silent until they got there. "Just remember one thing. It wasn't my idea."

"What—"

He opened the door, and the second she stepped in, Katie was greeted with a chorus of "Surprise!"

Streamers adorned the entry hall, and Jamie was right there with her chair that was also decorated with green-and-red streamers and balloons tied to the handles. He was grinning like an idiot and rolled over to her. "Sit down, Katie, love."

"Da, this is not—"

"Up for debate," he whispered to her as she settled into the chair. "It's your birthday, and you will have fun. Most of the family is here, love." He knelt beside her and waited for her to look him in the eyes. "Katie, five years ago we almost lost you. Every year we can celebrate your birth is a miracle. Please, for once let us be happy and love you. Okay?"

She wiped at the sudden tears and nodded, unable to conjure any words.

Her younger siblings rushed forward for hugs and laughs, taking over the handles to her chair and wheeling her farther inside, where she was immediately mobbed by the crowd of family and friends.

As they moved her down the long entry hall, she spotted a very familiar face at the end. Siobhan was wearing a party hat, slightly askew, and had a drink of some kind in her hand. She was laughing and talking to Mrs. Kerry.

"Well there she is," Mrs. Kerry said. She waved the kids away and stooped to give Katie a kiss on the cheek. "I was thinking you fell into the sea you were gone so long."

"Had I known you lot were here waiting for me, I'd have been gone longer," Katie said with a smile. "Thanks, Mrs. Kerry. You know I appreciate you coming over. Why don't you sit down awhile? You look tired."

Mrs. Kerry straightened and groaned a little as she sat. She winked at Siobhan. "Always looking out for everyone else, that one is. 'Bout time she let someone else watch out for her."

"Someone needs to watch over you, Mrs. Kerry. Why on earth are you all here so early? It's just past eight. I don't think I've ever seen Rory up before noon."

Mrs. Kerry laughed heartily. "That boy wasn't up and about when I got here. Me and Colm did the decoratin' before he ever opened his eyes. When he did and found out yer dads set up a surprise party, he nearly fainted. Started phonin' you straightaway."

"Ah, that explains things then. He was worried I'd be angry at you all for doing it. I was, the last time they tried this."

Mrs. Kerry patted her hand, her kind smile touching Katie's heart. "You're a dear one, love. We all care about you, so you make sure you let your dads celebrate when they want ta. It surely makes them feel better."

"I will."

Mrs. Kerry carefully got up, giving her body time to stretch enough so she was mostly standing straight. "Now I'm off to the kitchen to see what kind of mess Colm's made. Sweet man never could cook an egg right."

Katie smiled as she watched Mrs. Kerry wander into the kitchen.

"So, are you okay?" Siobhan asked.

"Aside from hating surprise birthday parties, yes. Why?"

"You're in your chair." Siobhan pointed out.

Katie touched the wheels with her gloved hands. "I might've overdone it a bit on me run today. Or yesterday." She absently rubbed her left stump, which hurt more than the right. "It happens sometimes."

"Is that why Jamie got you to sit down?"

"It is. He saw the blisters yesterday and got a bit fussed about it. I just didn't feel up to arguing with him with all the people around."

"Is there anything I can do to make you feel better?"

Katie seriously considered that, but swallowed back her first retort. Which was to ask Siobhan to kiss the wounds to make them better. She wasn't so sure Siobhan wouldn't run off once she saw the ugly blisters on top of the even uglier scarring.

"No. I need to get the blades off and take a shower. But that can wait." She saw the worry in Siobhan's eyes and reached for her hand. They needed a change in subject. "So, I guess I now know why I didn't see you on me run this morning."

Siobhan seemed to accept the change and said, "I had planned on being there, but I overslept. I went to the pub to wait for you to finish your run and ended up here helping to decorate. You could have told me today is your birthday."

Katie shrugged. "It's nothing special."

Siobhan squatted beside her so they were eye-level. "Bullshit. Every birthday is special, Katie. My granddad always said it was God's way of gifting you another year." She leaned closer and kissed Katie on the cheek. "Suck it up and enjoy yourself."

"You sound like me da."

"Your da is a smart man." She nodded in Jamie's direction. "And he warned me you'd be grumpy. I thought I could cheer you up." She sighed a bit dramatically. "Guess I was wrong."

Siobhan started to stand, but Katie grabbed her wrist and cupped her other hand around Siobhan's cheek. "Don't. I want you here. I promise. It's just a hard day for me." She pulled Siobhan gently toward her until their lips met in a sweet kiss. Were it not for the rowdy crowd, Katie might have pressed for more, but she released Siobhan instead.

"You want to talk about it?" Siobhan asked, her eyes searching for an answer.

"I don't think I've talked much about it. To anyone."

"It's okay. Just know that I'm here when you feel up to it. Okay?"

Katie nodded when words failed her. How did she get so lucky to meet a woman like Siobhan? Had Fiona ever been so kind to her? She must have, at one point or another. Otherwise, why did she spend six years of her life with the woman? Hard to believe that all the time she invested in their relationship fell apart in a matter of hours.

"Earth to Katie." Siobhan's expression turned to concern. "You okay? Did I say something wrong?"

Katie took Siobhan's hand in hers and placed a kiss across her fingers. "No. It's not you. Just an unpleasant memory."

Siobhan stood but didn't release her hand. "Then tuck it away for now. It's time to have some fun. You've got a castle full of people that want to see you and celebrate."

"Well, I'd prefer to celebrate after a shower and maybe something to eat. I can't believe they got so many people here this early in the day."

"Colm told me they've been planning it for weeks. He was so excited when I stopped by the pub earlier."

"He loves a party," Katie said.

"So I see. Go get your shower. I'll be here when you're done." Siobhan kissed her and pointed Katie toward her bedroom. "Maybe you'll let me take you out someplace nice for dinner? Someplace not in Cúnant?"

"Do you have any suggestions?"

Siobhan pulled a slip of paper from her pocket and waved it around. "Your da gave me some."

"Figures. I'll be back in a bit." Katie greeted a few people and steered her way to her room.

She made quick work of getting a shower and clean clothes,

anxious to return to Siobhan. For the first time in years, her birth-day was turning out to be fun. Not that she wasn't going to have a chat with her dads about this surprise party nonsense. But with Siobhan there, she found it all tolerable.

Siobhan was waiting outside her bedroom door, a big grin on her face. "That's more like it. Now, let's go mingle. You've got people to introduce me to."

Siobhan started to push her back into the fray, but Katie stopped her. "Wait. How do I introduce you? As my friend? Or— or as my girlfriend?"

Siobhan's laughter was gentle and sweet, and it made Katie blush even more than when she posed her question. "You're adorable, you know that? And after the kisses you gave me last night, I think we could safely use the 'g' word."

The smile didn't fit her face as Katie let Siobhan push her toward a mass of people. Her heart swelled, and for the first time in years, her birthday didn't suck.

"ARE YOU SURE you're good to drive," Katie asked for the fifth time.

Siobhan stumbled with the gears, again, but finally found first and took off. "I'm fine. No drinking at the party, or at lunch, or after lunch at the pub."

"I wasn't concerned about the drinking. I meant your, um, issue with driving on the left."

"Oh that." Siobhan flashed back to her near disastrous acci-dent with Katie and a ditch and grimaced. "I've been practicing. It's the shifting that's the problem. The gears are all backwards from what I'm used to. Well, not backwards, just that I feel like I'm shifting backwards. It's hard to explain."

"You ought to find an automatic."

"I asked the garage owner who sold me this one to be on the lookout. He laughed but promised I'd have first dibs."

"What garage?"

"Don't be surprised, but it was Cronin's Garage on the north end of the village."

"I'd be surprised if it was O'Malley's on the south end. I'd make you take this thing back right now if that were the case. But Cronin is good, and if he says he'll find one, he will. Might be a bit though. Not many of those around here. Maybe if you look closer to Dublin."

Siobhan spared her a quick glance before merging onto a

round-a-bout. It took her an entire loop before getting to the exit the GPS told her to take. "You sound just like him. He told me the same thing. And stop laughing at me."

"I'm not laughing at you," Katie said around her snickering. "I just find it funny that your GPS voice made fun of you for going around the round-a-bout twice."

"Stupid Stephen Fry voice. He always has some smart-ass thing to say about my driving."

"Well, he is a comedian. And a smart one, too. You might want to find another voice to use."

"Maybe." Siobhan stayed in the right lane for a few miles before she realized all the traffic was speeding past her. After very expressive hand signs from three angry drivers, she remembered the slow lane was the one on the left. She grumbled, "I wonder if I'll ever get used to driving here."

"You will. Da has a friend that's from Germany. Took him a year or so, but he got the hang of it. Just remember to always stay to the left. Especially on the motorway. And the round-a-bouts. Oh, and on the roadways."

"Ha-ha. Are you having fun over there?" Siobhan playfully slapped Katie's thigh. "It is your birthday, so I'm going to let your hilarity slide this time."

"This time? What will you do next time?"

"Oh, next time it's all going to be very serious. I'll have to get you back."

Katie laughed, and Siobhan smiled at the sound of it. Their playful banter was refreshing. Especially after the call from her mother the night before.

"I may have to do it again just to see what that's like."

"So you're a button pusher, are you? Hmm. I'll make a note of that."

Stephen Fry announced they had reached their destination as Siobhan pulled into the lot of a good-looking restaurant. Jamie assured her it was, in his words, "posh and romantic." She didn't care about posh; the romantic bit made Siobhan choose it. She'd had a nice long conversation with Mrs. Kerry about how Katie took care of everyone but herself. Katie deserved a lovely night out.

Siobhan parked and helped Katie out of the car. They strode hand-in-hand to the entrance, where a man dressed in black slacks, shiny black shoes, and white, pressed, button-up shirt, opened the door for them. He smiled politely and closed it behind them.

"Welcome to Rosalee's. Do you ladies have a reservation?"

"Yes," Siobhan said. "Landry."

"Please have a seat while I check on it. Would either of you like a drink?"

"Water for me. Katie, would you like something?"

Katie was looking at the interior of the restaurant with an expression that was hard for Siobhan to read. "I'll have a glass of white wine, please."

"I'll be right back." The waiter left quietly.

"White wine? I'd say that's a good choice, but I've only ever seen you drink beer. Have you been here before?"

"Just once," Katie said, staring at her hands.

Siobhan instantly regretted her decision to come here. She covered Katie's hands with one of hers. "I'm sorry. We can cancel—"

"No. It's a nice place, and I love that you thought to bring me here. Even if it was with a bit of pushing from da. He loves this place. Brings Dadaí here every year on their anniversary, birthdays, whenever he can get away with it. I'm not surprised he thought to send you here. I just didn't expect I'd feel this way when I got here."

Siobhan shifted so she was facing Katie and waited for her to meet her gaze. "I want this to be special. If bad memories ruin that, then we can go to my flat. I'll fix you something to eat there. I just want to spend time with you, Katie. Where we are doesn't matter to me."

Katie looked ready to cry. Instead she gave Siobhan a chaste kiss. "Nope. Here is fine. You'll love it, and I dare say you deserve some pampering, too. That's what me dads love about it. It costs a mint, but they're very good to their guests."

As if on cue, the waiter returned with their drinks. "You're a little early, so we're still prepping your table. Would you like to sit in the lounge? I can call you when it's ready."

"That'd be grand, thanks." Katie took Siobhan's hand and led her into the lounge. She found a two-seat couch, and they sat in companionable silence for a bit.

"Your dad said it was posh, but I don't think I've ever been in such a beautiful restaurant before. Leather couches, glass coffee tables, and a corner bar that looks like it cost twice as much as my car."

"More like ten times as much," Katie said, placing her drink on the glass table. "When Da says posh, he means it. There aren't a lot of places close to us like this one. They've gotten two Michelin stars since they opened ten years ago. Do you like steak?"

"As long as it's juicy and not cooked until it's rubber, yes."

"Then you're at the right place. Best damn steak you'll ever have."

"Is that the only nice thing here? The steak?"

"Everything on the menu is good. That's what Da says. And he's a picky eater so I'd believe him. But I think the company is more important." She turned on that smile again, and Siobhan felt her heart melt at the way the skin at the edges of her eyes crinkled. It would be so easy to fall for Katie. If she hadn't already.

"Ladies, your table is ready. You can leave your drinks here. I've put fresh ones out for you."

Siobhan was glad for the break in her thoughts and followed the waiter out of the lounge and to their table, which was tucked into a dimly lit corner. Katie held her hand until they had to let go to be seated. The waiter left them menus and promised to return shortly.

Siobhan was about to comment on the meal she wanted when her cell phone buzzed. She was so glad she'd remembered to turn off the ringer. She pulled it out of her pocket and stared at the screen. Of course her mother was calling. Her finger hovered over the phone before swiping left to ignore the call.

"Don't feel like chatting with whoever that was?" Katie asked. Her voice was kind, and Siobhan got the sense Katie was glad she hadn't picked up the call.

"It'd be rude to you. Besides, I really don't need to talk to my mother right now. I need to spend time with you."

"I like how you think, Siobhan." Katie set down her menu and took Siobhan's hand. It was so good to feel the contact again. "But if your mother is calling it could be important, right?"

"I doubt it." Siobhan jumped when the phone buzzed again. She was still holding it and almost dropped the stupid thing. "I really hate that she even has my number, but she nearly had a panic attack and I had to give it to her. In case of emergency. Only emergency she's called me with is whether or not I'd be home for Christmas."

"She must miss you," Katie said. "And she's fairly insistent on getting through to you. Why don't you answer and at least let her know you're okay? I don't mind. Seriously."

The phone started a new round of buzzing. Siobhan wasn't sure she should answer the call, but the look of encouragement on Katie's face was hard to ignore. She took a deep breath, slowly let it out, and answered. "Hello, Mom."

"Oh, I was so worried," Mary said, her voice raising an

octave as it always did when she was nearing a panic attack. "Why didn't you pick up? Is something wrong?"

"Nothing's wrong. I turned off the ringer because I'm at dinner, and I thought it would be rude to Katie if I answered the phone."

"Are you still at dinner? And who's Katie?"

Crap. "Yes, we're still at dinner, and Katie is the woman I'm dating. What did you need, Mother?"

"Why are you dating a woman? I thought you were past all that after Susan. I mean, that was years ago. You should be trying to find a man now."

Siobhan closed her eyes in an attempt to keep calm. She felt Katie's hand give hers a reassuring squeeze as she worked up a reply. "I'm dating Katie. If that's what you called about, then I'm going to hang up and get back to our nice dinner. It's her birthday, and I'd like her to have a nice time."

"Well, you don't need to be mean. I was calling to let you know I decided to get tickets for you and me to the mother/daughter dinner. I didn't want to lose the chance that we wouldn't be able to get them. Assuming you're still coming."

Siobhan hadn't wanted to go back to the states quite so soon. She'd been hoping for May when the weather was nicer. It'd give her more time to get settled into her new life in Ireland. But as usual, her mother assumed she'd be returning at a time convenient for Mary Landry. Siobhan, ever the good daughter, acquiesced. "I'll be there. I'll call you tomorrow for the date and time. I need to go now."

"Great. I'll let Susan know. She's in charge of the whole thing this year. She'll be glad you're coming home. I think she misses you."

"Goodbye, Mother." Siobhan hung up before her mother could say another word. Especially about Susan. Right then, had it not been for Katie's touch centering her, Siobhan might have thrown her stupid phone across the restaurant. Instead, she turned it off and tucked it into her back pocket again.

"That didn't sound like an easy call," Katie said after a brief pause.

"It wasn't. It never is. But that's all done now. Can we go back to having a nice evening?"

Katie hesitated before she released Siobhan's hand and motioned for the waiter. "Let's get some food. I'm starving."

KATIE LEANED BACK in her chair as if doing so would make a bit more room in her stomach. It didn't work. They'd debated for a few minutes about ordering the chocolate mousse for dessert, and since it was her birthday, they went for it. In fact, Katie went for it twice. Now that last bit of food was sitting uncomfortably in her belly.

She looked over at Siobhan, but she didn't look the least bit uncomfortable. Like all that food went through her without issue. She was probably one of those women that never gained weight, too. Not that it mattered to Katie, who now found herself drawn, again, to Siobhan's very girlie figure. Her hormones were raging like a randy teenager's. If Siobhan said the right thing, she was sure they'd end up at her flat in no time.

And then what? In a second, her brain doused the flames from her hormones. The idea of what Siobhan might do then still scared Katie. Even if her heart told her it was nonsense. This woman was different. She was sure of that, though they'd known each other but a few weeks. Siobhan wouldn't hurt her on purpose. But what if she did hurt Katie? Then what? Could she bounce back from that?

Why the hell was she thinking all this again? She longed for the days when self-confidence was a given. This wasn't how things should be. Always doubting herself.

"Hey, come back to me." Siobhan's gentle voice rooted her to the present. "I don't know where you go sometimes, but your face tells me it wasn't pleasant." Siobhan gradually moved her chair closer to Katie so their knees touched. "Do you want to talk about it?"

"And scare you off? No way." Katie tried to laugh it off, but she was sure Siobhan wasn't buying her act. "Just some stuff I need to work out. Nothing to do with you, I promise." She kissed Siobhan on the cheek. "It's been a wonderful evening, even if me belly is so full I can't move."

"Maybe dessert was a bit much?"

"Well, dessert was fine. Me ordering seconds on dessert wasn't." This time Katie's laugh was genuine, and Siobhan joined her. "I'm ready to go when you are."

"I already paid. Shall we head out?"

"When did you pay? I never saw you."

"While you were being frowny."

"Sorry for that."

"Don't be." Siobhan stood and offered her hand to Katie. "Need help getting up?"

"No, but I wouldn't dream of not accepting your offer." She took Siobhan's hand and rose from the chair. When they started out, Katie stopped dead. She couldn't believe her bad luck. A lump formed in the back of her throat, robbing her of breath.

Siobhan was speaking, but Katie couldn't make out the words. Not three meters in front of them stood Fiona. Her long, dark hair flowed over a fiery red evening gown that barely covered her large breasts. She hung on the arm of a handsome woman, dressed in a black tuxedo, complete with matching red cummerbund and bowtie. They were laughing about something until Fiona's gaze landed on Katie. The woman with Fiona said something, but Fiona waved her off and came to stand in front of Katie.

Fiona didn't pay any mind to Siobhan as she regarded Katie. "Hi," she said, her voice just as sexy as ever. The memory of that voice as they lay together after making love for hours sent a thrill down Katie's spine.

Katie cleared her throat. "Hi."

"It's good to see you up and about," Fiona said. It seemed to Katie she was startled to see her. Like Katie would be confined to the indoors. "I didn't think—I mean, you're walking."

"It's how I get from place to place," Katie said, finding her voice. "You'd know that if you had bothered to stick around."

"Fiona, darling, our table is ready." The tuxedoed woman put a hand on Fiona's arm. "Is everything okay?"

"We were just leaving," Katie said and gave a gentle tug to get Siobhan to follow her out of the restaurant. She was trembling, and as soon as they were at Siobhan's car, Katie leaned against it for support.

Siobhan's face was full of worry as she pulled Katie into a tight embrace. "I can guess that was your ex. I'm sorry, Katie. You didn't need that. Especially not tonight."

"I was just surprised is all. I haven't seen her since—since the incident."

"When you lost your legs?"

Katie nodded but didn't dare let go of Siobhan. The feel of her arms around her was like a balm on the wounds inflicted by Fiona. All she wanted was to stay there and feel safe. "Can we go to your flat? I don't feel like going home."

"Of course. But I have to let you go to drive there."

"Well that sucks," Katie muttered. As she pulled back, she saw a big grin on Siobhan's face. "You're very good at hugging."

"Then I'll hug you more when we get there. Okay?"

"Deal." Katie kissed her before climbing into the car. Once Siobhan was also in, she placed a hand on Siobhan's knee. "Thanks. It was a lovely evening. Despite how it ended."

Siobhan grinned at her. "It's not over yet."

SIOBHAN'S FLAT WAS up two flights of stairs, and by the time Katie got there, she was knackered. Two flights should have been easy for her, but the day's events had left her more tired than she expected. Her legs burned from the climb, and she was happy to be seated on Siobhan's couch.

"Would you like some tea?" Siobhan called from the kitchen area. The flat was open plan, so she wasn't more than a few meters away.

"No. I'll end up not sleeping. Water would be great though."

"Coming right up." Siobhan was there a moment later. Once she settled beside her, Katie found herself in an amazing cuddle. It was like their bodies were built for purpose as they fit together perfectly. Katie couldn't help the satisfied sigh that escaped her lips.

"Comfy?" Siobhan asked.

"I am. This is the perfect ending to the day. I really needed this."

"It was fun, and I'm more than happy to sit here and hold you. Trust me, it's not a chore."

"I'm sorry for the drama. I hadn't meant to speak to her, but when I saw her, I just froze."

"Don't apologize. There's no need. Don't let it ruin your day, okay?"

"That's a hard thing to do. I was serious when I said I haven't spoken to her in five years. After she found out I was alive and had lost one leg, she left. I never saw her again. She wasn't even there when I woke up. My dads were. But not Fiona." Katie felt tears forming and couldn't stop them. "We'd been together for six years. I thought I meant more to her than that. But I guess I stopped being right for her when my body stopped being whole."

"I wish we could go back to the restaurant so I could say a few things to her." Siobhan wiped the tears from Katie's face with her fingers. "She clearly had no clue how special you are, Katie. No woman with a heart would ever walk out on you like that. Especially if she was supposed to love you. She should love you, not your body or your imperfections, but you." Siobhan put her hand over Katie's heart. "This is the important part."

"What did I do to deserve a girlfriend like you, Siobhan?"

"I hope that's not a serious question." She kissed fresh tears from Katie's cheeks. "I'm lucky enough to be able to be supportive of you, and I'm going to do it. Katie, this feels like so much in such a short amount of time, but I can't help thinking we could be good together. Good for each other."

"You're off to a nice start. But let's agree to go slowly, okay? I feel it, too, and I don't want to make any mistakes."

"It's a deal. Now, what can I do for you right now? How can I help you?"

"Hold me."

"Done."

KATIE WOKE TO find herself wrapped in a quilt with a nice pillow under her head. She could tell by the feel of the material against her hand that she was still on the couch in Siobhan's flat. Her prosthetics were still on and that felt rather weird. She couldn't recall ever falling asleep with them on. One of her dads always managed to be there to remove them.

Her back was stiff as she sat up. And her head throbbed in that way she knew would end up as a migraine. Bugger it all, she thought. The first nice birthday she'd had in years, and it was going to end with a migraine that would probably shove her into bed for days. Fuck.

She stood on unsteady legs and nearly fell back onto the couch. Siobhan was suddenly there and holding her arms to steady her. "Did you get drunk without me knowing it?" she teased.

"Ha-ha," Katie said, grateful for the assistance. "I'm not used to waking up in me legs is all. Plus, I think a migraine is working its way in."

"Would breakfast help? I'm making pancakes."

Katie's stomach rumbled of its own accord. She patted it and laughed. "Apparently, I'm hungry. I'd love to join you for breakfast. Maybe it'll stave off this damn headache."

"Hope so. Have a seat at the table, and I'll get things started."

Katie did and watched with interest as Siobhan moved around the economy-size kitchen. She wore a too-large T-shirt and boxer shorts. Her hair was mussed from sleep, and she was beautiful. Katie couldn't take her eyes off her.

Siobhan said, "Do you get migraines a lot?"

"Depends. If I'm extra tired, run too much, have too much stress—there's a huge list of reasons the doctor gave me for getting them." She rubbed her forehead as if that would do any good. "I hate the bloody things."

"I imagine you do. I dated a woman that got them, and she'd be sick in bed for a couple of days." Siobhan turned to Katie with concern in her eyes. "Are you sure you should eat? I remember she got sick to the stomach sometimes."

"I'm sure. If I get sick it won't be for hours yet. When I get home, I'll take some meds and sleep. Hopefully prevent the worst of it from happening."

Siobhan presented her with two pancakes and placed butter and syrup on the table. "Eat up."

"Thanks." Katie dove in and practically shoveled the delicious food into her mouth. "Wow. I've never had pancakes like this. What do you put in them?"

"Bit of cinnamon and nutmeg. Nothing special." Siobhan set a plate down for herself and started eating. "Something my dad taught me to do. He wasn't a great cook, but he always made pancakes when we went camping. They were his specialty."

Katie noted the sparkle in her eyes when Siobhan spoke of her dad. She wished she could have met the man. "He sounds like a great guy."

"He was amazing. I mean, how many dads will sit with their four-year-old daughter and play Barbies for hours on end? Or let her do his hair and nails?"

"Not many. Though I remember one time Kyra painted Da's toenails green. Thing is, she didn't use nail polish."

"What'd she use?"

Katie laughed at the memory. "The same paint that Da used on the garden fence. Stuff you need turpentine to remove."

"Ick. Bet that was messy."

"Especially since she wasn't all that tidy about it. He was asleep, and she got most of it on his toes, some on his leg. She was only three at the time. She'd seen some girlfriend of Danny's doing it and thought it looked pretty. Well it did. Pretty messy. Took him a few hours to get it all off."

"Did he yell at her for it?"

"Nope. He was as sweet as could be. Kept telling her how special it was that she'd done that. Then he made damn sure she couldn't get into any more paint. After he got it all off, he wore socks and long pants until she forgot she'd done it. He didn't want to upset her that he'd removed it all." Katie finished her food and took a sip of her now cool coffee. "He's a special man, my da."

"He sounds like it. I'm not surprised, though, given that he and Colm adopted all of you. It takes special people to do that."

"Oh Dadaí, well, he's a different story, sort of. I don't tell many people this, but Da—Jamie—is my biological dad. I met Dadaí when I was seven, and he was the first man I approved of as a boyfriend for me da. And trust me, I was super picky. Not just any man would do for my da. He had to be perfect."

"That's so cute. What made you decide Colm was the right guy? Do you remember?"

"Oh yes," Katie said. "The first time I met him he got on his knees so we were eye to eye and asked me if it was okay if he took me da out to dinner. I remember staring at him and trying to figure out if I was okay with it. Before I could say anything, he took my hand and asked if I wanted to go along to make sure everything went well. The man was a mind reader. Or just good with kids. I guess I was scared my da wouldn't come back. So we all went to dinner. It wasn't long after that he moved in and I decided to call him Dadaí."

"Wow. That's amazing. And you right away started using the Irish word for dad for Colm. On your own?"

"Yep. I always called Jamie, Da, and if I was going to have two dads, I needed another name and that's the one that popped into me head. Probably because I'd had an Irish lesson that day in school. Who knows. But the kids that followed—they just used the same names."

Siobhan stood and began cleaning up. "I would have loved having two dads. I sort of had that with Dad and Granddad, but to grow up with parents as loving toward each other as you did—that's special."

"It is. Not special when you bring home a girlfriend and find yer dads necking on the same settee you were planning to use." Katie grinned at the memory. "It's all funny now, but it sure wasn't back then. I couldn't even go in the room for a week after that. Ick!"

"I bet you'd have the same reaction if you go home now and find them on the couch together."

"Probably," Katie said. She glanced at the clock on Siobhan's wall. It was well past ten. "I should get going. Me headache isn't going to get better, and I think I need to show up at home. I'm surprised no one's called me yet."

"Do you want me to drive you? I know it's not far, but you

look a bit pale."

Katie waved her off, even though she felt unsteady again when she got up. She grabbed her cell phone off the coffee table and checked it for messages. It was off. Battery completely dead. "Well, mystery solved. They've probably been calling for hours. I best get going."

"I could walk with you at least." Siobhan accompanied her to the door.

"Nah. I'll be fine. I promise."

Siobhan pulled her into a loving embrace. "Be careful and call me when you get home, stubborn girl. I want to know you're okay."

"I will." Katie searched Siobhan's gaze, comforted by the concern she found there. She closed the small gap between them and pressed her lips to Siobhan's in a soft, promising kiss. "I had a grand time. Thank you."

"You're welcome. Happy birthday."

Katie kissed her again before heading down the stairs. "It was indeed."

Chapter Eight

THE SUN SHONE brightly behind the black curtains of her bedroom window. She could see the outline as one of the curtains was pulled back just a touch. Katie slowly turned her head away from it, happy that the nausea was gone. Some bits of pain remained behind her eyes, but it was no longer agony for her to move. She tested the waters by sitting up.

So far so good.

She reached for her chair and hoisted herself into it.

The room didn't spin, and her stomach didn't complain. Except that she was hungry.

She wheeled into her bathroom to pee and get cleaned up, hoping the brightness of the sun indicated it was morning. Problem was, what morning was it? She couldn't remember getting home after waking up at Siobhan's flat. She remembered the sweet kiss they shared before she left. That was really the only thing she wanted to remember. Even though other things crept into her thoughts.

Like Fiona.

She'd acted like nothing ever happened between them. Like she didn't abandon her in a hospital in Boston, fighting for her life. Like she hadn't left and never so much as looked back. What kind of person does that?

Katie finished up and returned to her room to find Kyra sitting on her bed. Her youngest sibling smiled when she saw her. "Mornin', Katie. You feeling better?"

"Much, thanks. What brings you in here?"

Her smile faded just a bit. "I just wanted to say hi." She hopped off the bed and headed for the door, her usually happy disposition suddenly gone.

"Hey, wait." Katie rolled forward and blocked her path. "What's wrong?"

Kyra shrugged. Her usual answer to that question. Katie quietly cursed the lack of language usage among pre-teens. She tried to wait her out, but Kyra had a stubborn streak as wide as Katie's, so she gave up.

"Kyra, something's wrong. You never just come in my room. Not that I mind, but you never do. Not without knocking."

"I wasn't sure you'd be awake, and if I knocked, it might

make your head hurt more."

Katie realized what her sister was doing and was touched by it. "Sweetie, were you checking on me?"

Kyra stared at the floor, nodded once.

"Ah, that's very kind of you. But I'm okay. I promise."

"You slept more than a day." Kyra had tears in her eyes. "I don't want you to sleep that long. Last time you did" — her voice hitched as she choked back a sob—"you almost died."

"Hey, come here." Katie held her arms out, and Kyra fell against her. She was small for her age and could still fit on Katie's lap. Katie kept a tight grip on her as Kyra sobbed against her shoulder. "I'm still here. That was different before. When I sleep now, it's to get rid of the migraines. The only thing that cures them is the medicine I take, and that makes me sleep. A lot. I'm sorry it scared you."

"I've been coming in and out most of the night. Da told me to get some sleep, that he'd let me know if you needed anything, but I just couldn't do it. I couldn't sleep thinking you were down here and sick and..."

"Shh. I'm not goin' anywhere. You hear me? Nowhere. The migraines are bad, but they don't last." She kissed the top of Kyra's head. "But I tell you what. Next time it happens, you tell Da I said you could sleep in my room. That way you'll know if I need anything. Okay?"

"Promise?" Kyra asked against her shoulder. She sniffled a bit and wiped at the tears on her cheeks.

"I promise." Katie settled her more securely on her lap. "Hang on and I'll take us to the kitchen. I'm hungry."

"Good. Dadaí made a big breakfast. I was hoping you'd be awake enough to want to eat."

"There you go. You hoped and it happened."

Kyra wrapped her arms tighter around Katie as she wheeled them down the hall. She whispered, "I prayed, too. Da says that helps."

"It does indeed. Thanks, sweetie."

"I love you," Kyra said and kissed her cheek.

Katie swallowed around the lump in her throat, holding back sudden tears. "I love you, too."

SIOBHAN CHECKED HER cell phone for the fifth time in the last hour. She'd sent a few text messages to Katie but had yet to hear back from her. That was two days ago. She worried about the migraine. Would it be okay if she went to their house? Maybe she should stop at the pub and ask about her? Yes. That was it. She'd go to the pub.

It wasn't like she was getting anywhere with her painting. She'd been staring at the blank canvas, and not so much as a drop of color had landed on it. Frustrated, she blew out a breath, put her painting supplies away, and tossed aside the long-sleeved, green, oxford shirt she always wore. It'd been her dad's and, until recently, proved to be quite helpful to wear when she was feeling inspired.

It wasn't working today. Or yesterday. Or last week, if she thought about it.

She grabbed her wallet, phone, and keys and donned a jacket before heading out. The weather was rainy, as usual, but a bit colder today. She huddled against the wind and quickly made her way to the pub, not bothering with an umbrella as it was useless in the wind.

At the pub, warmth greeted her, and she was happy to remove her wet jacket.

She smiled a greeting to Colm as she wandered up to the bar.

"Well, hello there, stranger," he said in way of a greeting. "Fancy a pint?"

"Not really. Bit early for me." She slid onto a stool and accepted a Diet Coke instead. "I've been texting Katie, but she's not answering. Is everything okay?"

Colm shook his head. "She came home with a migraine that's lasted almost two days. Poor girl. I hate when this happens to her. She misses out on things sometimes. Like yesterday."

"What was yesterday?"

"Kyra had a school play. She was all excited about it and made sure everyone in the family had a ticket. Mind you, her part was very small, but she was thrilled to be in it. But Katie and Jamie weren't there, and she cried her eyes out over it. I was so proud of her for doing the play anyway, but a lot of the excitement was gone for her."

"Can I ask — I don't want to be rude — but do the migraines happen a lot? I mean, Katie sort of downplays those things. She looked awful when she left my flat, but I thought that might be from sleeping on the couch. Still, she wouldn't let me drive her home."

"She's a stubborn one, our Katie. Wait, she slept on your couch?" Colm raised one eyebrow, and his amused face caused Siobhan's to turn red. She could feel the heat coming off her cheeks.

"Yes. We fell asleep talking so I made her comfy and went on to bed."

"You're a dear one, Siobhan. A keeper for sure."

She was never going to stop blushing. "I don't know about that, but I do like your daughter. A lot."

"This I can see." He gave her hand a friendly squeeze. "How 'bout I call Jamie and see how she's doing?"

"That'd be great. Thanks."

Colm smiled kindly at her and left to make the call. Siobhan couldn't hear him, but she could tell by the way his shoulders lifted that it was good news. He was back in a few minutes.

"Well, seems Miss Katie is enjoying some late breakfast. She came out of her room with Kyra on her lap. Kyra's done that since Katie came home with the wheelchair, but I suspect the girl is getting too big for doing that much longer."

"Kyra's adorable. She was having such fun wheeling Katie around that party. They're cute together."

"Hard to separate them. Katie's more mother than sister to the younger ones, but it suits her. Even if they drive her mad."

"I'm so glad she's feeling better."

"Same here." Colm paused and leaned against the bar next to Siobhan. "Since I haven't heard, tell me how the evening went. Did you enjoy the restaurant?"

"It was perfect. Even if my driving drove Katie a bit nuts. I'm still not used to the whole using my left hand to shift thingy." She laughed and so did he. "The place was stunning. The food was amazing, and it ended almost perfectly."

"Almost?"

"If we hadn't run into Katie's ex, I think it would have been a magical evening."

Colm's expression fell, and she saw the anger brewing in his eyes. "Fiona? Was it Fiona?"

"Yes," Siobhan said it slowly, now wondering if she should have kept her mouth shut.

"Did she say anything to Katie?"

"Not really. Asked how she was doing, and Katie sort of told her off. Then we left." She paused to watch the conflict on his face. She could see he wanted more information, so she figured he ought to know some of what happened next. "I don't know what she did to Katie, exactly, but we went back to my apartment and spent some time on the couch because Katie needed it. She was pretty shaken up after seeing Fiona. I didn't press her for information, I just held her until she fell asleep."

Colm's eyes softened, and he leaned over enough to kiss Siobhan on the cheek. "I leave the story-telling to Katie. But like I said, you're a keeper. If that bitch ever comes near my daughter again, would ya tell me?"

"Will you kill her?" Siobhan half-teased.

"No. But I'll be happy to give her a piece of my mind. She broke Katie, and it's taken a lot of time for her to heal." He straightened. "And I hope you'll be the one to help her along."

The thought terrified her, but Siobhan said, "If she'll let me."

"There's that. If you'd like to see her, Jamie said you're welcome to come over. You didn't see much of the castle the other day, and I bet Katie might fancy giving you a tour."

"Oh, I'd love that." She took a sip of the cola she hadn't touched and gave Colm a warm smile. "Katie's a lucky woman to have parents like you and Jamie."

"We're the lucky ones."

She waved at him, donned her jacket, and headed into the rain, this time with a little more spring in her step.

SIOBHAN USED THE ornate door knocker and was startled by the echoing boom it caused. The knocker was brass and in the shape of a man's face. He had a handlebar mustache and his chin composed the "knocker" part. His wicked grin made her laugh.

The door was constructed of heavy oak and was over seven feet high and, since it was a double door, about half as wide as it was tall. The rain ran off the dark wood in fat drops, and she wondered if this door were original to the castle.

She was about to knock again or maybe ring the bell when the door opened, and she was greeted by a tall, dark-haired young man. His youthful face lit up with a very wide grin as he recognized her. She wasn't sure if this was Rory or Danny but was certain he was one of the twins.

"Hey, Siobhan. Come in." He gestured her inside and closed the heavy door behind her. "Sorry it took a minute. We almost didn't hear the knock. But I was pretty sure of it, even if Kyra and Katie are both deaf to it."

"Thanks. I didn't mind. I was going to hit the doorbell."

"Wouldn't have done you any good. We disconnected it years ago. Too loud for Katie when she's sick." He motioned her to follow him. "But she's in the kitchen shoving food down her gob if you want to see her."

"I do."

He led her down the long hallway and into the kitchen that also served as a dining area. Katie was gleefully eating while Kyra chatted away about something. Jamie was cleaning up but had a big grin on his face.

Katie looked up when Siobhan entered. "Rory O'Briain. Could you find the manners to hang up her jacket?"

"Oh, sorry." Rory helped Siobhan out of her jacket and wandered away.

Siobhan wanted to protest, but Katie's glance silenced her. Seems she was doing her "mother" bit with the boy.

Kyra patted the seat next to her, which was across from Katie. "You can sit by me, Siobhan. We're talking about my play."

"Thanks." Siobhan joined them. "I heard you were excellent in your role."

"You did?" Big green eyes widened as did her smile. "Seriously?"

"Yes. Your dadaí was bragging about you at the pub just a little while ago. Said he was very proud of you."

Kyra's blush was the cutest thing Siobhan had ever seen. But she seemed to accept the compliment well. "He's my dadaí. He has to say stuff like that."

"Oh, that's not true," Siobhan said. "My dad told me that part of being a good parent was always telling the truth and never exaggerating it. If he says he's proud, he means it. Besides, he was bragging to me, remember? Dads don't brag unless they mean it."

"Told you," Jamie said from behind them. "Now do you believe me?"

"Okay, okay," Kyra said. "I did okay. It was just a little part."

Jamie settled next to Katie. "Kyra wants to be an actress. This was her first speaking role."

"That's so cool. Congrats, Kyra." Siobhan held out her hand to shake Kyra's. "Did anyone get a video of it?"

Katie, who had so far been quiet, almost choked on the milk she'd just drunk. "Are you kidding me? There's video of all of us doing things that no one ever wants to see. Those two," she said and pointed to Jamie, "record everything. Have done since I was little and they discovered digital cameras."

"We love our kids so we want to memorialize everything. What's the big deal?" Jamie asked with a laugh.

"It's a sickness," Katie said with a teasing tone in her voice. "You didn't need to video the first time Rory came home drunk. Nor did you need to video him getting sick the next day."

"Oh yes we did. Taught him a good lesson those videos did. He hasn't done it since."

Kyra smirked. "That you know of."

"Kyra Marie..." Jamie's tone made Kyra duck her head before getting up from the table. "What aren't you telling me?"

"Nothin', Da. I think I need to go do some homework."

"It's Saturday," Jamie said, his eyes on her as she moved to the doorway.

"Yeah, well, it's maths. You know I hate maths, and we have a test." She was out the door before he could say anything else.

"Way to clear the room, Da." Katie finished her milk, and then to Siobhan she said, "Have you had breakfast? Da can heat something up for you. Are you thirsty? Sorry, but everyone here forgot their manners today."

Siobhan shook her head. "I'm fine. I really just wanted to make sure you were doing okay. You look a lot better than the last time I saw you." And she did. There was color to her cheeks, and her green eyes didn't have the lack of luster they'd shown the other day.

"I'm good. Especially since you're here."

"My cue to leave," Jamie said. He kissed Katie on the forehead. "I'm going on to the pub. Got a few deliveries coming in. You be all right?"

"I'm fine, Da. See you later."

"Okay, love. Nice to see you, Siobhan." Jamie waved on his way out.

And then they were finally alone. Siobhan moved to Katie's side of the table and sat next to her. She took Katie's hand in her own and placed a soft kiss across her knuckles. "I was worried about you when you didn't return my messages. I had no idea how bad those migraines could be for you."

"Well, this one was mild compared to some of the others. But I'm good now."

"Next time I offer to take you home, you let me do it, okay? Especially when you look like you can barely walk."

"I make no promises. If I can walk on me own, I will. But I thought the offer was sweet, if that's any consolation."

Siobhan kissed her, softly at first, before allowing the kiss to deepen into something more. Katie's tongue slid into her mouth, and a warm sensation went all the way to her crotch. They spent minutes exploring each other, warring for dominance as their tongues danced together.

Siobhan's hand wound around the back of Katie's neck, pulling her closer until she was nearly in Siobhan's lap. If the wheels on her chair hadn't been locked, they would have fallen over when Siobhan leaned against her. Katie stopped their kisses, keeping them a breath apart.

"Wow. That was...amazing. If we keep this up, something might happen."

"Like what?" Siobhan asked, letting her fingers run along the smooth, short hairs at the back of Katie's head. "Like more kissing? Touching?"

"Yes. Like that. I'm not sure..."

"It's okay." Siobhan kissed her again, resisting the sudden urge to put all the passion she felt into it.

"It's not really," Katie said when they parted again. "Because I want to. I really do."

Siobhan sensed something in Katie's demeanor. It wasn't just about the passion that was building between them. She knew Katie felt it, too, or she'd never have returned her kisses. But something else was weighing on Katie's mind.

"Sorry if that was too much. I've never done that before, but I just had this sudden urge...God that sounds pathetic."

"It's not. I promise you the feelings are mutual. But I can't risk another headache. I need to be training, and I can't train if I'm flat on my back because I'm sick."

"Sex gives you a headache? Isn't that a little backwards?"

Katie laughed softly. "That doesn't make the headache. At least I don't think it does. I wouldn't know. I've not been with anyone since the incident. No, I think it would be the physical exertion. I have to be careful for the next day or so. Otherwise, no running."

"And no running is really hard on you, isn't it?"

"It's my lifeline, Siobhan. The one real thing I have left of the life I had before. I can run again, and that means more to me than I can ever explain."

"You don't have to," Siobhan said. "I don't know what I'd do if I couldn't paint or draw. For me, art is like breathing. I can't do without it. Even when I find that I have no inspiration, the idea of never being able to do it scares me."

"Then you understand."

"I think I do. Why don't you show me the castle instead? I didn't get the chance for a tour at your birthday party. I'd love to see the place. I noticed a few paintings on the wall in your entryway, and I'm dying to check them out."

"Then let me be your guide." Katie led her out of the kitchen and back to the front door, where she pointed to the floor.

Siobhan hadn't noticed the exquisite tiled mosaic and knelt to get a closer look. "The colors are amazing. Is this your family shield?"

"Nah. It was here when we moved in. Belongs to the Murphy Clan. Came with the castle. I went to the library, not long after we bought the castle, and found information on it. Me dads thought it was a grand idea to give me a project, so I got to work restoring it. Had no idea what I was doing, took me two years to finish it. I found most of the tiles in a back room. The rest I painted to match the ones around them. I think I broke more than I fixed at first. Lucky for me we found a ton of white ones along with the ones that make the crest."

Siobhan ran her fingers over the smooth tiles. Closer inspection revealed the new ones, but the overall effect worked wonderfully.

"How old were you?"

"About Casey's age. Fourteen."

"I'd say this is pretty damn good for someone with no training. You've got a great eye for detail."

"That's what the gardai said when I first joined. I was hoping to make detective someday."

Siobhan placed her hand on Katie's thigh. "You'd have been great at it."

"Maybe." Katie backed up and motioned her to follow. "You mentioned the art we have on the walls here in the entry hall. They aren't original, but you might recognize them since you're so into art."

"Indeed." Siobhan took her time in front of each painting, identifying the marks that told her immediately the painting was not original. But even considering they were replicas, she could appreciate the work that went into them, especially the Vermeer.

Had she not been so good at her job, she'd never have known it was fake. *The Maid Asleep* wasn't his most famous, but she always found it interesting. The maid's ruddy complexion reminded Siobhan of a blush, while it was clear she was exhausted from her work. She enjoyed the detail of her face and the objects around her, though she was obviously the center of the piece. Siobhan could get lost in a painting like this and forced herself to move on to the next one.

Katie watched her, her hands folded in her lap. There was an interesting expression on her face, but Siobhan couldn't figure it out. "What?" she asked.

Katie shrugged. "Just enjoying the way you put so much attention into gazing at a painting."

"They're beautiful. Vermeer is one of my favorites, but even an unknown artist can catch my attention. I love to look at the way the artist uses the brushes and colors—whether or not they work well or if the subject is interesting. Though I'm partial to the old masters, I can appreciate some newer art."

"Like that Chinese guy that does all those weird things?"

Siobhan scrunched her face. "If you mean Ai Weiwei, no thank you. I'm not a fan. I'm not into him or Jackson Pollock or most of the modern expressionists. They just don't evoke any emotion other than ick."

"Ick? Is that an emotion?"

"Of course. Don't you ever feel ick?"

Katie laughed. "I suppose I do. Shall we move on? I think you'll like the sitting room. Da made sure to combine two large rooms so it's pretty damn big." She led the way to a room on their right, and Siobhan was indeed surprised by the size. It hadn't looked so big during the party, but then again, it'd been full of people. Now it was empty, and she could appreciate it.

On one end were windows she suspected faced out over the front of the castle. On the other was a fireplace large enough to store a small car. And she didn't think that was an exaggeration. Two long couches set up in a vee formation were placed on either side of the fireplace, presumably to get the most out of a fire should they light one. She suspected a room this size could get very cold in the winter. It was easily large enough to fit her entire apartment into.

Another set of couches formed a semicircle around a large-screen TV that was far enough away that it wouldn't bother you too much if you were curled up by the fire. She could see the appeal of sitting on a couch and being romantic. She chanced a look at Katie and wondered if she was thinking the same thing.

Katie's face was a careful mask, but Siobhan thought she might be right.

"We spend a lot of time in here in the evenings. Da has always been big on the family being together as much as we can. Gets harder as we all get older, but he and Dadaí make it work. You've seen that monster table we have in the kitchen, right? Da got that one to make sure we had room for girlfriends and boyfriends to sit with us for dinner. I imagine he'll get a bigger one once he senses that grandchildren might be coming along."

The thought made Siobhan laugh. "If my mother thought

grandchildren were in the picture, she'd buy a house here in Cúnant and force herself on me as a babysitter. Of course, she might change her mind when she realized that I wasn't having a baby with a man."

"Do you want children?" Katie asked and Siobhan sensed the seriousness of the question.

"I do. I've always wanted kids. Maybe it comes from being an only child, but I dreamed of having a big family someday. What about you? I bet you've had your fill with the younger siblings?" Siobhan held her breath, hoping hard that Katie would not say no. She took awhile to answer, and Siobhan finally had to release her breath.

"I didn't want them when Casey and Kyra were little. I ended up spending a lot of time with them because Danny and Rory are just too immature. Conor is, well, Conor. He's got his own agenda. When I was with Fiona we talked about it, but she wasn't into it. Couldn't see herself giving birth."

"What about you? Giving birth, I mean."

"I'd never do it." She looked away from Siobhan. "But I don't know if that means I don't want kids or not. I'm just not sure."

Siobhan moved until she was in Katie's line of sight and knelt in front of her. She took both of Katie's hands into hers. "There's a lot more to it than that, isn't there?"

"Yes, but I don't know if I'm ready to tell you."

"It's okay." She kissed both of Katie's hands and moved forward to press her lips gently to Katie's. "You'll tell me when you're ready."

"How are you so sure of that?"

"I just am. If it bothers you so much, eventually you'll tell me why. In your own time. I have to trust that you'll do that. If I can't trust you, there's no point in continuing this relationship. Right?"

"You've a good point." Katie squeezed Siobhan's hands before pulling hers away. "But I should tell you now that I've got a lot of baggage. You might not want to stick around with so much stuff to deal with."

"We all have baggage. You don't know the half of it from me yet, so I'd say we just need time to get to know each other." She cupped Katie's face in her hands and kissed her again, this time conveying how much she cared for her. "You're special, Katie, and I plan to spend a lot of time getting to know you."

"Get a room!" The cry came from the door behind them, and Siobhan glanced up to find one of the twins standing there laughing.

Katie closed her eyes and, with a shake of her head, replied, "I will kick yer arse, Danny O'Briain. You best run now."

"You can't catch me and you know it. Besides, I'm your favorite." He bounded over to them and planted a sloppy kiss on Katie's cheek. She immediately wiped her face clean.

"What are you doin' home so early?" she asked. "Don't you have a shift at the pub?"

"I did, but I talked Rory into working for me. I've got a date tonight."

"Tonight? It's not yet noon. What are you doing that takes you all day to get ready?"

Danny grinned. "Nothing much. Just didn't want to work today. Besides, Rory owes me. I covered for him yesterday so he could have time with Tabby."

"And how did that go?"

Danny shrugged, and Katie shot him a glare that said he wasn't being truthful. "Tell me what happened."

"I don't want to. You have to ask Rory." Danny sidestepped out of her reach and ran out of the room.

"What were you saying about having kids?" Katie asked, her smile taking the edge off of her words. "I might have to say yes only if they're girls. No boys. Boys are a pain in the arse."

"So I see. Maybe it's just those two boys. All boys can't be that bad, can they?"

"You've not met Conor properly yet."

"Then I suppose I should. I might need to do some research. Not like you can choose the sex of the baby, unless you're adopting, of course. Did your dads do that? Choose to have boys and girls?"

"Nope. Once child services realized they had two suckers on their hands, they were given more babies. Mostly they were emergency placements and didn't stay with us more than a few days. Took a couple of years after the twins came along to get Conor. Casey was a year later and two more years for Kyra. They're still on the list for emergency foster care, and sometimes we have a kid here. Once in a while it's a baby, not usually for more than a few days. I think now that Kyra is twelve they're thinking about adopting another kid."

"Six isn't enough?"

"Nope. Not for them. And they just finished the first floor, so that means there are two extra rooms available now. They only need furniture."

"Wait, two more rooms upstairs? How many rooms does this

place have?"

Katie thought for a moment. "Well, the second and third floors are mostly finished, and when they're done, that will make a total of twelve rooms. Counting the sitting room and kitchen/ diner. Da put in two full bathrooms on this floor and two on the first floor, even before all the rooms were done. We all have our own bedrooms."

"Are you independently wealthy?" Siobhan spoke without thinking and immediately regretted it. "I'm sorry. That's not any of my business."

"It's fine. And no, we're not. They first put all their money into the pub. It makes enough, but when the chance to buy the castle came along, they scraped all their savings together and bought it for practically nothing. It was derelict, and it took three years just to get the structure stable enough to start building. The pub pays for most of the expenses since Dadaí started catering to parties and such. Da has worked on and off as a builder, too.

"My parents work their arses off, so when I turned sixteen, I got a job and started helping to pay for things with the castle. We moved in when I was eighteen. The boys had to share a room, and for a while I was sharing with Casey. Kyra didn't come along until they had at least one extra room, so Casey and Kyra could eventually share. They always had the nursery in their bedroom. It must have been so nice for them to put the girls in their own room."

"Wow. So how do they manage to pay for things now?"

"I still give them money for the renovations, and the boys work the pub for free. That way they don't have to hire much help. It's very slow going. We've been here twelve years now, and there's still a lot to do. The old chapel is going to be a B&B eventually. As if those two haven't enough to do with the pub. But Da thinks they can manage it."

"Again, wow. They're really trying to build something here."

"They are and I'm damn proud of them."

"It's amazing that you're helping them financially. I don't know anyone in my family that would do that, except for Granddad."

"What else am I to do with it? They spent money to renovate two rooms on this ground floor so I could have my own space. I told them to consider it my rent. Trust me, it was hard to get them to accept the money."

"Can I see it?"

Katie's face turned a slight shade of pink. "You want to go to my room? Are you planning to seduce me?"

"Only if that's what you want," Siobhan answered softly. "But I'd like to see where you spend your time."

KATIE STOPPED INSIDE her room and watched Siobhan take careful steps into it. She slowly wandered around, taking everything in. Which wasn't a lot, Katie had to admit, but it was enough for her.

A two-person settee nestled into one corner, so she could be away from the daylight if need be. It's where she liked to sit and read. The bed was a double and took up much of the center of the room. Bookshelves designed for her to reach from her chair lined the wall opposite her bed.

The black curtain was still drawn against the sunlight, but Siobhan went right past it and into the wet room/toilet room. Almost twice the size of most family bathrooms, along the right wall was a counter low enough for Katie to use while in her chair. The work surface was about a meter-and-a-half long with a full-size mirror above it. The center had a sink she could roll under as she usually had her prosthetics off when she used the wet room.

The toilet was on the left side of the room and lined up with the hoist. Katie was mortified when she realized Siobhan took note of that as she walked farther in. A bench was positioned under the shower head. This is where the hoist ended. Katie could seat herself on the bench and use the shower controls that were at her height level.

The shower walls were tiled in a green-and-white pattern, the floor in stone. A gradual incline allowed the water to drain, but it wasn't enough that it would cause Katie problems in her chair.

Katie stiffened as she waited for Siobhan's reaction. It wasn't what she expected.

"This is so cool. Like you've got everything you could imagine in here." Siobhan came out but kept pointing back to it. "Is that thing on the ceiling a lift?"

"It is. When I first got home I couldn't walk, and I'm a bit too heavy for Dadaí to carry me. Da's the strong one, but he was getting no sleep taking care of me, so Dadaí found a way to get that installed. Along with the wet room." She stared at her hands, not able to meet Siobhan's gaze. It was still very embarrassing to her that she could be so feeble and weak. "I hated it. Still do. At least we don't need to use it very much. Just if I've had another bad migraine. I'm so weak from the medicine, I can't always get meself into the wet room. Da has to hook me up and help me out."

Siobhan's voice was soft in her ear, and her arms were comforting as they wrapped Katie into a gentle embrace. "It's good that they're here for you and thought far enough ahead to be prepared to help. You're so very lucky to have them in your life."

Katie felt tears welling up and couldn't stop them. She hadn't cried this much in years. "I don't know how I'd get on without them."

"Hey, why the tears?"

"It's bloody embarrassing is all. I hate feeling like a weak babe that can't wipe her own arse. It's hard and I think that's why Fiona left me in Boston. She knew what was coming, and she couldn't handle how hard it was going to be."

"She's not here, and she doesn't sound like the most stable person. Like someone you can always rely on."

"I tried to call her when I got home, after I felt strong enough. But she knew the state I was in. I'm sure of it. She never returned a call or text message and eventually changed her number. That was it. Not a single word. The last time I spoke to her she told me how much she loved me. What a damn lie that was."

"You're better off without her then. No matter how much it still hurts. If I saw her today, I'd probably knock her on her ass. I'm so sorry she hurt you, Katie. You don't deserve that. Especially not after all you've been through. But I can see one thing very clearly here."

She paused, and Katie had to look up before she'd speak again. "You are the strongest woman I've ever met. You're still here, fighting to do the things you love, adjusting your life to make it the best you can. Women like Fiona don't have that in them. When I say you're special, I mean it, Katie O'Briain. You're very special."

"Thank you." Katie swiped her cheeks dry with the back of her hand. "I didn't expect that. I thought you'd go running off once you came in here."

Siobhan kissed her cheeks, nose, then lips. "Why would I do that?"

"Because now you know my reality. Now you've seen how hard it can be for me. Not all the time, but some days are harder than others."

"I see the same thing I saw when I first met you. A sweet, strong, beautiful woman who deserves all my attention. Nothing you can say or do is going to scare me off that easily. Trust me,

I've had nightmare relationships, and I'm very sure this isn't going to turn into one. And it's weird because I've never been so sure of anything in my life. I'm usually the skittish one that's always afraid to say or do the wrong thing. But you don't make me feel that way. You make me feel strong."

"How on earth did I ever end up with you?"

"Who knows? Just go with it, okay?" Siobhan kissed her again, and this time the kiss was long and full of promises that Katie desperately wanted to believe. They parted breathlessly, and Siobhan said, "Do you believe me?"

"I do."

Chapter Nine

NOVEMBER CAME AND brought with it even more wind and rain. The temperature dropped, and Siobhan found herself in dire need of a warmer, water-resistant coat. She braved the cold and drove herself into Cork. On Colm's recommendation – she'd quickly learned he was her go-to guy for almost everything – she went to a well-known clothing retailer. Well known to the Irish. Siobhan hadn't heard of them, but she didn't feel the need to be picky. Just the need to get warm.

Indiana weather wasn't any warmer this time of year, but she wasn't used to the rain and cold winds that came in off the sea. The wet part sucked. Even if it made Ireland green, it sucked.

She made her way through the store, getting assistance in finding just what she needed. And there were a lot of choices. She could see why Colm told her to come here. She was trying on her third coat when she spotted a familiar face.

That alone was weird, since she didn't know too many people. And none from Cork. But she watched the woman while she sorted through a rack of sweaters. Her long blonde hair hung loose around her shoulders. She wore black jeans, grey, knee-high boots, and a tight, white sweater that showed off her assets quite well. Fiona.

Siobhan felt anger bubbling up and wanted to give the woman a piece of her mind, but her mother's voice stopped her. She couldn't make a scene. Not in a public place. Even if she wanted to more than anything at that moment.

She grudgingly went back to the jackets, though her interest was completely gone. She was about to give up and leave when someone spoke to her. She whirled around to find herself facing Fiona.

"Don't I know you?" she asked in a sex-kitten voice that grated on Siobhan's nerves.

"I doubt it."

"No, I think I do." She smiled sweetly, but Siobhan continued to stare her down. Then her expression changed. "You were with Katie the other night. Right?"

"It was almost three weeks ago, but yes. Not that it's any of your damn business. Excuse me." Siobhan started to leave, but Fiona stopped her with a gentle hand on her arm. Siobhan glared at her. "What?"

"Is she—is she doing well?"

"Seriously?" Siobhan pulled away from her, keeping her hands at her sides to avoid the instinct to take a swing. "If you wanted to know how she was doing, all you had to do was call. Or go see her. Not like her family is hard to find."

"You have no idea what happened between us. But that doesn't matter. I just wanted to know that she was okay."

"Better than when she was with you. At least now she's got someone that actually cares about her."

The slap to her face was such a surprise that Siobhan had no time to react to it. She willed herself to punch Fiona but just couldn't do it. No matter how much she wanted to, Siobhan couldn't make herself do it. And Fiona sure as hell deserved it.

"I loved her. You've no right to say otherwise."

"You don't walk out on someone you love in their worst time of need and never look back." Siobhan took a step away from Fiona. "You're a real piece of work and don't deserve someone like Katie. And you best stay away from her."

"Or what?"

"Or I'll find the nerve to knock your ass out." Siobhan stomped out of the store and was in her car before her pounding heartbeat slowed. She'd never been good with confrontation, and today was no exception. She didn't even tell Fiona half the things that she wanted to, but she was sure nothing she said affected the woman.

Her cheek still stung from the slap. And she was worried about what Katie would think of what she'd said to Fiona. It wasn't her place to make those accusations. Even if it felt good to do it. She shouldn't get involved in such things. She was sure she could hear her mother saying as much.

She put her car into gear and left Cork, abandoning her mission to get warm.

An hour later she was at the pub and plopped down into a booth near the back, away from the draft of the door. She put her coat onto the seat next to her and tried to smile when Tabby came for her order.

"Yer smile's like that of someone in pain."

Siobhan laughed. "Sorry. It's just been a bad day."

"A pint to get you settled then?"

"You know me well, Tabby."

Tabby's smile was much brighter than Siobhan's. "Well, it pays to know your customers. Be right back."

She waited for a few minutes, checking her phone to see if she'd missed any text messages from Katie. She was in Dublin with Jamie to get some adjustments done to her running blades. They'd seen each other last night, and Siobhan discovered that any time apart caused her to miss Katie terribly.

"So, did you find a nice coat?" Colm handed over her Guinness. He slid into the booth across from her.

Siobhan sighed. "I didn't. Found a lot to choose from, but I sort of had to leave the store before I could pick." She took a long swig of her beer, hoping it would calm her a bit. It didn't.

Colm patiently waited for her to continue.

"I ran into Fiona while I was there. We didn't exactly have a nice chat." She touched the cheek that Fiona struck. It didn't hurt anymore, but she could still feel it. "It didn't go well."

"Fiona's in Cork? I'm sorry, love. I wouldn't have sent ya there if I knew. Tell me what happened."

She did. His face went from angry to concerned to sympathetic all in the space of a few minutes.

"I never should have said anything, Colm. It's not my place."

"Like hell it's not. You were sticking up for your girl. It's your place, and don't you be forgetting it. You done good."

"Will Katie think so? I don't want to upset her, but I do need to tell her what happened. Last thing she needs is to find out from someone else. I have no idea if anyone there knows Fiona or Katie, but word can travel fast and —"

"Stop worrying. Katie will be just fine. I only wish Fiona would be out of her life forever. That she'd move to the continent or something."

"Colm, can I ask you something?"

He gave her a sideways smile. "Might not answer it, but sure. Ask me."

"Katie said that Fiona left almost right away after she got hurt. That she found out Katie lost a leg and then left her there, alone. Why would Fiona do that? Did Katie ever tell you?"

"I'm not sure that's my story to tell, Siobhan. But I'll say this much, Fiona didn't love Katie enough to stay by her side. I don't know if she ever loved my girl at all, but she left her and that's all I need to know."

"You're a good dad. You know that?"

"I do me best for all our kids. But even though it's what I should do, I can't ever forgive Fiona for the hurt she put on Katie. It was hard enough to lose her legs and have to learn to do even the simplest things all over again, but to have to do it without the

person you love right next to you—no one should go through
that."

Siobhan felt her throat tighten as a tear leaked down her
cheek. "I've never run out on anyone I cared about. Not even my
mother, and trust me, she's a nightmare. But if she needed me
today, I'd be on the first plane to Indiana."

"Yep. You're a keeper. Sure and certain." He patted her hand
and got up. "How 'bout some stew? You look like you could eat."

"That'd be great."

"And when you're done, I'll take you to another store.
Nowhere near Cork. You're gonna catch your death of cold in
that coat you got there."

She started to protest, but his expression stopped her. It was
a fatherly look. One that her dad might have used on her to get
his way. She gave him a genuine smile. "I'd like that. Thanks."

He headed to the kitchen, and Siobhan felt tears pooling in
her eyes again. In such a short time, she'd been accepted into the
big family O'Briain. She felt more loved now than she had in
many years. She closed her eyes and sent a little prayer hoping
her dad and granddad were watching.

"KATIE, LOVE, STOP fidgeting. We'll be home soon
enough."

"I hate my phone," she complained for the tenth time. "Damn
battery dies after a few hours. I need a new one."

"Then get a new one, silly girl." Jamie tapped her leg playfully. "Though you could have brought your cord to charge it. Or
just get an iPhone like Dadaí and me. You know we always have
charging cords on hand."

"I don't want an iPhone. I like my Android thank you very
much." She felt a bit grumpy, but it really had nothing to do with
her phone. She could tell by Jamie's look he suspected as much.
"Is it weird to be missing her?"

"Missing who?"

It was her turn to hit him. "Siobhan. I know it's only been a
few hours, but it's hard to be away. Especially if I can't send her a
text or call her."

"What horrible lives we led before mobile phones." He
moaned and clutched his chest but gave her a sly wink. "You're in
love with her, aren't you?"

Katie shrugged. She didn't want to admit it aloud, but she
was pretty sure that she'd fallen for Siobhan the first time they

kissed. Or maybe the first time she saw her.

"It's kinda fast. Is that the problem?"

She nodded, not at all surprised he could read her so well. "It's never happened like this before, Da, and it's scarin' the hell out of me. I mean, what if she suddenly decides that I have too many needs and just runs out the door? Then what? My heart's broken all over again."

"She's not Fiona."

"So far. But I never thought Fiona would leave me like she did, and we were together six years."

"Did you love Fiona the way you love Siobhan?"

Katie hesitated to answer. Did she? "It's different. You know that. Not every relationship is the same. But there's something about Siobhan I can't put me finger on."

"She didn't run off when she saw your wet room. She knows you use the chair as much as you use your legs. She knows you're a runner and that you're stubborn as hell. What more is there?"

"I don't know." Except she did. The last woman Katie dated had run away the moment she realized that sex was going to be a challenge. Not much of one, but Katie wasn't comfortable in her prosthetics and removed them. The sight of her residual limbs sent the woman out of her room and out of her life for good. She didn't fancy a repeat of that with Siobhan. But wasn't it inevitable? Could they really have this relationship without ever having the topic of sex come up? Every time they kissed, Katie felt the passion between them. She couldn't put it off forever.

"I can't help you if you don't talk to me, love."

She looked at Jamie, who gave her occasional glances as he drove. She knew she could confide in him. She always had. About everything. Even the woman that couldn't have sex with her. How many women could say they could have those types of chats with their father?

Katie leaned her head against the cool glass of her window. "It's going really good between us. I can feel that we're getting closer every time we're together. When she kisses me... Da, it's like magic. I've never had that before, and I'm scared to lose it. I'm tired of being scared, but what if she sees me stumps and the look of them makes her sick? She's only ever seen me in pants or shorts with them covered up. I've got other scars, too. What if I repulse her?"

"Oh, love, I don't think that's going to happen. Not with Siobhan. That other bitch, she wasn't any good for you anyway. She just wanted to hop into bed with ya. She was the repulsive one. Not you."

"You're my father. You'll not tell me I'm disgusting." She sighed heavily, steaming the window with her breath. "She's told me she gets how hard my life actually is. That my reality is not an easy thing to deal with. She had to care for her granddad when he was diagnosed with cancer. But it's not the same. I've got decades of life left in me. He was old, and it's sad, but he didn't last but a few months."

"If she loves you, she'll stick around. If she doesn't, then she doesn't deserve you. I really think this is a chat you need to have with her. Let her know how you're feeling. Okay? Get it out in the open before it becomes something that keeps you two apart."

"I'm sure you're right."

Jamie laughed softly. "Of course I'm right. I'm your da."

"Ha. That doesn't make you right all the time."

"Oh? And when wasn't I right?"

Katie straightened up and stared at him incredulously. "Let's see now. How 'bout the time you told me I could climb any tree I wanted to and I did and ended up falling down and breaking me arm? Or the time you told me it was okay to kiss Cassidy Byrne if I fancied her, except that she gave me a bloody nose when I did? Or—"

"Point made. You make me sound like a bad parent," he said, still laughing. "Though the look on your face when Cassidy came to apologize and kissed you on the lips was precious. What a sweet girl that one was."

"Sweet? She nearly broke me nose!"

"And she's still your best friend, yes?"

Katie knew when she'd been beaten. Jamie always won these types of arguments. "She is. Even if she up and ran off to Scotland of all places."

"Now, tell it right. She met the man of her dreams, got married, and moved with him for his work."

"Fifteen years ago. Thanks for bringing this up. Now I'm missing her, too."

"You brought her up," he said.

"Only to prove you wrong."

"You best stop now, love. You know you can't win this."

Katie sighed, but she had a smile on her face. "I love you, Da."

"I love you, too."

HER APARTMENT WAS small, but it seemed to Siobhan that it took forever to clean. Or maybe she just wanted everything perfect for when Katie showed up. They'd made a habit of spending most evenings on the couch, talking and watching TV. Sometimes Katie stayed the night, but never in bed with Siobhan. She claimed the couch was comfy enough. Siobhan didn't buy it.

They needed to talk, and she planned for that to happen tonight. After she told Katie about her run-in with Fiona. She certainly wasn't looking forward to that. Siobhan had just started the coffee when her doorbell rang. She practically ran the fifteen feet to answer it.

Katie stood before her wearing a red polo shirt and black jeans, her coat slung over one arm. Her hair was wet from the rain, but her smile was radiant. Siobhan practically dragged her in and, once the door was closed, trapped Katie against it and kissed her for all she was worth.

She may have been startled, but Katie returned the kiss, her lips parting to let Siobhan's tongue in as she tried to devour her. Siobhan had never been so turned on with just a kiss, but even the sight of Katie had her itching with need.

Siobhan ran her fingers through the long side of Katie's hair, keeping her close as their kiss deepened. Her other hand rested on Katie's side, where Katie kept it from going under her shirt.

They parted breathless, as always. Katie's cheeks were flushed, and her eyes dilated. Siobhan didn't need any further evidence that Katie wanted her. It was just a matter of convincing her it was okay.

"Hi," Siobhan said.

"Hi, back." Katie gently extricated herself. "I don't believe we've ever said hello like that before."

"It was overdue." Siobhan took Katie's coat, hung it up, and followed her to the kitchen table. "Coffee?"

"Sure." Katie settled onto a chair and accepted the mug without comment.

"Honey, we need to talk," Siobhan said and sat beside her. "First thing's first—I missed you today."

"I missed you." Katie shook her head. "Don't we sound a little pathetic?"

"Maybe, but I don't mind." Siobhan took Katie's hand in hers, softly rubbing her index finger over her tender skin. "I went to a store in Cork and saw Fiona there."

Katie started to pull her hand away, but Siobhan held tight. "No. We need to talk about this. About her. She and I had words, and it was ugly. I've never come so close to hitting someone in my life. Especially after she slapped me."

"She what?" Katie's face showed her indignation. "I'll —"

"You'll nothing. It's over." Siobhan carefully told her exactly what had happened between her and Fiona. "I wanted you to hear it from me. And I'm sorry that I let her get to me or that I spoke up. It's not my place, but I felt this incredible need to protect you."

Katie sighed, her gaze fixed on their hands. "It's okay. I don't know why she's decided to find out how I'm doing now, after all this time."

"She claims she loved you."

"Maybe she did. I don't know. Leaving me like that — especially when I was in a coma — how is that loving someone?"

"It's not. Not to me. But I've been thinking about it, and maybe it was too much for her. Maybe she did love you in her own way."

"You're not sticking up for her, are you?" There was a hint of hurt in Katie's eyes.

"Lord no. I just want to understand. I think it's something we need to talk about. Seems we both had long-term relationships that ended badly. But Susan — she hurt me by literally leaving after sharing an incredible night of love-making. She told me it was fun, but she was going back to her wife. I didn't know she had a wife. I was naïve and stupid, really." She held up her hand to quiet Katie as she continued.

"Thing is, I learned from that. I dated here and there, but I never let myself get close to anyone else. Until you. And I fought it at first, but I have to say that didn't last very long at all. Katie, we've got something here and I don't want to lose it. I don't want Susan or Fiona to get in our way ever again.

"That's why I decided two things. One — I will tell you anything you want to know about my overly boring past. Girlfriends, lovers, friends, whatever. I want you to know there's nothing you can't ask me and nothing I won't share with you."

"Number two?" Katie asked.

"That's the hard one. Number two is about you. There's something holding you back. I can see it in your eyes and feel it when you gently push me away. I don't want anything coming between us. We both need to open up, and I have to say I really want to know more about the incident where you lost your legs because I think there's something there we need to talk about." She brought Katie's hand to her lips and placed a gentle kiss on her fingers. "Let me in, Katie. Please."

Katie didn't reply right away, and Siobhan was scared she'd made a huge mistake as she was hoping that this might lead them to discussing Katie's reluctance at intimacy. Had she been horribly wrong? So much emotion passed across Katie's beautiful face that Siobhan wanted to hold her and tell her to forget it. She'd relay the details in her own time.

"I was in Boston, Massachusetts. You know I've been running marathons most of me life. Boston was on my bucket list."

"Oh God." Siobhan was stunned. She'd expected there'd been a car accident, but this was something she'd never considered. "You were there when they bombed — when the bombs went off? That's how you lost your legs?"

Katie nodded once, and Siobhan couldn't get her arms around Katie fast enough. "That's horrible. I'm so sorry that happened to you. I can't imagine — I can't put my head around how that must have been for you."

Katie leaned into her; her voice was barely a whisper. "I don't remember anything. I was doing pretty good, somewhere in the middle of the pack, and I could see the finish line. Fiona was in the stands, and I saw her waving at me. Then nothing. Doctors call it traumatic amnesia. I don't even remember waking up in the hospital.

"I was told that the bombs went off right at the finish line. I hit me head and lost my leg all in a few seconds. My right leg was pretty bad off, and they had to take it as well, later at the hospital. All this is stuff Da told me. I was in a coma for almost two weeks because they had to do that to keep me alive. I had internal injuries, too, and more surgeries than I care to count. Da was there when I woke up, but he says it took me three days to speak, and they weren't even sure I knew who he and Dadaí were.

"Fiona called them from the hospital. She got hit by something and needed her arm stitched up. Da got there about a day after — he couldn't get a sooner flight over. Fiona told him where I was, as much of what happened as she knew, and while he was in to see me, she left. He and Dadaí tried to get hold of her, but she was gone. Da says they didn't spend much time looking because Dadaí arrived in Boston, and they focused on me. They didn't much care where she'd gone off to."

"Colm told me they didn't leave your side, even after they were finally able to bring you home."

Katie shrugged one shoulder like it was no big deal. "I don't remember coming back to Ireland. I woke up one morning to find

Da asleep on a chair beside me bed in a hospital in Dublin. I'd apparently been awake off and on, but I don't know any of it. My head hurt like hell, and I couldn't figure out where I was. So there's about a month or so of my memory just gone. They tried again to find Fiona, but she wouldn't answer any calls or text messages. Da even went to our flat, but she'd moved out before we got back to Ireland. Took her all of two weeks.

"I remember crying me eyes out because I needed her so much." Katie choked out a sob. Siobhan held her tighter and wished she could make all the pain go away. Katie's voice cracked as she continued, "I needed her, Siobhan. I needed her so much, and she wouldn't come near me. Like I had the plague or something. I loved her so much I wanted to marry her. We were going to spend a week in the states, and I was going to propose. She's never told me why she left me. Not one call, text, email—nothing in five years. Like she's just forgotten me. I know she moved on. Seeing her with that woman made that clear."

Siobhan's own tears fell. Did Katie still love Fiona? Did she dare ask her outright?

Katie took a deep breath and pulled away from Siobhan. "I want to move on. Truly I do. I know I'm ready, but I never expected all this to come up. I never thought it would be so damn hard."

"I'm not going anywhere. I hope you know that."

"I do. But it still hurts. I mean, why couldn't she love me enough to be there when I needed her most? What's so wrong with me?"

"There's not a damn thing wrong with you, Katie." Siobhan cupped her hands around Katie's face. Their eyes met, and it hurt to see the pain there. "You're a beautiful, amazing woman. I know I keep saying it, but it's how I feel. And I thank you for telling me all this. I can see how hard it was for you." She placed a soft kiss on Katie's lips. "I care about you more than I can say. Please know that I think you're perfect for me. Okay?"

"You've not seen all me scars, dear. You don't know just how imperfect I am."

"I said you're perfect for me. I'm not worried about your scars. We all have them."

Katie took Siobhan's hands and pulled them away from her face. "No, you don't understand. They're ugly—you might be repulsed by them."

And finally Siobhan understood. She got up and gestured for

Katie to do so as well. "Then I want you to show me. I don't think we can move forward with our relationship with this lingering doubt on your mind."

"I don't know if I can." Katie looked so fragile. "You keep saying I'm strong and beautiful, but I don't buy it. I know I'm stubborn, and when I want to do something, I do it until I can't do it anymore. Like running. But this sort of thing—showing you me scars—I don't know that I have the strength for that."

"You don't need strength. Just faith." Siobhan took her hand and gently tugged Katie toward her bedroom. "I'm not asking for anything more than for you to show me what's got you so scared. Let me prove to you I'm not going to run out the door screaming. Okay?"

Katie didn't speak as they entered the bedroom. She settled onto the bed. Katie took off her shoes, and Siobhan placed them on the floor. Then she helped gently pull Katie's jeans off and over the prosthetics. Katie was wearing purple Lycra shorts underneath the jeans, and the color made Siobhan smile.

She turned away long enough to fold the jeans and put them on the nightstand. She held Katie's gaze as Katie's hands moved to remove the left leg. Siobhan was quiet as she took it and placed it against the nightstand, close enough that Katie could reach it. They repeated this with the right one. A single tear ran down Katie's cheek, and Siobhan gently wiped it away.

Nylon sheaths still covered her legs. Siobhan knelt in front of Katie and caressed the warm skin below the shorts. She moved her fingers to the sheaths and along the uneven surface of the remainder of Katie's right knee. Siobhan held Katie's gaze while she touched her leg, seeing the scars in Katie's eyes. She slowly removed the sheath.

Katie's breathing hitched when Siobhan's left hand touched the shorter of her legs as she removed that sheath as well. Siobhan leaned up and softly kissed Katie on the lips.

"You haven't seen them."

"What haven't I seen?"

"Me scars," Katie said, her voice deep with emotion. "You've only touched them."

"I can see them, Katie. When I look at you I see them." Siobhan placed small kisses on each leg before meeting Katie's eyes again. Her hands ached to reach under Katie's shirt and feel the warmth of her skin there. She wanted to push Katie onto the bed and show her exactly what she was feeling right then. In that moment, Siobhan realized how much she cared for the woman in front of her. How much she loved her.

Their lips met again, and Siobhan barely restrained herself. "No one has ever made me feel the way you do, Katie. I love you."

"Please, don't say that." Katie looked at her with scared eyes. "How can you be certain so soon? We don't know each other."

"You're wrong. I know you, and I'm sure that I love you."

"Can you love this?" Katie pulled up her shirt to reveal thick, diagonal scars across her tight abdomen. "This is me, Siobhan. Scarred. Forever. I can't take this away." She pushed back her bangs and showed another mark just above her temple. "This one means I get sick. A lot. I can't work. I'll never support meself because of all the problems I have. I have to rely on money from the council to live. I can't expect anyone to be part of my life. Or to love me."

"Bullshit," Siobhan said. "Your body isn't what I've fallen in love with. And I know you have problems. You showed me some of what it takes to get through your day. But more important, you've shown me what it feels like to really love someone. And to be loved back. I've never had this before, Katie."

"You're not hearing me. I don't have an easy life."

"Who does?" Siobhan stood and took a step back in frustration. "Nothing worth doing is ever easy. You get migraines that last for days. Sometimes you need help getting a shower or to the toilet. Sometimes you're fine and walk around as though nothing bad ever happened to you." She sighed wearily, not sure what to say but determined not to lose this particular battle.

"I'm not perfect either. I lock myself away for days and not just to paint, but to lose myself in another world and block out this one because it can be so damn frustrating. And hurtful. I never thought for a minute that I'd find a woman who would care about me longer than the time it took her to get me into bed. But here you are.

"I want to spend time with you. I want to learn about you. Most important, I want you to know that you have my heart and I'm not going to leave you. I've seen your scars. Tell me what more you need." She knelt before Katie again and took hold of her hands. "Whatever it is, you can tell me. I'll promise to always do right by you. Be by your side."

"You can't. You don't know what could happen later. You could change your mind."

"I won't. I'll prove it to you. Every day if I need to." She kissed Katie's fingers. "I love you."

"I don't know—I didn't expect this. I don't know what to say."

"Say nothing." Siobhan kissed her again. "Would you like me to help you get dressed?"

Katie's hands shook, and for a moment Siobhan thought she might decline. For just a moment, she saw a shimmer of passion cross over Katie's features. But it wasn't the right time. They both seemed to sense that.

Siobhan decided to lighten the mood a bit. "If I thought you were up for it, I'd rip off your remaining clothes and have my way with you."

"Seriously?"

"Yes. Oh yes. I'd make love to every inch of you." Siobhan emphasized that by trailing a finger along the scar on Katie's stomach. "You've shown me your scars. I only wish I could make the pain of them go away."

"Me, too."

"So, back to my question. Dressed or undressed?"

Katie finally smiled. "Dressed, please."

"Done." Siobhan helped her, finally pulling her off the bed so they were standing together. She wrapped her arms around Katie. "Thank you. I seem to be saying that a lot, too, but I know it wasn't easy. Thanks for trusting me."

"Thanks for not running away."

Siobhan responded with a kiss. "There is something I'd like to show you."

"Oh?"

Siobhan linked their fingers together and gave Katie a gentle tug toward the door. "In the other room. If you can show me yours, I can show you mine."

Katie laughed as they walked the short distance across the hall. Siobhan hovered near the door while Katie wandered into her art studio.

Boxes and crates still cluttered the place, and three easels had works in various stages, but it was the one painting she'd finally finished that she wanted Katie to see. Eventually, Katie made her way to the spot where the painting captured the waning sun outside. Sea-green eyes were the center of the piece. Katie ran with graceful strides, her blades not really touching the ground. The light reflected off a sheen of sweat on her face and highlighted the red in her hair.

Best of all, was how the morning sun had stretched across her face and showed its warmth in her eyes. Eyes that Siobhan could look into for the rest of her life.

She moved to stand beside Katie and wrapped one arm lightly around her waist. She longed to feel the soft skin that had been under her touch moments ago. It was important that Katie understood how Siobhan felt.

She heard a tiny sniffle. Katie was crying. Siobhan wiped her tears and kissed her cheek. "Is it that bad," she joked.

"It's beautiful. I've never seen meself in such a way. I look like — like I was born to run."

"Maybe you were. But it's how I see you. Graceful. Beautiful."

"You're biased."

"No, I'm an artist, and I paint what I see. And what I saw that day was this amazing woman running along the cliff like she belonged there. Like she owned the place." She turned Katie so they were facing each other. "I wanted to capture the moment in all its glory. Do you think I did?"

Katie stole another glance at the piece. "You're a talented woman, Siobhan Landry."

"Thank you. I've never really shared my work with anyone. My mom just criticizes my choice to be an artist, and Susan, well Susan didn't get it. I painted a lot of animals when I was in Indiana, and Susan hated them. Said there was no point since they weren't, as she put it, saleable."

"What a right bitch she was." Katie's fingers hovered just above the painting, as if she were afraid to touch it. "She had no idea what she had in you."

"Maybe not. But I'm glad to be rid of her. And I'm glad you like this. I was going to give it to you for Christmas, but I guess I could give it to you now."

"It's for me?" She turned her surprised face to Siobhan's. "But don't you want to keep it? It's fine work and all."

"Everything I paint has a purpose. Some are for sale, some not. This one is not. I'll get it into a nice frame this week and bring it to the castle for you." Siobhan laughed. "Maybe you can put it in the entry hall."

"No way. It's going in my room. I'm not sharing." Katie kissed her soundly.

Really, Siobhan could just throw the woman on her bed and stay there for the next week. Her libido needed to have a cold shower. They finished the kiss, and Siobhan was left breathless.

"You keep that up and there won't be any movie tonight."

Katie grinned and there was just the tiniest hint of mischief in her eyes. "No movie?"

"Well, maybe if you promise to cuddle."

"I promise."

"And promise not to eat all the popcorn."

"Um, not sure I can do that one," Katie said. "But I promise to make more if we run out."

"Fair enough. So, I've got Netflix all ready to go, and it's your turn to choose."

Katie took her hand and led Siobhan back to the living area. "Oh, then you know it's going to be an action flick. Lots of shooting and car chases and the like."

"I figured as much. Want some popcorn and a Coke to get us started?"

"Of course, but there's one thing I need more than that." Katie pulled her into her arms and kissed Siobhan in a way that left Siobhan with no doubts how Katie felt about her. No words were necessary after that.

Chapter Ten

THE RAIN HAD stopped, and Katie was ever so glad for it. She hated running in the mud, and while the path she used was a bit dryer, it still wasn't pleasant. Her blades slipped a few times, and she considered turning around and going back home. But that would mean she didn't reach her time for the day, and that wouldn't do. April would come soon enough, and she was determined to complete the London Marathon without collapsing. But first she had to complete the Clonakilty Waterfront Marathon. That would be a good test of her endurance. One last full marathon before London.

Her new blades were holding up well, and her legs felt very strong today. She'd already passed the spot where Siobhan sometimes sat to draw and was a bit disappointed she wasn't there. But she knew that Siobhan was working on a new painting and had warned her she might not come out of her flat for a while. That was a week ago. And Katie missed her terribly.

It was early December, and Siobhan would be leaving for the states in a few days. What would that be like with her so far away? She wasn't more than two kilometers from Siobhan's flat most of the time, and it was hard not to be with her. Thousands of kilometers would kill her.

Okay, that was an exaggeration, but Katie was already feeling the squeeze of her heart at the thought of not seeing Siobhan for a couple of weeks. Though she'd yet to say it, Katie was sure and certain she was falling for Siobhan. Sweet, loving Siobhan. Who hadn't run away when Katie showed her the scars. Or told her how she'd lost her legs. Or cried over the woman that broke her heart into tiny pieces.

They'd spent that night cuddled on the settee watching movies and laughing, with sweet kisses now and again.

Nearly every night since then she'd been to Siobhan's flat. Or Siobhan had come to the castle for dinner with the family. And oh did the clan love Siobhan. Dadaí doted on her like a daughter; she was pretty sure Conor had a crush on her, and Casey and Kyra fought over sitting next to her. Rory and Danny had been caught watching her in the way young men watched a beautiful woman. Katie'd had a mind to slap their heads together, but instead took it for a compliment. Siobhan was an amazing woman. She could share her just a little.

All her thinking had made the long trek back home go a lot faster than she expected. She looked to her watch to see she'd made her time, and that caused her to smile. Katie was just slowing down to jog the last few meters home when she spotted an all-too-familiar yellow VW Golf pull into the drive ahead of her.

She faltered but didn't fall as she increased her pace up the hill. Fiona was standing beside the car when Katie got to her. Her hair was tied back in a French braid, and her cheeks were red from the cold wind. She was leaning on the car with her arms crossed over her chest, either to keep her coat closed or because she was nervous. It was a habit Katie well remembered.

For a moment she was tempted to run past her and into the house. But that would have been cowardly, and lately, thanks to Siobhan's support, she didn't fancy herself a coward anymore. She slowed her gait until she was standing in front of Fiona. "What are you doing here?" she asked, getting right to the point. No sense in being nice.

Fiona hesitated. "I was wanting to see you."

"Why?"

"Can we go inside? It's bloody freezing out here."

Katie did a mental check of the family calendar to figure out who might be home. The young ones were in school, and she was fairly sure everyone else was at the pub. At least until lunch, which would give Fiona about half an hour to spit out whatever it was she intended to say. Katie nodded and led the way inside.

The front door closed with an echoing thud. Katie took a seat in one of the chairs in the entry hall and waited. "No one's home. Say what ya need to say."

"I—you've done a lot more work in here. It looks nice."

"Fiona, we both know you're not here to admire the work me da's done on the place. You've waited five plus years to come see me. Why now? What do you want?"

Fiona clasped her hands in front of her and kept her gaze on the floor. "You're right. I came here to tell you I'm sorry. I never should have left you in Boston."

"No, you shouldn't have. Not that I would have known you were there, but you could have at least kept in touch with me dads to see how I was doing. If I was even alive. I almost died. Did you know that?"

"I did. Katie, I was at your side the whole time. I don't remember the moment the bomb went off, but I remember getting hit in the arm with something and then running to you. There was this mass of bodies and people screaming and running around. It took me forever to find you." Fiona took a shaky breath but still didn't meet Katie's gaze. "When I did, a man was holding what was left of your leg and trying to stop the bleeding. There was so much blood—from your legs and from your head. Then I saw the stain spreading on your shirt, from the wound to your stomach. I had to move away because I got sick. And the smell...I can't begin to tell you about the smell.

"I rode in the ambulance when the paramedics took you to the hospital. I couldn't touch you because they were working on you, but I was there. I told them I was your partner, and they let me stay by your side until someone realized I was bleeding and made me get looked at. That's when I phoned Jamie. Then I called my ma, and she tried to get me to come home straightaway. She was terrified I'd be killed. By then it was all over the news."

"Da didn't tell me this."

"He doesn't know. I've never told anyone except my psychologist. I stayed with you until you had to go to surgery. I waited until Jamie got there, and I left. I was only going to the hotel to wash up. I was going to come back, but I got scared. Terrified. I couldn't stay there a minute longer. So I packed up and left. Got the first flight out, even though it meant spending the night at the airport."

"You left me." Katie's voice sounded small to her own ears. "When I needed you most, you left. I can understand being scared, but why didn't you call after me? Why didn't you come see me when I got back? Come here to help me recover? Hold me when I cried over a life I could no longer have?"

"Because I was in pieces, Katie. I could barely keep meself together. I quit my job and moved home with my parents. I didn't go anywhere for over a year. They finally forced me to get help. Even tried to get me to see you, but I couldn't."

"Because you didn't love me enough." Katie stood up and faced Fiona. "I get it. You were a mess. So was I. But five years?"

"I did love you, Katie. I loved you more than I've ever loved anyone before, and that's what scared me, I think. I couldn't bear the thought of losing you, and when I found out you were alive and—I just didn't have the courage to help you. And I'll always be sorry for that."

"I wish I could forgive you."

"You don't need to." Katie saw the sorrow in her eyes. She'd know if Fiona was lying, and she was sure and certain she was not. "I'm not asking for forgiveness. I only wanted you to know what happened and why. I still love you. I don't know if that will ever change."

"I've moved on, Fiona. At least I'm trying to. I have a woman in my life now who supports me and loves me more than I think you ever could."

"I wish it could be me," Fiona said and took a step toward Katie. "You have to believe that I never stopped loving you."

"Then where have you been?" Katie felt like a knife had been plunged into her chest. She'd spent the years vacillating between hate and love for Fiona. "I needed you."

"I know. I needed you, too. But I was broken, and when I managed to pick myself up...I didn't think you'd want anything to do with me. Time and distance seemed the only thing I could manage."

"Looked like you moved on pretty well when we saw you at the restaurant."

Fiona's face paled. "I thought I had. But after seeing you...I haven't seen Trina since."

"That's too bad."

"Is it?" Fiona was suddenly closer now, and Katie felt her heart speed up at the familiar sense of intimacy.

They were millimeters apart.

Fiona's hand caressed Katie's cheek, and Katie forgot to breathe.

It was all a dream. One she'd had over and over. Sometimes it ended beautifully, but sometimes—most times—it ended in a nightmare.

But then Fiona's soft lips pressed against hers, and Katie's body reacted to the feel of them. She put her arms around Fiona and deepened the kiss, allowing herself to have the one thing she'd craved for so very long.

After a few moments they parted, and Katie met Fiona's gaze, searching for a promise she wasn't sure would be there.

Finally, Katie said, "I think this is a mistake. I don't think you could fit into my life again."

"Why not? I love you, Katie. I'm sorry it took so long to come back to you, but I'm here now. Can't we try?"

"I don't know. I have Siobhan and she's—she's stable and good for me."

"Do you love her?"

Katie released Fiona and stumbled backwards. "I'm not sure. Yes. Maybe."

"Do you love me?" Fiona asked.

Katie couldn't answer that one either. "You shouldn't have come back. It was easier when you weren't here."

"That's why I came back. I don't want to take the easy way anymore. Please let me show you I've changed. Let me be here for you now."

Katie shook her head, trying hard to listen to all the reasons why she should kick Fiona out the door. "I've got scars."

"So do I."

"No, you don't understand. I've got horrible scars, and sometimes I can't even get out of bed. What would you do then? Stay at home and be my caregiver? Could you do that?"

"I would do anything you need me to do." Fiona sounded almost desperate.

Katie was startled when she heard her da's voice booming from the other end of the entry hall.

"You'll get yourself out of my house, and you'll do it now." He stormed to Katie's side, putting an arm protectively around her. "You've no right to be here."

"This is between me and Katie, Jamie. Please let us work this out."

Katie felt the anger coming off Jamie, and she held onto him, in case he decided to get physical with Fiona. "No. This isn't just between the two of you. It involves me and my family. You have no fucking idea what it's like for Katie every single day. Just to get out of bed and take care of herself takes a lot of effort. That she's walking at all, much less running again, is a bloody miracle. There are times she's bedbound for days. Can you cope with that? Think you can use the hoist we have to help her go to the toilet? To take a shower?"

"Jamie, I've done a lot of research on this—"

"You don't know a fucking thing, Fiona." Jamie and Katie glanced behind them to find Conor stalking toward them. His soft voice sounded loud in Katie's ears. What was he doing home so early? She wanted to ask, but Conor continued speaking. "I watched my sister crawl out of the deepest hole to get back on her feet and start her life again. She don't need you. She's got everything she could ever need right in this castle. You don't belong here. You need to leave and do it now. I'm not going to let you stand here and fuck with my sister anymore. You done enough damage, you bitch."

Fiona looked like she wanted to say something, but her mouth opened and closed without a word coming out.

Conor shoved past her, opened the door, and pointed.

Katie shook her head and also pointed to the door. Fortunately, Fiona had sense not to speak as she left. Conor slammed the door shut, and the sound sent knives through Katie's head. She felt Jamie holding her up, and in an instant, Conor was at her other side.

"You okay? Did she hurt you?" His gaze was a mix of anger and fear.

"Not physically, but I think I need to lie down."

Jamie must have sensed what was happening and scooped Katie into his arms. He carried her to her room and helped her get settled onto the bed. Conor was there to remove her blades, which he took to the wet room to clean. Katie held Jamie's hand for a moment and whispered, "I'm so proud of him. I've never known Conor to be so..."

"Protective of his sister? Oh, you've just not seen him when you're in here resting. He's like a sheep dog herding the little ones well away from your room. He's been known to yell at Rory for having the telly on too loud."

"How did I get so lucky?"

Jamie kissed her forehead. "You were born that way. Want me to help you get a shower before the headache gets worse?"

"Yes, please."

"Let me scoot Conor out. When you've rested up, I think we need to have a long talk."

"We do," she said and closed her eyes for a moment. She could hear Conor and Jamie quietly talking. Then Conor's soft voice was close to her ear.

"I won't let her hurt you again. I promise." He kissed he cheek and left before she could say a word.

Jamie helped her sit up and undress, then he carried Katie to the wet room for a shower. He put her wheelchair where she could get it when she was done and left her to it. Katie sat on her shower chair and let the water wash over her in hot waves, hoping to remove the dirt and the pain that Fiona brought back to the surface.

She'd kissed her, and it'd felt so good, but her brain screamed at her the whole time to stop. It was wrong. Fiona never really loved her. How could she have?

Was it even possible to love someone and stay away from them when they needed you most? Who does that?

Katie let the water run until her skin was red. She turned off the water, towel dried as best she could, and used the chair to return to her room. Jamie was waiting for her with clean undies and a nightshirt.

"Do you want your medicine now? Before the nausea starts up?"

"I guess so. Can you get me my phone? I need to send Siobhan a text. She leaves for America in a few days, and I don't know if I'll be able to see her."

"Soon as you're settled I'll bring it in. But if you can't reach her, I'll call her for you. Okay?" Jamie tucked her into bed much as he'd done when she was a kid. He smoothed back her bangs. "Fiona's made a right mess of things again. But I'll tell you now, that if you decide to give her another chance, I'll support you. I won't like it, and neither will anyone else, but you have to follow your heart, love." He put his palm on her chest. "This is what matters. Okay?"

"Okay, Da."

He fished her phone out of her running pouch. "Call. Don't text," he said and left.

SIOBHAN NORMALLY KEPT her phone turned off when she was painting. But the shrill ring tone that cut through her wonderfully silent world told her she'd managed to forget to do it this time. The call went to voicemail, and she was about to get started again when the ring tone broke her concentration. It must be her mother. She's the only one that would ignore voicemail and keep calling until Siobhan answered.

Two choices. Either answer the damn thing or turn it off. She hurried to the kitchen, intent on turning it, off until she realized it was Katie's number on her screen. She accepted the call. "Hi, honey. Sorry it took me a bit to get the phone. I was painting."

"It's fine." Katie's voice sounded far away so Siobhan turned up the volume on her end.

"Are you okay? You don't sound right."

"I'm not. Migraine is starting up so Da got me in bed and I just took my medicine. I'll be asleep soon."

"Oh, baby I'm so sorry. Can I do anything? Want me to come over?"

"It'd be grand to see you, but I don't know if I'll be awake."

"Won't matter." Siobhan was already stripping off her dad's old shirt. "I'll be there in twenty minutes. If you feel sleepy, just go with it. You need to rest. I'll be there when you wake up."

"Siobhan, there's something I need to tell you."

Siobhan grabbed her coat, keys, and wallet and was already

locking her door. "Tell me when I get there. I love you." She hung up and practically ran to the O'Briain home.

Jamie met her at the door and asked her in, immediately telling her to be quiet. He whispered, "She's asleep. Let me get you settled, and we'll talk."

She wordlessly followed him into the sitting room. She noticed Conor was seated in the center area, playing a video game. He wore earphones, so she doubted he'd heard them come in. Jamie left and returned with a cup of coffee and handed it to her as they settled on the couch by the fireplace. The flames warmed Siobhan who hadn't really noted how cold she was until then. She took a sip of coffee and waited for Jamie to speak.

His eyes were tired and his face was pale. "Katie really wanted to see you, but she fell asleep a few minutes ago. I had to put her phone away 'cause it was still in her hand." He gave her a tight smile. "She's had a rough morning."

"Anything you can tell me?"

Conor suddenly joined them, his eyes narrowed in anger. "That bitch came here."

"Conor Matthew Patrick O'Briain. I let it go when you used that language before, but you need to apologize to Siobhan. You know better."

Conor mumbled an apology. "But I'll not say I'm sorry to that — that woman. She's hurt Katie enough. Who does she think she is coming here?"

Jamie held up his hand to stop Conor's rant. "We don't know what's going on between them, Conor. I'm just as angry as you are that she was here." He looked to Siobhan. "Fiona paid Katie a visit."

"I figured." Something in her gut told her there was a lot more to this story. "What did she say?"

Conor scoffed. "That she still loves Katie and wants her back."

Siobhan felt a knot form in her stomach. Hadn't Fiona hurt Katie enough already? To just show up after all this time and ask her back was unbelievable. Worse yet, she was afraid to ask about Katie's reply. Would she even want the woman back in her life?

Katie's vulnerable right now. Siobhan could feel that, and that's what kept her at a slight distance. She didn't want to take advantage of it. She wanted Katie to love her, not feel obliged to do so, but because she truly felt it in her heart.

She was quiet for a while as Conor and Jamie continued to talk. She gathered that Fiona hadn't been here long, but it was enough to bring on a migraine. Jamie thought they caught it in time, and it wouldn't be as bad as some.

"Conor, I want you to go to the school and tell your sisters to head over to the pub for a bit. I'll let you know when they can come home. Ask Rory and Danny to stay there, too, please. Let's give Katie some space."

"Sure, Da." His dark eyes seemed to lighten up a bit. "I'm glad you're here," he said to Siobhan. "She's gonna need you. Thanks for coming over." Then he was gone.

Siobhan didn't know what to say to that. "Katie told me we needed to talk, but I thought it was best to tell her to go to sleep. Would it be okay if I sit in there with her?"

"It could be hours before she wakes up," Jamie cautioned. "And she might not be in much shape to talk."

"I know. I promised her I'd be there, and I meant it. I've got a million things to do at home, but this is where I plan to be until I know she's going to be all right."

Jamie said, "You're a good woman. The room will be totally dark because the light makes the pain worse. Do you like to read?"

"Whenever I get the chance."

He stood and headed for one of the many bookshelves that lined the walls of the room. He returned with an e-reader. "It's the family bookstore. I would be surprised if you couldn't find something there to keep you entertained for a while. We all use it, especially when we're keeping an eye on Katie. The light isn't bright enough to disturb her."

"You're well prepared."

He shrugged. "Have to be. Have you eaten? I can fix you something."

"I had breakfast, but that's it. I was painting and sometimes I lose myself...and track of time."

"I'll get you something and bring it in."

"Thanks." Siobhan left him and went to Katie's room. She was careful with the door, surprised that it didn't make a noise as she opened and closed it. She used the light on the e-reader to find the couch, where a thick, soft blanket and pillows lay, beckoning her over. It didn't take much to get comfortable.

For a long time she sat there and listened to Katie's breathing. Slow and steady. She wanted to be closer so she could touch her but worried it would wake her. Siobhan would have to be content to be on the couch.

Jamie came in and gave her a plate with a sandwich and a

glass of water. He left without saying a word. Siobhan settled in and waited.

Chapter Eleven

THE BUZZING OF her phone brought Siobhan out of the quiet of Katie's room and into the entry hall. It took a moment for her eyes to adjust to the sunlight that streamed in from a window above the door. Was it afternoon or evening? Time seemed to stand still while keeping watch over the frail form on the bed. She swiped her screen and accepted the call without looking to see who it was. Though the moment she heard her mother's voice, she sorely wished she had.

"Where have you been?" Mary said, her voice sounding oddly loud in the entryway. Siobhan wandered farther down, toward the front door. "I've been calling you for hours."

"Mom, first off, you know I turn off my phone when I'm painting. Secondly, I don't live with my phone attached to my ear. So, what is it you need?"

"You mean you don't know?" Her mother was clearly aghast. "Siobhan, your flight has been delayed. We got two feet of snow overnight, and Indianapolis Airport is at a standstill because under the snow is four inches of ice. Nothing is moving. You won't be getting in until Sunday morning."

"Oh. I haven't checked my email. But don't worry. I'll still get there. I promise to check it tomorrow."

"Tomorrow? Your flight leaves tomorrow. Siobhan Landry, what's going on? Aren't you ready to go?"

"Tomorrow?" Siobhan pulled the phone from her ear to get the date. Shit. It was Friday, and she was supposed to be on the plane tomorrow morning at ten a.m. Somehow she'd lost an entire day.

She glanced at the door to Katie's room. There was no way she was leaving. "I'll call the airline and see what I can do. Did the news say when the weather's supposed to let up?"

"Sunday."

Siobhan did some quick calculations. She honestly didn't think Katie would be much better tomorrow, and she was hesitant to leave. "Let me see when I can get a flight. I might try to come out on Tuesday instead. I'm sorry, Mom, but my girlfriend, Katie, is really sick. I don't want to leave her just now."

"Sick? Is she in the hospital?"

"No. But I need to be here for her."

There was a deadly silence on the other end, and Siobhan waited for her mother's tirade. It never came. "Let me know the flight number so I can come get you. I have an appointment on Tuesday, but I'll see if I can change it."

"It'll be in the evening, so you should be fine. I've got to go. Goodbye, Mom." Siobhan hung up quickly. She started to check her email, but that was when the phone decided to give up and die. The battery was dead. "Shit."

"Problem?" Colm said from behind her.

"Sort of. I'm supposed to fly out tomorrow to see my mom, but my flight got delayed. Except I forgot I was flying out tomorrow, and I never checked my email and my mom was a little beyond annoyed with me."

"Ah, well if you need to go it's fine. We'll be looking after Katie. No worries."

"I know but..."

Colm's smile was kind. "But you want to be here."

"Yes. And I'm going to be. I just need to run home so I can rebook my flight for Monday. And get the cord for my phone — probably should get a shower and change." She sighed. "I really had no idea it was Friday already."

"Don't worry. You get yourself sorted. If Katie wakes up I'll let her know you'll be back."

"Thanks, Colm." She kissed his cheek and left.

Two hours later, freshly showered and in clean clothes, with her overnight bag as well, Siobhan returned to the O'Briain's. She'd packed her suitcases and left them in the bedroom so she'd be ready to leave on Monday.

Colm laughed when he saw her bag. "So, you've come prepared, have ya?"

She was a little embarrassed but shrugged it off. "I'm not leaving until she's better, so I figured it was best to bring some clothes and toiletries. You don't mind, do you? I probably should have asked."

"Why would I mind? You're family. Just tell me what you need to be comfy. Right now Kyra is in there with her. Apparently they made some kind of pact that she got to sleep in there when Katie wasn't feeling well. I'm afraid she's already taken residence on the couch."

"It's okay. I suspect she needs to be close to her sister."

"You are a keeper," he said for probably the tenth time. "How 'bout I get you settled in one of the guest rooms? You can get some proper sleep. Katie woke up enough to take more medicine an hour ago, so she'll be out for a bit."

"I'd love to get some real sleep. That couch is only comfy in the short run."

"Follow me." He picked up her bag and headed for the stairs.

IT WAS BLESSEDLY dark when Katie opened her eyes. She hated this but knew it was part of her life now. Just once she'd like to have a normal headache — take a pill and have it be gone in an hour. She suspected that after the two times she recalled waking up, at least that many days had passed.

A gentle snore drew her attention to the settee. She couldn't make out who it was, but the small form made her suspect it was Kyra. She was glad Da let her stay in the room. Though she did seem to remember Siobhan being there. Or was that a dream?

Katie pushed the blanket off herself and sat up. The pain was gone, and this time without residual nausea or dizziness. She lifted herself into her chair and headed for the wet room. When she was done, the light from the wet room showed her it was indeed Kyra asleep on the settee. Katie pulled on some clean undies, Lycra shorts, a fresh T-shirt, and left the girl to slumber.

She rolled toward the kitchen in search of food and found the rest of the clan gathered around the table. Danny was telling some tall tale about a drunk he had to toss out of the pub, and she waited for him to be finished.

She crossed her arms over her chest and said, "And you think we believe that your skinny arse could toss anyone out of the pub?"

Danny's grin was too big for his face. "Believe what you want. Or ask Quinn Greaves how his arse feels after it hit the sidewalk. I'm sure he'll tell ya all about it."

"I'm sure he will." She laughed at his antics, knowing full well he'd never toss Quinn out on his arse. He'd have shoved him out the door, sure, but never hurt the old bugger. Her gaze took in all the happy faces around her, landing lastly on Siobhan's. Katie's heart did a little flutter.

"How you feeling?" Siobhan asked.

"Better. Much better. Looking for some food."

"Coming right up." Colm was out of his seat in a hurry and started working his magic at the stove.

Katie said, "How is it all you lot are here? No one working today?"

Jamie moved behind her and wheeled her to a place at the

table next to Siobhan. "It's Sunday, love. No one's working."

"Ah. I hate this losing-time stuff."

"I know." He kissed her cheek. "Colm, honey, I think the rest of us will take our breakfast in the sitting room. I'm sure there's something for us to watch on telly. I'll go wake Kyra."

"Okay." Colm waved them all away and soon only he, Siobhan, and Katie were in the room.

Katie took Siobhan's hand. "How long have you been here?"

"Since you called me." Siobhan placed a soft kiss on her fingers. "I eventually went home to pack some clothes and stuff."

"But wasn't your flight supposed to leave yesterday?"

"I got another flight on Tuesday. My mom's not happy, but she'll live."

Katie said, "Wait. You changed your flight to America to stay here with me?"

"The original flight was canceled due to weather, but I'd actually forgotten I was supposed to be on it. I had to reschedule anyway. You shouldn't sound so surprised. I told you I'd be here when you woke up."

"Well, I do remember you being here at least one of the times I woke up. You could have left then." Katie didn't know what to think. Fiona would have left.

"I guess, but you weren't exactly talkative, and I was worried about you. Jamie showed me what to do when you woke up—if you were still sick—and I did that. Kyra and I have been taking turns in your room." She squeezed Katie's hand. "I wasn't about to leave until I knew you were okay. That's why I made the flight for Tuesday, but trust me, I was ready to change it again if need be."

"You didn't have to do that."

Siobhan kissed her lips when Katie started to protest more. "I did. I love you and I wasn't going anywhere."

They stopped their quiet chatting when Colm presented them with a full Irish breakfast of eggs, bacon, sausage, potatoes, and veggies, with toast to round it out. He poured them each a cup of coffee. "You two eat up. I'll take some out to the clan." He winked at Katie before wandering away with a tray loaded up with food.

"Are they going to use their fingers?" Katie asked to his back.

"Your da already took care of that," he called out.

"I hadn't noticed," Katie mumbled realizing that once she saw Siobhan her focus had solely been on her. "I still can't believe you stayed."

"I know." Siobhan released her hand to start working on her food. "And it makes me sad."

"Sad?"

"Yes. Sad that you have such trouble trusting that I'm not going to take off."

"I see." She pushed her food around, her appetite waning. "It's hard. Especially since Fiona showed up at me doorstep."

"I heard." Siobhan was also not eating and turned to face her. "Whatever happened between you two, you need to know that I'm different. I'm not Fiona. I'm not going to leave you. Ever. Well, except to visit my mom, but I'm coming back to you. Every time. If I say I'm going to be here when you wake up, I mean it. Hell, I wish I could be there every morning that you wake up." Siobhan showed a sudden interest in the hands in her lap. "I don't want to push you, and I'm sorry if I did. That all just kind of came out in a rush."

"No, you're not pushing. And I wish I could just trust you and say I'll never doubt a thing you do. Maybe that'll change with time. Can you wait that long?"

There was the hint of a smile on her sweet face. "I'm sure I can. I'll earn your trust. You can count on that."

"Thanks. You said you were in the room one of the times I woke up. I barely remember that."

"I was. I helped you into the wet room so you could pee then gave you another dose so you could sleep. It wasn't easy doing things in the dark, but we managed."

"I get fuzzy-headed with the damn meds. Wait. You never turned the light on? How'd you know where to take me?"

Siobhan smiled. "I followed the nightlights Jamie told me about, but that was only good enough to find the toilet. Then again, it's not like you don't know where your parts are." She looked down as her cheeks colored a light pink. "Anyway, Jamie said to keep the lights off. When you were done, I helped you get back into bed."

"Did—I don't remember. Did you have to use the hoist?"

"No, you managed mostly on your own."

"Thanks."

Siobhan kissed her cheek. "You don't need to thank me."

"I do, actually. You stayed and had to help me with something as basic as going to the toilet. You have to know that being with me—it's going to be like that a lot. I'm going to need help sometimes."

"I'm still not going to leave you. Your parents have things

down to a science and have been more than willing to show me what to do. We'll be fine." She took Katie's hand. "Please, trust me."

"I'll try," Katie said. "Now you best be eating your food before it gets cold. Dadaí is likely to come in here and have a fit if we're not feeding our faces."

"Well, we wouldn't want to disappoint Dadaí, now would we?"

"You have no idea," Katie said around a mouthful of delicious eggs and potatoes. "Best you never find out."

THE FLIGHT TO Newark/Liberty Airport was dreadfully long. Siobhan had been so excited when she flew to Ireland the first time that she hardly paid attention to how long it took. But now, her mind back in Cúnant with Katie, it seemed to take days. She looked at her watch for the hundredth time, wishing she could make the damn plane go faster. Too bad they no longer used the Concord. That would have been so much better.

And she still had to catch a connecting flight to Indianapolis.

The moment the plane touched the ground, Siobhan gathered her carry-on items and was one of the first people to line up in the aisle. She had to be patient as she was behind an older couple ambling through the narrow halls that took them to immigration.

She held onto her patience when she saw that same couple having trouble with the kiosk that was used to find out if you had anything to declare. They were again ahead of her when she offered up her paper and passport to the immigration officer.

Done with that, she re-checked her bags, got through Security without issue, and hustled to her gate with an hour to spare. Just enough time to get a bite to eat and call Katie. It was around six in the evening in Ireland so she should be up and about.

Their parting was bittersweet, and Siobhan worried about how quiet Katie was. Jamie drove her to Cork Airport, and when they dropped her off at Security, Siobhan got the feeling that something was very wrong with Katie. She didn't always meet her eyes, and their kiss was—well it wasn't full of the passion that most of their kisses were. It had her concerned. Had Fiona really gotten to Katie? Despite everything, was there a chance they would reunite?

Siobhan found herself terrified she'd be that in-between woman again.

She'd be in Indiana for a month. More than enough time for

Fiona to work her way back to Katie.

She gave herself a mental shake and dialed Katie's number. She picked it up on the second ring. "Hi, darlin'."

"Hi," Siobhan said. "I just got to Newark and stopped to eat. My flight to Indy leaves in about forty-five minutes."

"Well at least you don't have to wait around. The flights are on time?"

"So far. The snow let up for now. There's more coming in, but not until Thursday. Most snow we've had in a long time."

"I would love to see that someday. I've not had the chance to see a lot of snow."

"Maybe we'll make a trip here," Siobhan said, her hand tightening on the phone. Assuming they had a future together. "Are things okay there? You feeling better?"

"Much," Katie said. It sounded like she was at the pub, and Siobhan could hear a lot of talking in the background. "I did me run today after we got back from Dublin. Didn't go as long as I wanted, but it's better than nothing. I'm still getting used to the new blades."

"You'll get there." Siobhan hesitated. She desperately wanted to know if Katie was feeling okay now that some time had passed since Fiona's visit.

"Thanks. I need to go. I told Dadaí I'd help out tonight. It's Karaoke and Conor's been grounded."

"Grounded? What'd he do?"

"Skipped half a day of school because he didn't think he needed to be there. He scored a ten on his last tests in maths and science and thinks he knows enough to come and go as he pleases. He's a hard one to figure out."

"I'm sure you've got your hands full, then. I'll call you tomorrow. I love you."

There was a brief pause before Katie said, "Take care. Bye now."

The call was disconnected, and that's exactly how Siobhan felt. Disconnected. She'd meant it when she told Katie that she didn't expect her to say "I love you," back, but it was getting harder not to hear it.

Everything in her being told her Katie was the one. She was that one special person that Siobhan could spend the rest of her life with. But what if that wasn't what Katie wanted? What if she decided to spend her life with Fiona?

Siobhan wanted to slap herself for all these confusing thoughts. Everything was going well before Fiona showed up, and she really wished she'd been there that morning. The itch to punch her was much stronger now.

She boxed up her barely touched dinner and hurried to the gate for her flight. In a few hours, she'd be back in Indiana and she needed to settle down. She didn't want her mother to get a hint of any problems with Katie. That was a conversation she refused to have.

IT WAS JUST above freezing when the plane landed at Indianapolis International Airport. Siobhan made her way to Baggage Claim and had her luggage in record time. Her mother said she'd be at the baggage claim area, so Siobhan began searching for her once she had her stuff on a cart. Lots of people were milling around the area, but she didn't see her mother. Siobhan was about to call her when a very familiar woman approached her.

"I'm sorry I'm late. I got caught in traffic," Susan said. She ran her fingers through her unruly curls and smiled brightly. "Looks like you got your bags already. My car's in the garage, but it's not far."

"Why are you here?" Siobhan finally found her voice. "Mom was supposed to pick me up."

"She didn't want to drive on the roads. There's still some icy spots, so I volunteered." Susan took control of the cart and started for the doors. "C'mon. I don't bite."

Siobhan had no choice but to follow her. Though she did consider getting a taxi.

Susan was the last person she wanted to see. She wanted nothing to do with the woman. Ever. Except that Mary Landry adored her. They got to Susan's Rav 4, and she deftly put the luggage in the back.

Siobhan climbed in and was quiet as they left the garage.

"How was your flight?"

"Long."

"You want to stop for a bite to eat?"

"No."

Susan was nonplussed at her one word responses. "You sure? I don't mind. I can find a drive through if you'd like."

"Why are you doing this? I mean, really. You told me you didn't want anything to do with me and went back to Candice like I never existed or mattered. Now you're what? My mom's bestie?"

Susan didn't reply right away. She kept her eyes forward as

they merged onto the interstate. "I'm doing it as a favor to your mother, yes. Mary's a sweet woman who misses her daughter. And I never said I didn't want anything to do with you. I told you we were over."

"Well, you remember it how you want to, then. I was only there for you to be with until you went back to Candice. But it doesn't matter anymore. I just don't get why you keep hanging out with my mom."

"I told you, she's a sweet woman and we sit together in church."

"Does Candice go to church? Or would that alert Brother Bob and everyone else that you're a lesbian? I mean, we did manage to hide it when we were together."

Again, Susan went quiet. This was so not something Siobhan needed. She wondered if her mother had done this on purpose to maybe get a friendship with Susan going again. Not a chance in hell of that happening.

"We can't be friends? You and me?"

"I doubt it. You were the last in a long line of women that stepped on me, Susan. I'm not going to let that ever happen again."

"I didn't mean to hurt you. We could be friends. I'm willing if you are."

Siobhan didn't believe her.

"I can't be friends with someone I can't trust." Siobhan watched the familiar landscape go by, and a part of her was glad to be back in the place where she'd spent her entire life, but a bigger part of her longed for the rainy weather and smells of the sea in Cúnant. And Katie's arms wrapped securely around her.

She realized Susan had been talking, but she'd not heard a word of it. "I'm sorry. I wasn't listening."

"I said I'm sorry. I'm asking you to forgive me." Susan's grip on the steering wheel was white-knuckled, and Siobhan didn't think it was the driving conditions. She really did want to mend things between them.

"I don't know that I can forgive you, Susan. Even though I know it's the right thing to do. Why don't we just make a pact to be civil with one another? I'm sure we're adult enough to do that."

Susan hesitated but eventually gave her a tight nod. "Deal. You sure you don't need anything to eat?"

"Yes. I got something in Newark. I just want to get to Mom's and go to bed."

"Okay." Susan was quiet for the remainder of the drive to Mary's house. She helped Siobhan with her luggage and carried it upstairs to the guest room once inside Mary's modest, two-story home.

Mary happily greeted them both, giving Susan a kiss on the cheek for picking Siobhan up and giving her daughter a brief hug. She peppered Siobhan with questions about the flight and offered food and drink to both women.

Siobhan was quick to decline. "I'm sorry, Mom. I'm exhausted. Would it be okay if I just get a shower and go to bed? We can talk more tomorrow."

"Of course, dear." Mary turned to Susan. "You'll stay for some coffee?"

Susan looked to Siobhan for a second before responding. "I'd love to, but I need to get home. Thanks for the offer." She hugged Mary, waved to Siobhan, and left.

Mary locked the door behind her and secured the deadbolt, handle lock, and slide lock as if she were trying to keep out zombies. Siobhan shook her head at the obvious overkill. Mary'd seen a news story a few years ago about a home invasion and ever since had locks installed on all the windows and doors, as well as an alarm system that got tripped every time she went to the bathroom in the middle of the night. At least that part was fixed in a hurry.

Mary stopped her as Siobhan started to go upstairs. "I'm glad you're home, dear. We've got a lot to talk about."

"In the morning. I promise." Siobhan gave into the urge and kissed her mother before heading to the guest room. She plopped on the double-size bed and tried to let herself relax.

She'd be there for four weeks. That's it. Then she'd go home to Cúnant and Katie and move on with her new life. Four weeks never felt so damn long.

Chapter Twelve

SIOBHAN STARED AT Mary with what was probably a deer caught in the headlights look. "You did what?"

"I told Brother Bob you were coming in and that you'd be happy to join him. It's a formal affair for all the local preachers. Something the Churches of Christ do every year to thank them for their service. It'd be nice if he didn't have to go alone."

"Why me?" Siobhan felt the eggs and bacon she'd been eating trying to work their way out of her stomach. She wished her mother had sprung this on her before she'd left Ireland. Then again, she probably wouldn't have made the trip.

"Because you're available," Mary said, as if that was the most obvious answer. "I've found a dress that you'll look stunning in. We just need to do a few adjustments, but Joanne can help with that. We'll need to buy you some shoes, a slip, and pantyhose, but that won't be a big deal. We have until Saturday."

"Oh goodie. Mom, I don't want to go on a date with Bob."

"It's not a date. You're just going as a friend." Mary smiled at her, and Siobhan knew that cunning expression. "Maybe it'll be a date by the time the night is over."

"No, it won't be a date. Not ever. I'm gay. I date women, not men. Specifically, I'm dating Katie O'Briain."

"Nonsense. Once you go out with Brother Bob, you'll change your mind."

"What if I say no?" Siobhan said the words without thinking. It'd always been in her nature to just go along with whatever her mother said. Do what she wanted, no questions asked. But she couldn't—wouldn't do that anymore. At some point in her life, Mary Landry had to understand there were boundaries. And she'd just crossed one.

Mary was quiet as she gathered her thoughts. Siobhan bounced one leg, anxiously awaiting a reply.

"You would make me look bad in front of the entire church? Do you hate me that much?"

There was a hint of tears in her eyes, and Siobhan felt the guilt coming at her in waves. "I don't hate you, Mom. I just don't like being told that I'm going out with someone I barely know, in a week, with no warning. Why couldn't you have asked me first? I might have had plans."

"You and I both know you don't have plans. The only friend you ever had was Louise, and she lives in Nashville now. You haven't contacted her in years. Susan was the only one you ever went out with so I know you're not doing anything. Susan would have told me."

"Did you not hear me when I said I'm gay? That I only date women?"

Mary waved a hand at her as if she could swipe away the thought of her daughter being a lesbian. "You need to date men. You'll see how wrong you are when you do."

"What about Susan? You could have set her up with Bob."

"Susan is Bob's distant cousin. That would be a sin."

Siobhan ignored the cousin comment. "She and Candice are lovers, yet you seem like you enjoy Susan's company better than mine."

"You have no right to say such things about Susan and Candice," Mary said, her tears gone and vehemence powering her words. "They are lovely girls, and they're good to me. They help me whenever I need them. And they go to church every Sunday."

"And I go to mass three times a week," Siobhan countered. "I'm no less a Christian than you or them." She stood, no longer interested in finishing her breakfast. "I didn't come here to fight with you. I'll go with Bob to this party thing, but you need to understand you can't set me up like this again. I'm not interested in him, and a forced date isn't going to change that."

Mary hesitated, then a slow smile formed on her lips. "Why don't we go shopping today? I know where we can get you some nice shoes, and we can stop at Joanne's to fit the dress."

As it had been for most of her life, Siobhan's words had gone unheard. Mary Landry was skilled at picking out what she wanted. That her daughter was gay was never part of her retention. Siobhan sighed, agreed to go shopping, and went to her room to change out of her nightclothes.

She took the opportunity to call Katie. It went straight to voicemail. Her message was brief. "Mom set me up on a date with Brother Bob. Can you believe that? I'll call you later today. I really need to vent."

KATIE LISTENED TO her voicemail once she could get a break from the kitchen. Her legs were killing her, so she sat down in the office for a bit. She wanted to ring Rory's neck for blowing off his shift again. She didn't want to keep him from being with

Tabby, but she'd be damned if she'd keep covering his arse at work. She needed to have a talk with him.

But for now she wanted nothing more than to chat with Siobhan. The phone was answered on the first ring. Siobhan's soft voice soothed her nerves and removed a lot of the day's stress.

"Hi, Katie. How are you doing?"

Katie closed her eyes and leaned back on the tattered settee. "Tired and pissed at Rory, but that's nothing new."

"Oh dear. Let me guess. He didn't show up for his shift again."

"You must be psychic. How could you tell?"

"You're tired, it's evening, and if you're pissed at him it's because you had to work in his place. Honestly, I'd like to slap him upside the head. He needs to get his shit together. You shouldn't have to keep covering for him. If he doesn't want to work at the pub, he should say so and let your dads hire someone."

"Wow," Katie said with a laugh. "All that from thousands of miles away. It's almost like you're right here."

"I wish I was." Siobhan's voice got quieter. "My mother sent Susan to pick me up at the airport. I knew this trip would suck, but that was not how I thought I'd start out." There was some mumbling as Siobhan spoke to someone else. "And Mom's demanding to know who I'm speaking to, because we're supposed to be shopping for shoes."

"All this on your first day? Aren't you knackered from the flights?"

"Exhausted, but I wanted to get this over with. If I don't do this now with Mom, she'll want me to go with Susan and I sure as hell don't want to do that."

"What is with your mother and your ex? Was she mean to you when she picked you up?" Katie didn't know much about their relationship, only that Susan had stomped on Siobhan's heart. Something she and Siobhan sadly had in common.

"No. She was very nice, and we came to terms, sort of. We agreed to be civil. There's no way we'll ever be friends, but I can play nice. But this thing with Bob...Katie it's just weird. It's like Mom thinks that if I go on a date with a man, I'll suddenly be heterosexual and the world will right itself."

Katie stifled a laugh. "I know it's not funny, but your mother is mad."

"Don't I know it." Siobhan released a long, suffering sigh. "I'll pretend I'm with you, and that'll get me through the evening."

"Aww, that's sweet. I will be there in spirit."

"Oh and it's a Churches of Christ event. Just the kind of thing a good Catholic girl wants to go to. Ugh. It's going to be a bunch of hillbillies decrying gays, liberals, blacks...whatever happens to be the worst thing at this moment. It's going to suck."

"I would gladly join you and kiss you in front of all of them."

That got a laugh from Siobhan. "I would so enjoy that. And not just because of their reaction to it, but because I miss you. I want to kiss you."

"And I want you to kiss me. But we'll have to wait. Eighteen days and counting."

"You're counting?" Siobhan asked. "That's adorable. And I miss you that much, too."

"I know. But, me break is over so I need to get back to cooking. Call me when you wake up tomorrow?"

"I will. I love you."

Katie felt her heart melt every time she heard those words. She so wanted to say them back, to affirm her love for Siobhan. But her throat tightened at the idea of it. She simply said, "Until tomorrow," and disconnected the call.

She didn't move from the settee for a few minutes, digesting the conversation. Siobhan never failed to tell Katie how she felt. If she was upset, angry, sad, happy...her feelings were laid out on the table. But Katie was hesitant to do that. She could share her happiness, sadness, anger...but there was one major thing she couldn't bring herself to share.

Her heart.

Fiona had broken it so completely that Katie feared it would never be the same. Worse yet was her fear that dear, sweet Siobhan would eventually give up and move on. Then what would she do?

"Go home."

The words startled her, and Katie turned to see Jamie in the doorway. He was not a happy man, but she knew instinctively his anger wasn't toward her.

"I'm fine, Da. Just needed a quick break. I can finish the shift."

"No. It's not yours to finish. Besides, Rory is in the kitchen now."

"No date with Tabby?"

"I cut it short," Jamie said. "He needs to grow up. He says he wants to work here and that he'd like to take it over someday. If that's the case, he has to take responsibility. Not showing up and messing up your day is not the path to being a successful publican. I just don't know what to do with him."

Katie stood and removed her chef's jacket. "I'm sorry, Da. I wish I could help you there. But he's a hard one, Rory. I'd love it if he had his life together like Danny does. All figured out where he's going, got a girl he's probably going to marry. But Rory's too much like a little boy. He got all the looks and not a drop of common sense. But you know he's not going to stay this way. I know he'll grow up. Just taking him a bit longer than Danny is all."

"You know you'll make a great mother someday, right?" Jamie said. "I can't wait for that to happen."

"If it happens, Da. If."

He stopped her when she turned to leave. "Sounds like you've talked about this. I didn't realize you were that serious with Siobhan."

"I am. Well, she is. Anyway, we did talk about it. You know I won't get pregnant, but she seems to be into it. Likes the idea of little ones running around us."

"But?"

"But that's all we did. Just a bit of talk. I don't know if I like the idea of her being pregnant. If we even get that far."

"It's not likely that anything bad will happen to her. You know that. What happened to your mother — it was horrible, but it doesn't mean you can't have kids."

"I won't get pregnant," she said with a little too much emphasis. "I won't take the chance of dying and leaving my child without a mother. Maybe I'll just get her to adopt."

"And that would be fine. Katie love, don't pass up the opportunity to enjoy bringing a life into this world. Watching you grow inside your mother's belly was the best time of my life. Holding you when you were born was magical. I would hope all my kids could get to enjoy that. Just don't discount it, okay?"

"I'll think about it. If we get that far."

"You will." Jamie winked at her. "Siobhan loves you. And I can tell by your face when I say her name that you love her, too."

"Am I that easy to read?"

"To me you are. Just don't wait to tell her, okay? A woman needs to know she's loved, Katie. And you both deserve that." He wrapped her into a bear hug and released her with a kiss to her forehead. "Now get on home. I need to have a chat with your brother."

Katie hung up her chef's jacket and left the pub, feeling more confused than ever.

Kids. She wanted kids. She wanted to raise a small brood and enjoy them as they grew up, went to school, played sports — hopefully rugby — and had families of their own. She'd fill Castle O'Briain with little ones if she could. She loved kids and loved the idea of having them. So did Siobhan. That should make her happy.

Instead she was apprehensive. What if Siobhan wanted to get pregnant? What if there were complications? Oh hell, what if the world stopped spinning on its axis. Katie was damn tired of the conflicting emotions and thoughts pulling her in all directions. Siobhan loved her. And truth be told, she loved Siobhan. So what the hell was the problem?

As if by divine intervention, her question was answered when she saw that damn yellow VW Golf in the drive. Would the woman never give up?

Katie braced herself for another confrontation and marched up to the car. Fiona stepped out when Katie got there. Fiona spoke first. "I'm sorry that I bombarded you the other day. That wasn't fair. And I had no idea how much your family hates me."

"They don't hate you. They just don't like what you did to me. Fiona, I don't know why you're here now, or if there's some grand plan behind your visits, but let me tell ya now that I'm not going to go back to you. That ship has sailed. You broke my heart into a million pieces, and I'm just now putting it back together.

"My family helped me learn to walk again, supported me when I started running again. Hell, my dads took out a loan on the castle to be able to afford to build that wet room for me. They spent money meant to renovate more of the house to put in a hoist to help me when I could barely move.

"Where were you? I know you were traumatized. So was I, even if I don't remember anything. Last thing about Boston I can remember is you kissing me and saying you loved me right before I started the race. Then I woke up in a hospital in Dublin and only me dads were there. And that's my reality. My family is right to be angry with you, and so am I."

"I don't know — I'm wanting to fix things, Katie. Truly. That's why I'm here now." Fiona's hands were shaking, and tears streamed down her face.

Katie wanted to hold her and reassure her because somewhere deep down inside she still loved the woman. She wasn't in love with her, but there was still love for her. "You can't, Fiona. The damage is done. We can't be together again. I have Siobhan now. And you should go back to Trina. We need to move on with our lives."

"I never wanted to hurt you. Please believe me."

"I do. I really do." Katie gave in and pulled Fiona into her arms. She held her as she sobbed, wondering how the hell they'd gotten to this point. In some ways, it felt good to be talking to Fiona. Like she was finally able to release some of her hidden emotions. Stuff she'd tucked away but was constantly eating at her.

When Fiona was done, they pulled away from each other. Her face blotchy and eyes red, Fiona was still beautiful. "You'll be fine," Katie said. "You're stronger than you think. And I don't hate you. I never did. Someday, maybe, we can be friends again. Just not right now. I need space, and I think you do, too."

"That's more than I deserve."

"No, it's exactly what we both deserve. No sense tossing away those years we had if we can manage to salvage them, right? Let's start fresh. When Siobhan gets back from the states, we'll have coffee so you can meet her properly."

Fiona's face was priceless. "You want me to meet your girlfriend? The one I slapped? Sure and certain?"

"I do. I want to mend fences, not tear them down. All this stress is eating at me, and I don't want it anymore. What do you say? Can we try to make it work as friends?"

"We can." Fiona sniffled and reached into her purse for a tissue. "Call me when you're ready."

"I will." Katie held the door for her as she got back into the car. "Call Trina. She seemed like a nice person, even though I only saw her for a few seconds."

"She's amazing. I'll give her a ring." Fiona started the car, and Katie closed the door. She watched her drive away and felt a great big weight being lifted from her shoulders. She couldn't wait to talk to Siobhan.

IT WAS NEARING four and Siobhan was growing anxious. Bad enough she and Katie had missed each other on the phone because Joanne had to adjust the stupid dress one last time, but now Bob Johnson was late. And Siobhan had enough anxiety about the stupid dinner without him being late.

Mary made plenty of excuses for him, but all of it went in one ear and out the other. Siobhan didn't care. The only thing on her mind was that she had fourteen more days in Indiana before she could go home. Why the hell had she decided to visit for three weeks? Next time it would be two, tops. Or maybe just one.

A black Bronco from too many decades ago pulled into the driveway. Mary excitedly announced it was Bob. Without waiting for her mother to comment more, Siobhan grabbed her coat and met him in the driveway.

"Hi, Bob."

"Good evening, Siobhan." His eyes were nowhere near her face as he spoke. She cursed her mother for the low-cut dress. Siobhan didn't have large breasts, but the dress showed off what she did have. She wondered if she could keep it and wear it for Katie sometime.

"We should go," Siobhan said. "Traffic is going to be difficult, and it'd be nice to be on time."

He cleared his throat and opened the passenger door for her. She watched him move around the vehicle as she buckled her seatbelt. The car was old, but it was in excellent condition, especially the interior. At least she wouldn't get dirty.

Bob slid into the driver's seat, smiled at her, and pulled out. He was wearing a solid black suit with a sky-blue Oxford shirt. His shoes, she noted, were shined to perfection and so not good if the sidewalks near the convention center were icy.

Bob wasn't an ugly man, and Siobhan could at least appreciate his apple face and vibrant blue eyes. What she knew of him was that he was decent to his parishioners and well educated. And that he was a bigot and homophobe. She tried to come up with something safe for them to talk about.

"Your mother," he said, "tells me you're determined to live in Ireland."

"I have temporary residency and asked for permanent status a few months ago. I plan to make it my home."

"May I ask why?"

She hesitated, not sure how much she should tell him and if he'd take what she said right back to her mother. "I love it there. They have a gentle pace, and nothing is 24/7. The people are amazing, and I love living by the sea. I'll never run out of things to paint."

"Hmm. You can make a living painting?"

"Can you make a living preaching?"

That caught him off guard, and he almost smiled. "I can and I do. I've got many blessings in my life."

"So have I," she said as she thought of Katie. She totally had to keep the dress. It did fit her perfectly and added a bit of shape to an otherwise boring body. "Bob, you should know before we get to this banquet that I'm seeing someone. I don't know what my mother may or may not have told you, but I'm not interested in dating you."

She could tell by the uncomfortable shifting in his seat and the drop in his expression she'd hit a nerve. Her mother had let him expect that something could come of this evening. "Your mother told me you were single."

"Single as in not married? Yes, I am. Single as in not dating someone? No."

He was quiet for so long that she thought they'd make the remainder of the hour drive in silence. "Siobhan, your mother seems to think that you're interested in — in women."

"She said that?" Siobhan could hardly believe it. Maybe some of what she'd told her mother had finally sunk in. "Wow. I didn't think she even knew the word lesbian, much less how to use it in a sentence."

The knuckles of his hand whitened as he gripped the steering wheel. "Well, she didn't exactly use that word, but yes. That is what she said."

"Good. Then you know why this isn't a date. I agreed I'd accompany you because she set this up and I didn't want her to look bad."

"But it's okay for me to look bad?" he asked, the words spoken so softly that Siobhan had trouble hearing him. "You should have declined."

"I tried, but Mom insisted. She seems to think I'll enjoy it enough to become straight." She watched him grow pale. "This is uncomfortable for you, so we should probably change the topic."

"No, we need to turn around. I'll take you home. Your mother needn't worry. I won't say a thing, but this is wrong. I can't go through with this."

"Wrong how? It's just two people going to a banquet. So it's not an official date. I can still go with you. I'm sure there are other things we can talk about. I know you've got several degrees, one of them in art. We can always talk about art."

"You don't understand. I don't think I should be seen with you."

He took an off ramp that would get them turned around and back on the expressway to her mother's house. Siobhan took a deep breath before speaking again. "Afraid I'll embarrass you in front of your church friends? Scared that my gayness might rub off on you?"

"No. Listen, what you do in your private life is up to you. But

I consider it a sin, and I can't take you to a banquet and pretend I don't know."

"Hold on a minute." Siobhan turned enough in the seat that she could see his profile. He refused to look at her, staring straight ahead. "Didn't Jesus dine with the sinners? Didn't he say that they were the ones that needed him? If what I do is a sin, why are you so upset? Shouldn't you try to counsel me?"

"I don't think it's appropriate. Not right now."

"Pope Francis says that homosexuals should be accepted by the church. He seems to think it's appropriate."

"I'm not Catholic," Bob said.

"Well, nobody's perfect." Siobhan turned back in her seat and enjoyed the next ten minutes of their ride. He dropped her off at her mom's without so much as a goodbye.

Mary met her at the door. "What happened? Why is he leaving?"

Siobhan stepped around her. She went inside and hung up her coat. "Mom, we need to talk."

"Did something happen?"

"Yes." Siobhan entered the living room and sat in one of the matching, pale-green recliners. "Please, sit down."

Mary did, her face a little pale, her expression one of confusion. "I don't—"

"Let me talk first." Siobhan carefully related the conversation she'd had with Bob in their short ride toward Indianapolis. "I get that you don't like that I'm gay. You've never accepted it, not like Granddad did."

"He spoiled you."

"Maybe, but he also understood me in ways I don't think you ever will. But I'm happy with the way I am. I'm in love with a woman who makes me happier than anyone ever has. I can see myself marrying her and having children."

"You can't have children with another woman."

"Physically, no. But one of us can carry a child from a sperm donor or we can adopt. Mom, it's the twenty-first century. Things have changed, and you need to change with them."

"I don't need to condone something I know is wrong under the eyes of God." Mary choked back a sob. "I don't need to tell everyone that my only child is going to hell."

"You don't know that. No one does. And it's not your call to make anyway. Mom, the only thing I have ever wanted from you was unconditional love. You don't have to like that I'm gay, but when I do have kids, I'd like them to have you as a grandma. And

I will have children. Will you shut them out, too?"

"Shut them out? I don't shut you out." Mary was sufficiently horrified at the suggestion.

"You do. You call me to tell me all your woes and the goings on here, but you never ask how I am. Or if you do, you roll right over whatever I have to tell you. And there is so much I want to tell you." Siobhan sighed, wishing she could open up to her mother. It would make things so much easier on both of them.

Mary kept quiet. She reached for some tissues to wipe her tears away.

Siobhan watched her, and for a moment, she wondered what her dad would do if he were here. He knew she was gay, and he hadn't cared. He still loved her just the same. But her mother? Mary had thrown a fit, threatened to toss Siobhan out of the house, and started a prayer chain to pray for her daughter's soul.

Now she was silent and refused to acknowledge Siobhan, and Siobhan felt all the old hurts bubble up to the surface. She wanted to fix this but knew it wouldn't happen overnight. She needed her mother to understand her to some degree. To know about her relationship with Katie and how Siobhan hoped they would be together forever. She wanted her mother to share her dreams of being an artist. She hoped that someday her mother would see one of her paintings and cry with pride.

None of that seemed attainable. Siobhan decided to speak her piece. "Mom, I love you. That will never change. But I don't feel like you love me, and that hurts in ways I can't explain. I need you to know that. You're all the family I have left."

"Then why did you leave me?" Mary sounded like a frightened and hurt child. It scared Siobhan to hear it. "If I'm your only family, why did you move to the other side of the world?"

"Because I wanted to follow my dream. I've always wanted to live in Ireland and see all the things Granddad told me about. To paint the beautiful, luscious green hills, the seascapes, the quaint villages."

"You don't have to live there to do that," Mary said.

"No, I suppose I don't. But I fell in love with Cúnant the moment I got there. It's hard to explain, but it feels more like home than this place ever did. I found where I belong. Maybe it's the slower pace, or that they don't care if I'm gay or not. They only care that I'm an American with an interesting accent that they poke fun at. They like to talk politics and religion with me but not in a nasty, fighting kind of way. It's refreshing."

"You couldn't get that here?"

"No. There are few places in the US you can get that, other than big cities. Cúnant is this small village where everyone knows everyone else, and they don't care that I'm gay. I can walk with Katie down the street holding her hand or give her a kiss, and we don't get harassed for it. Maybe because they all know Katie or maybe because they genuinely don't care. Either way, we feel free there."

"I don't understand."

"You don't have to." Siobhan rose and knelt beside her mother, who was seated in the matching recliner. "I only ask that you love me. It's the only thing I need right now. To know my mother loves me."

Mary finally looked at her, and Siobhan thought she saw a flicker of resignation in her eyes. "Of course I love you."

"Thanks." Siobhan kissed her on the forehead. "Can I keep this dress?" she asked as she stood. "I do like the way it fits me."

"Sure. I have no use for it," Mary said, and that's when Siobhan heard the familiar disappointment she'd been expecting.

"Thank you," she said and made her way upstairs. She quietly shut the door to the guest room and removed the dress so she could carefully pack it away. Unexpected tears came to her eyes, and she wondered if she should leave right then. Her mother said she loved her, but there wasn't any love in the words. Like she said them by rote. Like she was required by law to love her because she'd given birth to Siobhan.

That idea hurt her more than anyone ever had.

She curled up on the bed, still wearing her slip, and cried herself to sleep.

KATIE REACHED THE top of a particularly difficult hill and wiped the sweat that dampened her brow despite the near-freezing temperatures. So far, her run had been great. She was making good time, her legs were feeling strong, and the new blades worked a treat. If everyday would go so well, she'd be in perfect shape for Clonakilty, then London. And if all that went well, she would go back to Boston. It was a terrifying prospect, but lately Katie couldn't get it out of her head. She needed to go to Boston and finish the race.

So lost in thought she was that she didn't realize her mobile was ringing. The song it shouted told her the call was from Siobhan, so she quickly tapped her Bluetooth to answer it. "Hi, sweetheart."

"Hey," Siobhan said.

Katie immediately picked up that she was upset. "Talk to me. What happened? Was it something with Bob?"

Siobhan sniffled. "It's a long story, but for now, let's just say that after tonight my mother isn't probably going to want me around. I'm going to find a hotel until I can get a flight home."

"I'm so sorry," Katie said, unable to understand what Siobhan's mother's issue was. How could she not want her own child around? Especially someone as sweet and loving as Siobhan. "Please, talk to me. Tell me the whole sordid tale."

Katie continued to run as she listened to Siobhan's story. It sounded like Siobhan had been crying for a long time, which Katie suddenly realized must be the middle of the night for her. "Have ya slept at all?"

"For a little while. I cried myself to sleep, but then I had to pee. I just got into my jammies and crawled back to bed. I'm starved because I never had dinner, but I don't want to go downstairs and risk waking Mom. I can't take another confrontation."

"Perhaps you should get yourself out of there. I don't understand why she's doing this, but you need some space to yourself. I'm almost home. I'll start up my computer and see what I can find for you in way of a hotel. Maybe if you stay somewhere else, it'll help her put things into perspective."

Siobhan choked out a laugh. "I'm not sure it'll help, but I think you're right that I do need to stay somewhere else. At least until I can get a new flight."

"This is going to sound mad, and you have to know that I miss you fiercely, but I think you should stay."

"Okay. That does sound crazy. Why?"

Katie waved to Mrs. Kerry as she rounded the corner that would take her to the castle. "If you leave early, you'd be running away. At least if you stay, you can know that you gave it a try. You might not fix things straightaway, but I think you need to do all you can while you're there. She's your ma. You only get one of those." Katie reached the front door and stepped inside. "Trust me, Siobhan. A ma is a precious thing."

"I used to think so. When I was a kid. My parents were amazing, and I thought they hung the moon. Then Dad died and my mom changed. Like she didn't care about anything that didn't have to do with her church. She even got mad when I moved in with Granddad to take care of him. She thought he was using me as a nursemaid. Even though I told her the idea had been mine. He didn't want me to put my life on hold for him. But she wouldn't hear it. It only got worse when he left me the bulk of his money. As if that mattered at all to me."

"I know. But there has to be some part of her that still loves the babe she gave birth to."

"I kinda doubt it."

"Try anyway. For me?"

Siobhan was quiet for a moment. "Why is it so important to you that I make amends with my mom?"

"Because it's important to you." And because I love you, she wanted to add. Instead she said, "And because I never knew mine, and I don't want you to lose yours, too. I shouldn't be telling you this on the phone, but it's time you knew. My ma died giving me life."

"Oh, Katie. That's terrible. No wonder you were so adamant about not being pregnant. I'm so sorry I brought that up."

"No, don't be. Just know that, for me, being a mother is important. To have a little one to nurture through life—I can't imagine not doing that. And I can't imagine having a ma to talk to and not being able to. Does that make sense?"

"It does."

Katie rested on her settee and started removing her blades. "So you'll try to talk to her again? Or as many times as it takes?"

"I will."

"Good." She reached for her laptop and started it up. "Now, let's find you a hotel."

SIOBHAN WAS PACKED and ready to leave by eight the next morning. She'd stayed on the phone with Katie as long as she could before Katie had to go to the pub. They'd both had to charge their phones because they talked so long. It felt good to hear Katie's voice reassuring her that she was doing the right thing. Even if it felt horribly wrong. But that was probably her projecting the guilt that her mother would soon lay upon her.

Trying to be resolute, Siobhan grabbed her suitcases and headed down the steps. The smell of coffee was welcoming, and she hoped to get an infusion of caffeine before heading out. The hotel they'd found was only a few miles away, so Siobhan would be able to get to her mother's house in a hurry if she needed to. She placed the suitcases near the door and ventured into the kitchen.

Dark bags lay beneath Mary's eyes, a clear indication she hadn't slept any better than Siobhan. Mary sat at the table, staring at the coffee in her cup, her thoughts clearly very far away.

"Hi, Mom." Siobhan poured a cup and joined her at the table. "I decided to get a hotel room at the Best Western on Fifth. I'm still close by, but I think you and I need a break for a day or so. I'm sorry that I hit you with all that last night. It's just been on my mind for a very long time."

Mary continued to stare at her drink. "You're probably right. Are you going back to Ireland?"

"Not for two more weeks. We still have time to see each other. I think that maybe being under the same roof is a bit much for both of us. But I want to spend time with you. It's why I'm here."

"I'll take you there. Let me check on the road conditions first. No sense having an accident on the way."

Siobhan wanted to protest, saying she could call a cab, but let her mother get up and turn on the small TV she kept in the kitchen. The news was on and reported that most major roads were clear. The temperature would soon rise above freezing, though they did expect more snow later in the week.

"Okay. I'll get dressed and take you." Mary directed her gaze toward the front door. "I see you've already packed."

"I had to do something. I couldn't sleep."

"Neither could I." Mary headed for her room.

Siobhan sipped her coffee and tried hard not to cry. She'd hurt her mother. Even if Mary had been hurtful to Siobhan for years, it didn't assuage the guilt one bit. Worse part of it was Siobhan had no idea if her mother was being manipulative or genuine.

A few minutes later, Mary returned wearing her coat and holding her car keys. She gestured toward the door, and Siobhan followed her out into the cold morning, carrying her luggage. She placed the bags into the trunk of Mary's red Buick Century and got into the passenger seat.

The ride took all of ten minutes, but time stretched in the thick silence between the two women. Mary pulled up to the entrance and waited. Siobhan hesitated before getting out. "I love you, Mom. Please don't forget that." She leaned across the front seat and kissed Mary on the cheek. "Let's have lunch tomorrow. Give us some time to process all this. Okay?"

"I'll call you," was all the response she got.

Siobhan got out of the car, collected her bag, and considered this a good start.

Chapter Thirteen

KATIE STARED AT the ceiling in her bedroom and willed the pain to stop. Of course, it refused. Pain was her constant companion these days.

Pain from legs no longer there.

Pain from the head injury that nearly killed her.

Today was a high-pain day. And that wouldn't do. The Clonakilty Waterfront Marathon was two days away. But she couldn't get out of bed. She turned her head to see outside, but that made her migraine worse. Now she closed her eyes, tried to relax. The bright sunshine burned through her closed eyelids and into her brain.

This was hell.

Then the bright light was extinguished, and Jamie was kneeling at her bedside. He placed a cool cloth on her forehead.

"I'm sorry, love. I brought your meds."

"Don't want them. It'll make me sleep." She felt and sounded like a petulant child. "Need to—" The nausea slammed into her, and Jamie helped her sit up, a bowl ready to catch her vomit.

When she was done, he helped Katie settle on the bed again, cleaned her up, and placed another cool cloth on her forehead.

Someone came into the room, but Katie couldn't bring herself to open her eyes. An ice compress softly covered her eyes and forehead. The cold seeped into her skin to soothe the pain. Her empty stomach started to calm down.

Jamie whispered, "I'll be right here, darlin'. Try to rest. Once we get some soup in you, I'll give you a pain pill, long as your stomach stays calm."

Katie was devastated. Tears rolled down the sides of her face. Jamie wiped them away. His voice was soothing. "I know, love. But there will be other races to run. I promise you we'll get you to another one."

"It's not fair."

"I know. Try to be still. No more talking." He took her hand and softly kissed the back of it. "Let your da take care of you."

She squeezed his hand and let the tears fall.

SHE WOKE A few times, only to have Jamie give her some

soup and another pain pill. The hours were running together. This time, Kyra was on the settee, reading from the family e-reader. She glanced up and smiled sweetly at Katie. "You need to get up? Go to the toilet?"

"No, thank you. I'm feeling a bit better."

"Enough to eat?"

Katie thought about that for a moment. She wasn't particularly hungry, but she wasn't nauseous either. It was one of those times when food was an uncertainty. "Maybe a bit of soup."

"I'll get it." Kyra jumped up.

"Before you go, could you fetch me phone?"

Kyra hesitated. "Da said not to have it here in your room."

"It's okay. I just want to call Siobhan."

"She's called four times already," Kyra said. "She really likes you."

"Good thing, since I really like her back."

"I'll get your phone." Kyra left in a hurry and was back in two minutes with the phone. "I asked Da to heat up some soup. Want me to leave you alone so you can call her?"

Katie couldn't stop the smile on her face. "When, exactly, did you grow up?"

Kyra giggled. "Danny always makes me leave when he calls Maria. Says he wants privacy. I don't get it, but whatever."

"You can stay if you like. Nothing I got to say is all that private." Katie had to squint to see the phone, but eventually got Siobhan's number and hit Send. She closed her eyes and waited for her to pick up.

"Hi there." Siobhan's voice was like a balm, and Katie felt the pain in her head fade a little. "How are you feeling?"

"Like I been at the bottom of a scrum. Otherwise, fair enough."

"I'm sorry you'll miss the race tomorrow."

Katie tried to sound nonchalant. "There'll be others."

"Doesn't make it any easier, does it?"

"No. It doesn't. How is it you know what I'm thinking when you're on the other side of the pond?"

Siobhan laughed softly. "I'm in love with you. Everything that matters to you, matters to me. Marathons matter to you. That's all I need to know."

"You're a sweetheart, Siobhan Landry."

"Please tell that to my mother, would you?"

"Oh, things not going so well there?"

Siobhan paused. "Not really. You sure you're up for talking

about this stuff? No sense making your headache worse."

"What matters to you matters to me," Katie said.

"Touché." Siobhan sighed as she said the word. "We had lunch today. I was hoping we could talk, but mostly all we did was eat. She met me at a restaurant down the road from the hotel. The only thing she really talked to me about was how it wasn't safe for me to walk there and insisted on driving me the entire half a mile to the hotel. We were together almost two hours, and that's the most she said to me. I'm really worried I've messed things up. Maybe I shouldn't have ever said anything to Bob. Then I'd have gone on the stupid date, and all would be fine."

"No, it wouldn't. He'd think you were sweet on him, and the next thing, your ma would have you two married off. It'd only get worse from there, and when you finally had the talk, it would be horrible. Darlin', I think you did exactly the right thing at the right time. I'm just sorry your mother can't see that."

"Me, too," Siobhan said and got quiet. It wasn't an awkward silence. Sometimes they simply had nothing to say, but Katie wanted to put her arms around Siobhan in the worst way. She needed comforting, and Katie wanted to feel the reassurance of her love.

Jamie came in then with a steaming bowl of soup. Katie managed to sit up, and as soon as she did, Kyra was there with a white tray to settle over her lap. Legs on either side of the tray steadied it. Jamie placed the soup on it, along with a glass of water. He kissed her forehead before he left.

Kyra went back to the settee but kept a watchful gaze on Katie.

"I'm being tended to like I'm a hotel guest in a five-star resort."

"As you should be," Siobhan said. "I heard Kyra's been staying with you. She in there now?"

"She is. Watching me like a hawk."

"Tell her I said thanks." Siobhan's voice lowered a bit, and the very sound of it sent shivers through Katie. "I love you so much. I should be there taking care of you. I want to be there taking care of you. Always."

Katie glanced at Kyra, who now pretended to be reading. "You've got things to tend to. It won't be long before you're home. Do your best to mend things with your ma. Please."

"I'll do what I can. I'm just never sure how to handle her."

"Just be yourself. Don't try to handle her. Be her daughter. That's all you need to do."

"And this is why I love you." Siobhan blew a kiss into the phone.

Katie returned it, aware that she was now blushing. "I'm going to eat and probably sleep some more. Call me tomorrow?"

"Of course."

They said their goodbyes, with one last "I love you" from Siobhan before hanging up.

Katie had just scooped a bit of chicken soup into her mouth when Kyra spoke up.

"Why didn't you tell her you love her?"

Seriously. When had the child grown up? "It's not easy to do."

"Sure it is." Kyra moved to the bed, where she gently sat so she was facing Katie. Her eyes held so much more maturity than Katie had ever seen before. Was she so wrapped up in her own world that she'd missed this new development with Kyra?

"It is for you and me. I'm your sister, and I love you dearly. When you're older and you find a boy or girl that you fancy, you'll realize how hard it truly is. You can't just bandy such words about like they're candy. You have to mean it with all your heart."

"I know. Like Danny and Maria. Or Da and Dadaí. They love each other, and they say it all the time. You love Siobhan, but you didn't tell her just now."

"I've never told her."

Kyra's young face fell, and for a moment Katie thought she'd yell at her. It shocked her. "What is wrong with you?" Kyra asked.

"Excuse me?"

"You have to tell her, or she might think you don't and leave, and that would be awful because she's the best thing that's ever happened to you, and I don't want you to get hurt again and cry all night."

Wow. Where had all that come from? She had to wait for Kyra to take a breath to get any words in. "I wish I could better explain it to you, but I can't. Yes, she's the best damn thing that's ever happened to me in my whole life. But we've only known each other a couple of months. These things take time."

"You're just making excuses." Kyra stood, hands on her hips, and glared at Katie. "I didn't think you would ever be so stupid."

"Kyra—"

"Don't tell me I don't understand. We all do. Every one of us has heard you crying, Katie. I was too young to get it when you first came home. I only knew that you almost died, but that you were home and even if you might still be sick, you'd be okay eventually. That's what our dads said. Me and Casey spent most of the time in the sitting room when you would get so sick you couldn't come out of your room. Conor would come and tell us what was going on, but all I knew was you were hurting and we couldn't help you.

"But you got better. I didn't get why Fiona wasn't around anymore, and if I asked, I didn't get any answers. No one wanted to talk about it, and 'cause I'm the youngest, everyone thought I wouldn't understand. But I do. I understand when you're heart is hurting so much you cry all the time. And you did. So did the dads."

Katie, stunned by her baby sister's impassioned speech, could only stare at her. Why had it taken so long for her to realize the impact her injuries had on the rest of the family? How her being sick took such a toll on them all?

"I'm sorry, Kyra. I don't think anyone meant to keep things from you. Just no one knew how to tell you or Casey or Conor what was going on. Yes, Fiona left me and stomped on my heart in the process. It's part of why it's so hard for me to tell Siobhan that I love her. Part of me is afraid she'll do the same thing."

"She won't," Kyra said with more conviction than Katie had. "She's sweet and kind and perfect for you. She draws amazing pictures and promised to let me see her paintings sometime. She should live here with us and be part of our family. I want her to live with us."

Out of the mouths of babes... Katie held her hand out to Kyra, who hesitantly took it. "When I tell Siobhan that I love her, and I will, it needs to be in person. Not over the phone. Okay?"

"You promise?"

Katie nodded, suddenly sure that she would be telling Siobhan this the moment she saw her again. Or very soon after. "I do."

"Okay." Kyra resumed her spot on the bed. She crossed her legs, leaned back, and regarded Katie as she ate. "Can I ask you something serious?"

Katie almost laughed. As if their conversation wasn't already serious. "Of course."

"What happened in Boston?"

"You don't know?"

"I'm the youngest, remember. No one tells me anything."

Katie contemplated what she should or shouldn't tell her.

Kyra may sound mature, but she was still twelve, and Katie didn't want her to be afraid of ever going out or doing anything for worry that there'd be a bomb. Not that it hadn't happened enough lately, as those sorts of things seemed to be increasing.

But Kyra had to know at some point. It shouldn't be a secret. So Katie carefully launched into her story.

Kyra didn't interrupt, which was a rarity with her, and when Katie was finished, she remained quiet. Katie could see from her expression she was thinking about what she'd just been told. Though Katie spoke of the bombing, she left out the more explicit details that Fiona recently gave her.

"Even though this happened, you still run the marathons. Aren't you scared?"

"No. Just determined. You know how I've been doing marathons most of me life, right? It's very important for me to keep doing that. I can't be a garda anymore, so I need something to do."

"You mean something to do that you did before Boston."

"Exactly."

Understanding showed on her features. "Can I run with you sometime? I like to run. Maybe I can do a marathon, too?"

Katie's heart was full to bursting. How did she ever get to be so blessed? Were it not for the lap tray, she'd pull Kyra into a bear hug. Instead she said, "That would be great. Soon as I'm feeling better, we'll get you started. Short runs at first, until you build up your stamina. Then we'll work you up to doing the racing. Deal?"

Kyra's smile didn't fit her face, it was so big. "Deal. I'm gonna go tell Da I need new shoes." And she was off. Katie could hear her running down the entry hall, halfway through her story before she was out of earshot.

She picked up her spoon and finished her soup in peace, feeling as though her heart had finally mended.

SIOBHAN AND HER mother spent most afternoons together. Their conversations were improving, and on the day before she was to leave, Siobhan suggested they go shopping and have dinner afterward. She could use some new jeans, and the prices in Indiana were a lot better than the ones in Cúnant.

Halfway through the second store, Mary stopped browsing a section of dress shirts and turned to face Siobhan. "You're in love with her?"

Siobhan was caught off guard but answered quickly. "Yes."

"Does she love you?"

"I think so."

Mary nodded but didn't say another word. She went back to her browsing and left Siobhan to wonder about it. They hadn't spoken a single word about her sexuality or Katie. Not since the incident with Bob. They'd even managed to go to the church's mother/daughter dinner without fighting. Siobhan hadn't enjoyed it much, other than giving Wilma, her high school art teacher, a set of souvenir playing cards. Mary seemed to have a good time. At least she smiled a lot.

Maybe she was turning a corner, and this would mean they could have an actual relationship.

"I still don't like it."

"I know, Mom. You don't have to like it."

"I can't support what you're doing," she said, never taking her eyes off the blouses, though Siobhan doubted she was actually looking for or at anything.

"You don't have to." Siobhan stilled Mary's hands. When their gazes met, Siobhan saw fear in her mother's eyes for the first time in her life. "Just be my mother. I want you in my life. I want you to be part of it. I want you to come visit me. And I'll come visit you."

"You want me to come to Ireland?"

"Of course I do. My apartment's not very big, but you can sleep in my room, and I'll take the couch. I think you might like it there. It's beautiful, even when it's raining. And there's a lot to see and do. I know you like museums, and in Dingle there's the oldest standing church in the world. I know you'd love that."

Mary seemed to consider it as the fear faded from her face. "Dingle? Is that a real name?"

Siobhan laughed. "It is. And it's a nice place. Wonderful people, and the food—oh the food is too much. I always have to watch what I'm eating."

"Would she be there?"

Siobhan knew exactly who her mother meant. "Only if you're comfortable with it. Though I do want you to meet her. You might actually like her. Can I tell you about her?"

Mary shrugged.

"She's a marathon runner. Has been for years. Though for a while she wasn't able to do any running at all."

"Why not?"

Siobhan hid her smile. Her mother was actually interested or at least listening. "Because she lost both her legs in the Boston

Marathon bombing." Mary Landry paled. "She wears prosthetics now and ran her first full marathon in October in Dublin. It was a huge achievement for her. She'd been doing half marathons last year, but this was the first full one since Boston. Twenty-six miles. I can't imagine running across this store, much less twenty-six miles."

"That's amazing."

"She is. She's had to deal with a traumatic head injury, too. But she's got this incredible family, and they would do anything for her." She paused, certain she had Mary's full attention. "So would I."

"I don't know if I can afford going there. Betty Farmer told me it was thousands of dollars."

"Only if you fly first class. But I have Granddad's money, and I'm sure he wouldn't mind me spending it on you so you can visit me. I know I wouldn't mind."

"That's your inheritance. You need to save it."

"And I am. But there's enough for a plane ticket for you. Mom, let me do this. Please. I can hardly expect you to be part of my life if I can't at least bring you to my new home."

Mary nodded and went back to her browsing. "As long as you're sure."

"I am."

"I'll check my appointments, but I could probably come over this summer. Is it very hot over there?"

Siobhan was sure they'd discussed the weather on many occasions during her year in Ireland, but she didn't mind repeating herself. Granddad would be shocked that Mary was considering a visit to his hometown. Mary, who never went farther north than Indianapolis or farther south than the Ohio River to visit the casinos with her church friends.

"It can get pretty hot, but it just depends on when you come over."

"I'll check my calendar when we get home," Mary said. "Are you done? I'm hungry."

And with that, Siobhan knew they would figure this out. It wouldn't be easy, but eventually she would have a decent relationship with her mom. Katie would be proud.

Chapter Fourteen

KATIE PACED THE small waiting area at the Cork Airport. She was jittery and anxious and nervous and had no fecking idea what she would say to Siobhan when she saw her. Other than she loved her. And she was trying hard to work up the courage to tell her.

One minute she was sure the words would just flow out of her mouth. The next she was even more certain they'd get caught in her throat.

She checked the time on her phone. Two minutes had gone by. This was killing her.

"Why don't you tell me what's troubling you?" Colm asked from his seat on the S-shaped settee. "And don't tell me you're just excited to see her again. I know there's more to it than that."

Katie didn't stop. "Do I have a sign on me forehead that tells everyone my thoughts?"

"Yes. And right now it's telling me you're scared. But why? Are you worried she found a new girlfriend in America?"

"Of course not. Siobhan wouldn't do such a thing."

"I know. So tell me what it is."

Katie didn't want to. Didn't really have the right words to explain her reticence. "I love her."

"This I already know."

"But *she* doesn't. I've never told her in so many words."

Colm got up and blocked her path. "You don't have to. You've told her with your actions. With all the hours of phone calls. The way you can just sit there and be quiet while she tells you her troubles, then you help her work them out. I'm sure she already knows how you feel."

"You think so?"

"I do. Why else did she call every few hours to check on you last week when you had a migraine? Why else would she call me at the pub just to make sure you weren't overdoing your running, that you were eating right and taking care of yourself?"

Katie narrowed her gaze at him, wondering if he was exaggerating. "She did that?"

"Every couple of days. We talked about other things, too, but we always came back to you."

"Why didn't you tell me?"

"I just did." He led her to the settee and urged her to sit. "And I've seen how she looks at you—how you look at each other. Your da says I'm a hopeless romantic, and I know that's true, but I know she's right for you."

"She's a keeper," Katie parroted his words. "But I have to tell her."

"Then why don't you?"

"I'm afraid. Things will change when I do. I'm scared of how they'll change."

"It'll be for the best. You'll see."

"You're not a psychic, Dadaí. You don't know that."

Colm pointed toward the Arrivals area. "I do know that. Now go get your girl."

Katie followed his pointing and saw Siobhan standing near the waiting area, her backpack slung over one shoulder and her roller bag at her feet. She looked exhausted, but as soon as Katie got near her, Siobhan's smile grew and her eyes lit up with joy.

Katie moved slowly to her, savoring her face, the love in her eyes. Eyes the color of the sky. Her golden hair was tied in a ponytail, much the way it was when they first met. Katie's arms trembled, and her stomach tightened. Why on earth had she waited so damn long to do this?

Then she was in Siobhan's arms, holding on for dear life. Katie inhaled the familiar coconut scent and closed her eyes for a moment. She was never letting this woman go. Never.

Siobhan pulled back enough to press a sweet, welcoming kiss to Katie's lips. It was a kiss she felt all the way to toes she no longer had. A fire ignited inside her, and it was all she could do to keep from ravishing Siobhan right there in the airport.

As the kiss ended, Siobhan peered at her with such fondness that it melted her heart. "I love you," Katie said.

Siobhan stared open-mouthed at Katie. Right there, in the middle of the hallway of a busy airport, Katie had finally told her how she felt. People pushed and shoved around them, but Katie blocked out every single, ambient sound. The only thing she wanted to hear, the only thing she wanted to remember was Siobhan's response.

"I love you so much," Siobhan said, choking back tears. She put a hand to her mouth as if that would stop her sudden crying. Her hand was shaking when Katie reached for it. "I didn't expect—I mean, I was sure, but to hear it..."

"I should've said it a long time ago. I'm sorry it took me so long, love. But you have me heart. All of it."

Siobhan rested her free hand on Katie's chest and leaned closer for another amazing, loving kiss that marked a new beginning for them. She returned the kiss, pointedly ignoring Colm's discreet clearing of his throat.

Siobhan sighed and rested her forehead against Katie's. "We really should take this somewhere else. Somewhere less public?"

Katie grinned. "Welcome home?"

Siobhan laughed and the sound warmed Katie's heart. "Best welcome ever."

"Hey! Do I not get a hug?" Colm had joined them and held his arms out to Siobhan. They hugged in the same way Colm hugged all his children. How quickly Siobhan had been accepted into the family. It was rare and Katie knew it meant something special.

"Let's get my bags so we can head out of here. I'm beat."

Colm took hold of her roller bag, and Katie grabbed her backpack. Katie said, "We're at your disposal, ma'am. Lead the way."

Siobhan laughed, took Katie's free hand in hers, and headed toward Baggage Claim.

COLM DROPPED THEM off at Siobhan's apartment but insisted on carrying her luggage up the steps before he left. With a fatherly kiss to her cheek, he was off and they were finally alone. Siobhan practically fell onto her couch and patted the seat next to her. When Katie settled, she put her arm around her and held her close. It was so good to be in the same room with her.

"I'm never going on an extended trip again without you," Siobhan said.

"I'm glad for that because I missed you terribly."

"My mom's going to come visit us this summer."

Katie turned to her with shock on her face. "Seriously? She's visiting *us*?"

"She is. We turned a corner yesterday. I told her about you and how much I love you."

"And she didn't get mad?"

"Nope. She was genuinely curious." Siobhan stifled a yawn. "It's something I'll never understand about her, but for the first time in my life, I felt like she was actually interested in what I had to say."

"That's amazing, sweetheart. We have so much to talk about, but I think a nap is in order for you."

"I think so, too." She got up and held her hand out to Katie.

"Would you join me? I've missed you so much, and I really just want to hold you."

Katie took her hand and got up. Siobhan could feel her nervousness. For a moment, Siobhan thought she'd decline.

Before Katie could say anything, Siobhan pulled her close for a kiss meant to push all her fears away. She wanted Katie to know just how much she loved her and needed her. Siobhan held her close and continued to kiss her until she thought they would both sag back onto the couch. "I'm not asking for the moon, love. Just to lie there and hold you."

"All right," Katie whispered against her cheek. They held hands as they walked the few steps to Siobhan's bedroom.

"I can lend you a T-shirt to wear if you'd be more comfy. I suspect you've got those Lycra shorts on under your jeans."

"I do indeed, but this shirt will be fine, thanks." Katie rocked back and forth on her heels, obviously nervous.

Siobhan grabbed a T-shirt and sleep shorts and ducked into the bathroom, hoping the privacy would put Katie at ease. She was back quickly and found Katie still standing at the side of her bed. She tossed her dirty clothes on the floor, went to Katie, and held her hand. "Are you still worried about what I'll think of you without your prosthetics?"

"Maybe. Probably." Katie squeezed her hand. "It's stupid. You've already seen me."

"It's not stupid." Siobhan gently touched Katie's cheek and turned her so they were facing each other. "Never say that. Nothing that's bothering you is stupid. You tell me and we'll work it out. Always."

There were tears in Katie's eyes, and Katie wiped them away with the back of her hand. "I've never felt this way before. Not even with Fiona. I'm scared that—that we'll be in bed and you'll find it—difficult."

"Let me prove you wrong," Siobhan said, as their lips met in a feathery kiss. "I love you. Let me hold you and prove it to you."

Katie didn't argue when Siobhan pulled the covers back and urged her to sit on the bed. Siobhan helped her undress, and once Katie was lying down, joined her. Without a word, Siobhan put one arm around Katie's waist and Katie turned to her side. They spooned as if they'd done it a million times before.

Siobhan rested her chin on Katie's shoulder. "We fit nicely, don't you think?"

"I do." Katie linked her fingers with Siobhan's. "Are you sure this is okay?"

Siobhan kissed her shoulder, her neck, and her cheek, and snuggled as close as she possibly could. Their legs touched, and she dared to put her leg between Katie's. "I do. This is perfect. Thank you."

"For what?"

"Trusting me."

Katie sighed and just as Siobhan was about to fall asleep she heard Katie say, "I love you."

KATIE WASN'T SURE what time it was, but she was still cuddled safely in Siobhan's embrace. It was everything she'd imagined. She was safe, loved, accepted. What more could she possibly want?

She turned carefully so as not to disturb Siobhan. She needed to lie on her back for a bit. When she got comfy again, Siobhan's arm resettled across her stomach, as if to make sure Katie wasn't leaving. One look at the peaceful woman beside her told Katie she didn't have any desire to go away. Not ever.

She'd never been the type to fall in love quickly. It'd taken her over a year to say it to Fiona. But Siobhan managed to capture her heart in a few short weeks, and Katie knew, deep down, she was the one. Was it too soon to move in together? Maybe even ask her to marry her?

"What's got you so deep in thought?" Siobhan's sleepy voice asked.

"I love you," Katie said with a big smile on her face.

"I know." Siobhan leaned over her, her face hovering just above Katie's. "Still doesn't answer my question."

"That's what I was thinking about." Katie's hand traced the line of Siobhan's jaw, along her cheeks, across her full lips. "I know you Americans tend to go fast and all. Get a moving van after the second date. I'm not like that."

"I never asked you to be. And it's the third date," Siobhan laughed softly. "You can come and stay at my place whenever you want for as long as you want. I can do some work to make it more accessible for you. Maybe put in a walk-in shower."

"You are amazing," Katie whispered. "But that's not neces-sary. I've got all that at home. Would it be too much to think you might want to live in a castle with me? We've got a lot of rooms, and there's one that looks out over the sea. Lots of light. Could be good for your painting."

"You're serious?" Siobhan's eyes filled with tears. "You want me to move in with you?"

"Yes. I love you, and after the last few weeks, I don't want to be without you for a minute. And I don't want you to just move into the castle. I want you to move into my room. Live with me." Katie paused and tried to read the answer in Siobhan's eyes.

Siobhan's tears came in earnest, and she choked back a sob. Katie was hopeful those were tears of joy. She wiped them away as best she could. Siobhan kissed her hand, then her arm, working her way to Katie's lips. When they settled into the kiss, it meant more to Katie than any kiss had in her entire life. Her world suddenly righted, and she needed nothing more than the woman she held in her arms.

Siobhan nestled on top of her, and their kiss sealed them together as if they were suddenly one person. She whispered, "Yes," against Katie's lips and kissed her again, parting her lips as their tongues danced together.

It'd been so different with Fiona, and Katie wanted to slap herself for doing a comparison. But it was hard not to. She'd loved Fiona, certainly, but what she felt for Siobhan went beyond love. It went into the world of soul mates. Katie felt whole. All the hurt and damage done to her over the last few years faded into the distance when Siobhan began exploring her body.

Siobhan traced delicate fingers along the scars on Katie's abdomen; soft kisses followed the same line. Then along her thigh, to the remainder of her right knee, and back again to the apex of her legs.

Eyes so blue they matched the color of a summer sky held hers while Siobhan's hand continued its exploration. How she'd dreamed of this when she first saw Siobhan sitting in the pub, her eyes far off in the distance. That first date where they'd barely touched. Then all the fleeting moments where their kisses grew as they discovered the passion that lay between them.

Katie hardly believed this was happening. But then Siobhan found the spot where Katie was wet with anticipation and began a slow, steady massage. All other thoughts faded as she elevated Katie to a place she'd never been. She was higher than the sky, drunk on her love for this amazing woman who was doing incredible things to her body.

Fingers entered her and began a slow and steady rhythm, taking her higher and higher until Katie fell into a delicious well of ecstasy that only the safety of Siobhan's arms and the steadying of her heartbeat could raise her from.

She relaxed into Siobhan's embrace and looked into the eyes

of the one person that would always hold her heart. "I love you, Siobhan Landry."

"It's all for you, sweetheart. Everything I do. I only want to please you — let you know that you can always trust me. I'm never going to leave you."

"Let me show you how I feel, love. Let me please you."

Katie gently pushed Siobhan onto her back. She had to use one hand to keep herself propped up, only able to steady herself with her right knee. Her left thigh brushed against Siobhan, and she felt her shiver. It alarmed Katie until she saw the passion in Siobhan's eyes and realized how wet she was.

Katie's body didn't disgust her.

She'd just loved her like no one in Katie's life ever had.

Katie bent to pull a taut nipple into her mouth, eliciting a soft moan from Siobhan. With her free hand, she started her own exploration, enjoying this first meeting, excited to find out what her lover liked best. One look at Siobhan's beautiful, loving face, and Katie decided she would spend a lifetime figuring these things out.

Her hand rubbed along Siobhan's thigh as she switched to the other nipple. Siobhan's fingers were tangled in the long side of her hair, holding her close as she suckled.

Fingers acting of their own accord pried open the sweet entrance to a very wet, special place. She wanted Siobhan to feel her love, and as she worked her fingers around the soft, moist folds, Siobhan pushed her hips forward, rocking in time with Katie's movements.

Her lips traveled the length of Siobhan's neck to her mouth and pressed in for a deep, passionate kiss as Siobhan's body squirmed beneath her. She came loudly and faster than Katie expected. Her fingers still deep within Siobhan, Katie paused in her kissing to take in the pleasure on Siobhan's face.

She was smiling at her.

"You're beautiful," Katie said.

"It's all for you, baby. All of it."

Katie wiggled her fingers, and Siobhan reacted immediately to her little tease. "All of it?" she asked.

Siobhan squinted at her but couldn't hold the face when Katie got more serious with her movements. "That's not fair," Siobhan barely managed to say. Her fists twisted the sheets beneath them. "You're...cheating."

"Am I?" Katie stopped and enjoyed Siobhan's face. "I could keep going..." She did, just a little. "Or I could stop," which she did. "Up to you."

"If you stop, you will regret it," Siobhan apparently meant to sound threatening, but her giggle ruined it. "Is it always going to be like this?"

Katie worked her fingers again, this time intent on bringing Siobhan over the edge. She whispered softly against Siobhan's lips, "I hope so."

Chapter Fifteen

SIOBHAN STRETCHED OUT languidly and put her arms around Katie, spooning her. One hand rested on Katie's firm abdomen while the other tickled her butt. Katie giggled and snuggled closer to her.

"'Morning, love."

"Good morning." Siobhan kissed the soft skin behind Katie's ear. "So, I've been thinking."

"Oh? So early? Couldn't it wait until we're more awake?"

"Nope. My brain is active right now."

"Then by all means, tell me what you're thinkin'."

"About us and how perfectly we fit together."

"This is why you're tickling me?"

Siobhan laughed softly. "No. I just like playing with your butt." She ran her fingers along Katie's shapely curves. "But I'm serious about how well we fit together. Like our bodies were made for it."

Katie turned around so they were facing each other. "We are, love. Made for each other."

"Hmm." Siobhan responded with a tender kiss. She closed her eyes just as their passion started to heat up again...and then her phone rang.

Siobhan pointedly ignored it. She was naked and in bed with the woman she loved. No phone call was more important than that. Whoever it was could just leave a voicemail.

Only they didn't. The phone rang again and again...

Katie gently stopped their make-out session. "Honey, you need to answer that or turn it off. It's a bit distracting."

Siobhan groaned and fumbled for the stupid phone, which was somewhere on her nightstand. She grabbed it and had her finger on the button to turn it off but stopped. Five calls missed — all from her mother. "Shit."

"Your ma?"

"Yes, and if I don't call back, she'll freak out and keep calling until I do." She gazed apologetically at Katie. "I don't want to talk to her."

"But you have to. Don't make her worry. You two are on the mend. Don't spoil it."

"I love you," Siobhan said.

"I know." Katie pointed to the phone. "Go on."

Siobhan made the call. "Hello, Mom. Sorry I missed your calls."

"Are you in bed? Did I wake you?"

Siobhan hesitated to answer that one, gently slapping Katie when she giggled. Apparently she was close enough to hear what Mary was saying. "No, I was just awake, but it's very late or, rather, early for you. Why are you up?"

"I'm packing. My plane leaves at six, and I'd like to be three hours early. That's what the TSA thing says, to be three hours early."

"Flight? You didn't tell me you were going away? Did something happen?"

"Yes, it did." Mary paused long enough that Siobhan thought the call had been dropped. "I realized that I need to know more about my daughter. I also need to meet the woman that—that she's in love with." The last bit was spoken so quietly Siobhan could hardly hear her.

"That's great, Mom, but—"

"I'll be in Dublin around five o'clock in the evening. I've emailed you the flight information, so please be there to pick me up."

"You're coming here?" Siobhan's head fell back against the pillow. She closed her eyes as if that would help her sort out this crazy phone conversation. "Wait. You are literally flying to Ireland today? In a few hours?"

"Well, to Newark and then Dublin. But yes. I've wasted enough time already. I don't want to waste a minute more. Susan is just pulling into the driveway. I'll see you soon."

Mary disconnected the call while Siobhan opened her eyes to stare at the screen.

"She's coming here."

"I heard that." Katie took the phone from Siobhan and placed it on the nightstand. "How about I get Da to set up a room for her? You can stay with me while she's here. I think she'd be more comfy there than here in your little flat. Yes?"

Siobhan shook her head. "I can't believe she's coming here. Just like that. My mother never does anything impulsive. Ever. And she's always so careful with her money. She still cuts out coupons from the newspaper, even though she doesn't really need to. I mean, she's got Dad's pension and...and she's coming here. Holy shit!"

Katie situated herself on top of Siobhan and leaned her

elbows on the bed so they were face-to-face. "Love, I can see it's a shock, but it's happening. We'll get things together for her. I promise. Maybe she's changed. Sounded to me like she's really wanting to reconnect with you. I think it's lovely."

"I do, too, but it's the short notice. And she's spending all that money for a last-minute ticket. I can't help but wonder what exactly happened that prompted her to do this."

Katie kissed her softly, her eyes holding Siobhan's. "She loves you. That's what happened."

"Do you think she'll be comfortable at the castle? Maybe I should rent her a room. I never asked if she's done that already. I didn't even ask how long she'll be here!"

"Stop freaking out, love. It'll be fine." Katie sank her body so they were once again touching each other fully. She rested her head on Siobhan's chest, and Siobhan wrapped her arms around her, still reeling from the shock.

"Talk about a mood killer," she mumbled.

Katie's hand cupped Siobhan's breast as her lips caressed the nipple. "My mood's just fine. Don't know what you're talking about."

Siobhan moaned and smiled at the amazing woman in her arms. "Well, if you keep that up, I suppose the mood will return."

"You suppose, do ya?" Katie gave her a playful nip. "We'll see about that."

Siobhan's next words died on her lips when Katie's hand slid between their bodies and rested at the apex of her legs. A gentle nudge moved Siobhan's legs farther apart, and soon she forgot all about her mother.

KATIE HELPED GET things arranged with Jamie to settle Mary into a room at the castle. They chose one that wasn't close to the kids' rooms to give her privacy. Katie kept very busy to hide her own nerves, not wanting to worsen Siobhan's.

One very important thing would come out of this time with Mary Landry. Well, two things. First, she would do her best to make Mary like and accept her as Siobhan's partner. Second, it would be a nice chance to see how good a fit she and Siobhan really were. They'd be living together, and that, as Katie well knew, was the best way to know if your relationship would last.

Even if she'd been wrong about Fiona, they had lived happily together for almost six years.

She had just put fresh linens on her own bed when a very familiar set of arms wrapped around her from behind. Katie smiled and leaned into Siobhan. "Hello there."

"Hi. I came to let you know that your da is amazing."

"Well, this I know, but is there a special reason at the moment that makes you say this?"

"He just got off the phone with Briana O'Hearne. He's decided we need a welcome party for my mother and has it set up for this Saturday at the pub. He wants Mom to meet her Irish relations."

"I'm not surprised." Katie turned around and kissed Siobhan's lips. "He's been wanting to have this party for a while now but never could get it together. I guess your mom's visit got him into the party mood. It'll be a grand affair, I promise you."

"I hope she has fun," Siobhan said. "I've never seen her at a real party. Just those stodgy gatherings her church puts together. I've kinda wondered if my mom was capable of having fun."

"She must be. You share her DNA. There's got to be something good about her. She is your grandda's little girl."

"I think the fun gene skipped a generation."

"I don't believe that for a minute." Katie untangled herself from Siobhan and finished making the bed. "Don't worry, love. The O'Briain clan will show your mom a great time. We might even get her to smile."

That got a chuckle from Siobhan. "I look forward to seeing that. Right now I need to get to Dublin to pick her up."

"Shall I go with you?"

Siobhan hesitated. "I don't know."

"Then I'll be going with you." Katie took hold of her trembling hand. "But I think I'll get Da to drive us. You're too nervous, and his car's a bit bigger than yours. Could be your ma packed a lot of suitcases."

"Oh, she probably did."

"It's settled then. Let's go."

AN HOUR LATER they were standing in the Baggage Claim area of Dublin Airport. Siobhan had a grip on Katie's hand that was so strong Katie knew she'd have a bruise before it was over. At least the woman stopped trembling. Katie gave her hand a reassuring squeeze as she looked at the Arrivals board.

Jamie sported a big grin, having spotted the same thing Katie did. Mary's plane had arrived, and folks were getting off. Katie took a few deep breaths and did her best to continue to keep her nerves hidden from Siobhan. One look at Jamie, though, and Katie could tell he knew. His smile was gentle and a little bit cocky. He was going to enjoy this first meeting. He'd probably exaggerate the details later at the pub, getting a chuckle from anyone that would listen.

She rolled her eyes at him. Jamie laughed.

"What's so funny?" Siobhan asked.

"My da's a git is all. Ignore him."

Jamie kept quiet, but the grin never left his face.

"She'll be here soon." Siobhan shifted from one foot to the other.

"It'll be fine," Katie said. "No matter what happens, I will be kind and polite to your ma. No one will say a cross word to her, and the kids have orders to treat her like a queen when she gets to the castle. Everything will work out. You'll see."

Siobhan stared at the area where passengers would soon be streaming into Baggage Claim. Her face was a mask, until the color drained from it like she'd seen a ghost.

Katie followed her gaze to the group of people ambling toward them. Most of them looked exhausted, especially the man with two rambunctious boys who were wide awake and full of energy.

Then she spotted a petite woman with soft blonde hair that she wore in a very feminine, short style. While most people looked rumpled and sleepy, this woman was well dressed and her hair was perfect. And Siobhan was staring right at her. As she got closer, Katie recognized Mary Landry from the photos Siobhan had shared.

She didn't look the least bit intimidating. Though she did remind Katie of the head mistress of her secondary school. She was all business, and once she spotted them, came to their little group with short, purposeful strides.

"Hi, Mom." Siobhan let go of Katie's hand and hugged her ma. It wasn't the kind of hug that Katie gave her dads, but she could still see some affection there. Siobhan turned to Katie and Jamie. "I'd like you to meet Jamie O'Briain and his daughter Katie. My girlfriend."

Mary shook hands with Jamie then held her hand out to Katie. They shook and Katie was shocked at her strong grip. Piercing blue eyes drilled holes into her as she was clearly sussing Katie out. "It's a pleasure to meet you, Mrs. Landry," Katie said.

Mary released Katie's hand. "I'm glad to meet you both. Now, if you don't mind, I'd like to get my bags." To Siobhan she said, "Is it far to your apartment? I couldn't sleep on the plane, and I'm exhausted."

"It's about an hour or so, depending on traffic." Siobhan led the way to the carousel. "But you're not staying at my apartment."

"Oh? And where will I be staying?"

Katie suspected there was something else Mary wanted to say but held it back.

Siobhan either didn't notice or chose to ignore it. "At the O'Briain's. Remember I told you they are turning part of the castle into a B&B? Well, they have two rooms completed, and you're going to be staying in the one that has an en suite. I'm going to stay there, too, so we can spend more time together."

Mary straightened her shoulders a bit, like she was trying to stand taller. "Well, I suppose that will be fine. I can only stay two weeks. I have a doctor's appointment that I can't miss or I'd stay longer."

"It'll be fine, Mom. Two weeks is great. I'm...I'm glad you're here." Siobhan gave her mother a one-armed hug. "We'll get you settled into your room, and you can rest. Tomorrow I've got a surprise for you."

Mary was clearly startled, but she didn't say anything. She gave Siobhan a tight smile and pointed out her bags as they came along the carousel.

SIOBHAN PACED THE length of Katie's room, her mind spinning. Mary had been very quiet on the ride from the airport. Not that Siobhan expected her to be overly chatty. It was too dark to see the countryside, and when they got to the castle, Mary went right to bed. She probably wouldn't be up and about until tomorrow morning.

Siobhan glanced at her watch. It was now ten at night. She should also be sleeping.

As if she read her mind, Katie sat up and patted the bed next to her. "My bed's a bit smaller than yours, but I promise you can still sleep in it. C'mon, love."

"I don't know why I'm so damn nervous. She's either going to love it here or hate it. I can't do anything about how she feels. But I'm still antsy. I can't believe she literally hopped on a plane and came over."

"Do ya think she hopped? On one leg or two?"

A smile crossed Siobhan's face. "Goofball."

"I accept that new name with honor. Now come over here and cuddle with your woman. It'll all be sorted in the morning."

"Promise?" Siobhan pulled the sheet back and slid in beside Katie.

"I do." She held her arms open and Siobhan settled into her embrace.

"I want her to like you."

"I think she will," Katie said. "I'm adorable. How can she not like me?"

"You're incorrigible." Siobhan's heart already felt lighter. "You're also the only person who can get me calmed down. Thanks." She placed a feather-light kiss on Katie's cheek.

"It's my duty."

"Good to know. And thanks."

"For what?"

"For hanging up the portrait I did. I noticed it when I walked in, but I was too freaked out about Mom to mention it."

"Of course I hung it up. What'd ya think I was gonna do? Sit it in the closet?" Katie kissed her forehead and snuggled closer. "Silly woman. It's beautiful and the only likeness of me that I can stand to look at. I still can't believe how amazing it is. It's one of the best gifts I've ever gotten."

"That's high praise indeed."

"Well deserved. Now, go to sleep. Plenty to do in the morning."

Siobhan placed her head on Katie's shoulder and closed her eyes as sleep overtook her.

THE NEXT MORNING, Siobhan awoke to the smell of fresh coffee. She and Katie were still cuddling in nearly the same position as when she'd fallen asleep. Her right arm was stiff and the left one a little numb from lying on it. She pushed herself into a sitting position and found Katie smiling up at her.

"Have you been awake long?" Siobhan asked.

"I have. Just waiting for you. I figured you needed the sleep more than I need to pee."

"How very noble of you." Siobhan kissed her then got up so Katie could get into her chair "But you shouldn't do that. I would have happily moved out of the way."

"Maybe I liked holding you," Katie said, an impish grin on

her face. "You're quite soft and cuddly. Like a real-life teddy bear."

"A teddy bear? Seriously?"

Katie laughed and disappeared into her wet room. A few moments later, she emerged a bit more presentable. "Your turn. And don't take too long. I smell bacon."

"Far be it from me to get between you and food." Siobhan went in to clean up enough for breakfast. She was done in a few minutes, and they were on their way to the kitchen.

Siobhan stood in the doorway for a moment to take in the spectacle in front of her.

Mary was seated at the kitchen table, flanked by Kyra and Casey, both talking excitedly about something to do with school. Siobhan caught a bit about reports and a science fair. She stopped in the doorway to listen.

"But that wasn't the best part," Kyra was saying. "Rory hadn't a clue what the thing did. He stood there like a statue and kept tellin' Miss Ryan that the really tiny ball was a moon and the great big ball was a sun and the other balls were the rest." She giggled with glee, despite the glaring look Rory was giving her. "He's such a git! He didn't know it was the solar system."

"How could he not know that?" Mary asked. "Didn't he help build it."

"No. Danny did and he was gonna give the report, but he got sick, so Rory did it."

"But Miss Ryan didn't know it was Rory," Casey added. She pushed back her brown, curly locks and tucked them behind her right ear. "See, Miss Ryan never could tell them apart. But everyone knows Danny is smarter 'cause he pays attention in school. Rory never listens and he got it all messed up. Miss Ryan was so fussed at both of 'em she made them stay after school for a month."

"And she never got them mixed up again," Kyra concluded.

Mary, to Siobhan's amazement, looked at each girl in turn and joined in their giggles.

"Hey, Katie!" Casey announced. "If you marry Siobhan, would that make Mary our grandma?"

Siobhan nearly choked. Panicked, she looked to Katie, who was grinning. She reached up to take Siobhan's hand. "I believe she'd be closer to an auntie, sweetheart. She'd be my ma-in-law. Not actually related to you."

"Oh," Casey said with clear disappointment.

Mary patted her on the shoulder. "But if that happens, you

can call me whatever you want. Ok?"

Casey brightened then and gave her a hug. "Thanks. Da, can you take me to football practice now? I don't wanna be late." She was halfway out the door before Jamie formed a reply. He shrugged and followed her out.

"Would you like some more coffee, Mrs. Landry," Rory asked.

"That'd be nice. Thanks." Mary held out her cup and finally caught Siobhan's gaze. "Are you two going to have breakfast, too?"

"Um, that was the plan." Siobhan tightened her grip on Katie's hand before letting go. She sat beside her mother. "How are you feeling? Did you get enough rest?"

"Yes, thank you. I wonder if I could speak to Katie for a while. Alone."

Siobhan didn't bother to hide her surprise when she turned to Katie, who had rolled up to the table across from them. Katie gave her a slight nod.

"I'd love to, Mrs. Landry. Do you mind if I'm eating while we chat? I'm quite hungry."

"Of course not."

Rory placed a plate of food in front of Katie. "Siobhan, how 'bout you and me go to the great room? I'll bring your plate out for you."

"Thanks, Rory." After one last look at Katie and Mary, she left the room.

KATIE SWATTED RORY'S butt as he walked past her.

"Hey! What's that about?"

"Proud of you for being so polite. Good on ya."

Rory grumbled playfully and carried Siobhan's plate of food out of the kitchen.

Now that they were alone, Katie started to speak, but Mary held up her hand.

"Please, let me go first. I think you already know that it's been very difficult for me to come to terms about my daughter's sexuality. I would be lying if I didn't say that I hold out hope that one day she'll marry a man and have a family. It's how I was raised and how I raised her. I don't understand what's happening, but I'm not willing to lose my only child over it. Which is why I'm here.

"I will admit that your rather — unconventional — family is

delightful. Your fathers have treated me with kindness since I walked in the door last night. I have no siblings, but I can see how much your family loves each other, and I'm glad to know that Siobhan is around such good people. Even if you are Catholic."

Katie couldn't suppress a grin. "Thank you."

"I flew out here to meet you and your family and decide if I think you're good enough for my daughter."

"I can understand that, but it's early days. I don't expect you've made a decision."

"I haven't."

"You will. And I suspect you'll approve." Katie dug into her food and let Mary think about that for a moment before she continued. "Mrs. Landry, I'm deeply in love with your daughter. I know that our time together has been short, but when it's right, it's right. I've been through a lot, and Siobhan is the first person outside my family to see beyond the fact that I don't have legs."

Mary held Katie's gaze for what felt like forever. Katie couldn't tell what the woman was thinking, but she was obviously mulling over something. She wasn't sure what she'd expected to hear. Hell, she hadn't even been sure what to say. It was clear, however, that Mary was receptive.

"She's my only child, and while she doesn't know it, I'm very proud of her. I wanted her to make something of her life. She was doing that by working at the museum, but now? Now she's trying to sell her art and maybe make a living. My father left her a lot of money, but it won't last forever. Art is the only thing she knows. What happens when the money runs out? Or her art doesn't sell? Is she going to just work in a grocery store? Will she have to give up her dreams?"

"I can appreciate that you're worried. I've been ma to this brood of kids here since I was a teenager. I worry about them all the time. I still want kids of me own, and it's hard because you want the best for them, but you can't make their decisions for them. No matter how much you want to." Katie set her fork down and folded her hands in her lap. "I'd like to take care of Siobhan. I've already asked her to move in with me."

"Live here? At your fathers' home?"

"Yes. They love Siobhan and she'd be welcome here. They've unofficially adopted her." Katie laughed. "Those two would adopt every stray they met, if they could. But understand that if she moves in here—and I'm pretty sure she will—she'd always have a place to live." Katie paused, not sure if she should proceed or not. But it was too important not to. "I think that, eventually,

I'll be asking her to marry me. I want to spend my life with her, Mrs. Landry."

Mary's face was tight and her lips pursed. Katie held her gaze, intent on making sure the woman understood how important this was to Katie.

"I think it's because of you that she stood up to me," Mary said. "Siobhan always did what I told her to without question. After a short time with you, that all changed. Or maybe it's the influence of your family, or being away from home for so long. She's a different person now."

"Is that a good thing or a bad thing?" Katie asked.

"I don't know. It's different. I don't know how I'd feel about her living here with you. It's a sin."

"That's your take on it. We're in love and love can't be a sin." Katie leaned forward a bit and rested her hand on Mary's, which was still grasping her full mug of coffee. "Let's not debate this. We'll not come to agree with each other. Don't try to understand why Siobhan is gay. Just love her. Accept her and accept me. My ma died giving me life. I don't want Siobhan to be without her ma, especially since her da is gone. She's part of our family, and we want you to be part of it, too."

She felt a slight tremble in Mary's fingers. Katie removed the hand from the coffee mug and gently held it.

Mary took an unsteady breath and gripped Katie's hand. "I can't promise anything. Just that I'll try."

"That's all I ask." She let Mary go and leaned back in her chair. "So, my da set up a party at the pub in your honor. Siobhan and I found your da's cousin, Gavin Byrne. He and his wife would love to meet you. Gavin's wife is a love, and she's probably going to give you more hugs than you can stand."

A smile crossed Mary's face. "Too bad Dad isn't here to meet them. He'd have loved it."

"He's here in spirit." Katie crossed herself and said a brief prayer for Fergus Byrne.

"Are you really going to ask Siobhan to marry you?" Mary asked.

Katie didn't have to think about her answer. "I am, in due time. Will you be okay with that?"

"Maybe. In due time."

Katie laughed. "Touché, Mrs. Landry."

"Call me Mary, please. You make me sound old."

"Mary it is. That's my name, too. Mary Katherine Cecilia O'Briain."

"Cecilia is the patron saint of music, right?"

"She is. I thought you weren't Catholic."

"I was raised Catholic and went to Catholic school. I became a Protestant later in life," Mary said. "But my full name is Mary Josephine Michael Byrne-Landry."

"Michael? The Archangel?"

"Yes. I always liked his story, and my father seemed pleased that I chose that name for my Confirmation, even though my mother was upset that I chose a man's name. Maybe I did it in defiance."

"Maybe." Katie fingered her St. Michael's medallion. "You know he's the patron saint of police officers, yes?"

"I do." Mary's attention was drawn to the medallion. "You're a police officer?"

"I was, yes. Until I lost me legs."

Mary's demeanor changed then as her expression softened. "There was a time, when I was eighteen, that I wanted to be a police officer. But they told me I'd probably never be on patrol and stuck behind a desk because women don't make good police officers."

"Bullocks. Did you never try again?"

"I didn't. I had Siobhan and became a mother and housewife. I don't regret that, but I don't want that for my daughter. I want her to follow her dreams."

"Mary, have ya ever told Siobhan this?"

"No. It's never come up."

Katie sighed. "I think it's time it did. Maybe you can do that today, while it's on your mind. Not like we have plans. The big party is tomorrow, and it's probably best you rest up so the jet lag isn't so bad."

"Perhaps you're right." Mary reached out and touched Katie's hand. "Thank you, Katie."

"For what?"

"Being you."

Epilogue

Four months later...

"ARE YOU NERVOUS?" Colm asked Katie for the tenth time since they'd arrived at the starting line for the race.

"Dadaí, I'm fine. You're the one that's nervous." Katie continued her stretches and wished she could allay his fears. He was pale, and she'd never seen him in such a state before.

"I can't help it." He paced around her. "Are you sure it's safe?"

"Colm," Siobhan said, "there are more cops here than when the president shows up." She was returning with Jamie from getting Katie's number. She helped Katie pin the giant yellow sheet to her chest. 4854.

Katie stared at it for a moment and soaked in the fact that she was in Boston again, getting ready to run the marathon she'd never finished. She'd planned to go to London, but something pulled her to go to Boston instead. It felt as though she had to conquer this last demon before she could spend her life with Siobhan.

And they would have such a wonderful life. Once Siobhan moved into the castle, Jamie and Colm announced they were going to scratch plans for a B&B in the chapel and give it to Siobhan and Katie. It would take a lot of work, but they'd just been given a grant from a restoration society. Her dads considered it money well spent.

With them and Siobhan at her side, Katie knew she could to this. Most of the time, anyway. There was still that little voice in her head that nagged at her. Was it really safe, as Colm had asked? Would she have the stamina to finish?

Siobhan must have sensed her apprehension because she kissed her lightly on the lips. "Trust me. There's no way anyone is going to get in here. We barely got in, and you had permission to bring us as your support team. They've run five marathons since the bombing without any incident. And you'll run the whole thing this time. I'm sure of it."

"We'll be at the finish line waiting for you," Jamie said. He hugged Katie, winked at her, pulled Colm into the crowd, and disappeared.

"I've got your chair and spare blades," Siobhan said. "Do you have the sprocket and Vaseline?"

Katie nodded and patted the pouch at her back. "And two protein bars. I'll grab bananas on the course."

"Good." Siobhan stood with her hands on her hips. "You'll use the Vaseline?"

Katie didn't need to look up to see the serious expression on her face. "Yes. I promise I'll stop and use it."

"It doesn't matter what your time is. Remember that, love. Please finish the race without hurting yourself. That's all I ask."

Katie sat on the ground to do more leg stretches. "That's all you're asking?"

"For now. I'd rather like it if you could walk around without pain when you're done. Mom's going to be here soon, and we did promise to take her sightseeing tomorrow."

"So we did." Katie didn't want to waste time adding Vaseline or double-checking her blades to make sure they fit securely and were in good working order. That always took too long. But the concern on Siobhan's sweet face made her realize it wasn't just about her, Katie O'Briain. It was also about Siobhan, and she didn't want to add any worry to her. Even if it meant losing a few minutes.

"I promise," Katie said as she stood up.

"Good. Now get lined up." Siobhan kissed her soundly. "I'll see you at the halfway point."

"See you there." Katie waved to her and joined the crowd at the start line. As she did, several runners took notice of her blades, each one giving her a nod of appreciation. One man, who was oddly familiar, made his way to her as they waited for the start.

"Mind if I run with you?" he asked.

"I'm a lot slower than you'll probably be. If I can make it in under seven hours, I'll be pretty damn happy."

His smile was genuine. "I don't mind. My name's Trevor, but I don't think you remember me."

"Sorry. My name's Katie."

"Katie. I don't think I ever got your name."

"When did we meet?"

He glanced away, and when his eyes met hers, she could see the sorrow in them. "Near the finish line. Five years ago. I was behind you and saw you go down. I did what I could to stop the bleeding..."

"Holy shit. That was you?" What were the odds of her meeting the man who saved her life? "I don't know what to say except thank you." She normally would never do such a thing to a virtual stranger, but Katie threw her arms around Trevor and hugged him for all she was worth. "You saved my life."

He shrugged as if it were no big deal, but his eyes belied that idea. "I noticed you a few hours ago, when you were getting out of your car. It took me a while, but I actually remembered your hair."

She laughed and ran a hand through the long side of it. "I had more red coloring in it then."

"So you did. But it's pretty distinctive. Anyway, when I realized it was you, I decided to follow you and get in the pack close to you. I hope that doesn't sound creepy, but I'm so stoked to see you here. I never stopped running, even after the bombing, but this is my first year back in Boston. Now I know why I had to come here this year. To see you."

"That's amazing, and I'm happy you're here. I'd be proud if you ran with me, Trevor."

In perfect timing, the starter gun went off and the marathon began. Katie and Trevor fell into an easy, steady rhythm, as if they'd been running together for years.

JAMIE AND COLM paced nervously at the finish line. Siobhan sent them on to find something to eat a few hours ago, but now they were back. It didn't help her nerves that they were like two cats locked in a tiny room. They took turns pacing, even though she told them Katie was doing well.

She had chatted with Katie briefly at the halfway point. She'd found someone to run with, and that made a huge difference to Siobhan. The guy looked nice enough, and he clearly could have outrun Katie, but he seemed determined to stick with her. That was three hours ago. Katie was on pace, probably thanks to her running partner, to finish in under seven hours. She would be so pleased to hear that.

The pack of runners she was in was due to arrive at the finish line soon. Most of the runners were done, of course, and that meant the largest part of the crowd had dispersed. Siobhan was glad for that. Even if it gave Jamie and Colm more room to pace.

She kept her gaze on the curve about two blocks from where they stood. Half-a-dozen people were there, and when they started cheering, she knew Katie was coming.

Sure enough, Katie and a pack of about ten runners rounded

that corner and hit the straight stretch to the finish. Katie was still beside her new friend, and they were both smiling.

Siobhan moved to the center of the road, a few feet behind the wide, blue line that marked the end of the Boston Marathon. She hadn't expected to cry, but she did as Katie got closer and closer. Her vision blurred a bit, but she could still see her proud, strong, lover racing toward her.

Siobhan's arms opened wide, and Katie ran right to her and melted into her embrace. Katie also had tears in her eyes, and they held each other for what felt like forever. Siobhan whispered over and over to Katie about how proud she was and how much she loved her.

The man who'd run beside her was there, standing right behind Katie. He looked like he was holding back his own tears.

Siobhan released Katie and was introduced to Trevor. Once she heard who he was, she enveloped him in a bear hug. "Thank you, Trevor. Thank you for saving her. I can't begin to tell you how much she means to me. And thank you for running with her. That was so sweet."

"I did it for myself, too." He put his hand on Katie's shoulder. "I'm here because of you, Katie. I came back to the city I love, to the race I always looked forward to, because somehow I knew you'd be here."

"And we finished this time, Trevor. Got across that line."

"We did indeed."

Colm and Jamie came forward and got their hugs, crying and telling Katie how proud they were of her. Mary held back for a moment, but when Katie spotted her, she pulled her into a hug as well. Siobhan almost laughed at the shock on her mother's face.

Katie whispered something to Mary, and her face went from shock to surprise to something Siobhan couldn't read. Katie then moved to Jamie and held out her hand. He placed something in it and put his arm around Colm, pride beaming from his eyes.

Siobhan almost lurched forward to catch her when Katie suddenly got down on one knee. The noise of the crowd faded away, and the only thing Siobhan heard or saw was Katie.

"Siobhan Landry, would you make me the happiest woman ever and do me the honor of becoming my wife?"

"I—I love you, Katie. Of course I'll marry you." Katie took Siobhan's left hand and gently placed a silver ring with a single, shimmering diamond on her finger. It fit perfectly.

Katie's smile filled her face as she got up and wrapped her arms around Siobhan. "I love you! I love you! I love you!" She kept up her chant, even when she stumbled as she twirled with Siobhan in her arms.

Siobhan never let her gaze stray from Katie's eyes. "My heart couldn't get any fuller. Because of you, Katie O'Briain, I finally feel like I've found my home."

"You have, darlin'." Katie brushed her lips across Siobhan's. "Welcome home."

Siobhan smiled. "Best welcome ever."

About the Author

Patty is the Goldie Award-winning co-editor of *Blue Collar Lesbian Erotica*, with Verda Foster. She and Verda also co-edited *Women in Uniform: Medics and Soldiers and Cops, Oh My!* and *Women In Sports*. Her first novel, *Souls' Rescue*, was a finalist for the Ann Bannon Popular Choice Award. Patty is a retired paramedic and currently resides in The Netherlands with her wife, Sandra, and their kitties.

OTHER YELLOW ROSE PUBLICATIONS

Anna Furtado	Tremble and Burn	978-1-61929-354-0
Pauline George	Jess	978-1-61929-139-3
Pauline George	199 Steps To Love	978-1-61929-213-0
Pauline George	The Actress and the Scrapyard Girl	978-1-61929-336-6
Melissa Good	Eye of the Storm	1-932300-13-9
Melissa Good	Hurricane Watch	978-1-935053-00-2
Melissa Good	Moving Target	978-1-61929-150-8
Melissa Good	Red Sky At Morning	978-1-932300-80-2
Melissa Good	Storm Surge: Book One	978-1-935053-28-6
Melissa Good	Storm Surge: Book Two	978-1-935053-39-2
Melissa Good	Stormy Waters	978-1-61929-082-2
Melissa Good	Thicker Than Water	1-932300-24-4
Melissa Good	Terrors of the High Seas	1-932300-45-7
Melissa Good	Tropical Storm	978-1-932300-60-4
Melissa Good	Tropical Convergence	978-1-935053-18-7
Melissa Good	Winds of Change Book One	978-1-61929-194-2
Melissa Good	Winds of Change Book Two	978-1-61929-232-1
Melissa Good	Southern Stars	978-1-61929-348-9
Regina A. Hanel	Love Another Day	978-1-61929-033-4
Regina A. Hanel	White Dragon	978-1-61929-143-0
Regina A. Hanel	A Deeper Blue	978-1-61929-258-1
Jeanine Hoffman	Lights & Sirens	978-1-61929-115-7
Jeanine Hoffman	Strength in Numbers	978-1-61929-109-6
Jeanine Hoffman	Back Swing	978-1-61929-137-9
Jennifer Jackson	It's Elementary	978-1-61929-085-3
Jennifer Jackson	It's Elementary, Too	978-1-61929-217-8
Jennifer Jackson	Memory Hunters	978-1-61929-294-9
K. E. Lane	And, Playing the Role of Herself	978-1-932300-72-7
Kate McLachlan	Christmas Crush	978-1-61929-195-9
Lynne Norris	One Promise	978-1-932300-92-5
Lynne Norris	Sanctuary	978-1-61929-248-2
Lynne Norris	Second Chances	978-1-61929-172-0
Lynne Norris	The Light of Day	978-1-61929-338-0
Paula Offutt	Butch Girls Can Fix Anything	978-1-932300-74-1
Patty Schramm	Because of Katie	978-1-61929-380-9
Schramm and Dunne	Love Is In the Air	978-1-61929-362-8
Surtees and Dunne	True Colours	978-1-61929-021-1
Surtees and Dunne	Many Roads to Travel	978-1-61929-022-8

Be sure to check out our other imprints,
Blue Beacon Books, Mystic Books, Quest Books,
Silver Dragon Books, Troubadour Books, and Young Adult Books.

VISIT US ONLINE AT
www.regalcrest.biz

At the Regal Crest Website You'll Find

— The latest news about forthcoming titles and new releases

— Our complete backlist of romance, mystery, thriller and adventure titles

— Information about your favorite authors

Regal Crest print titles are available from all progressive booksellers including numerous sources online. Our distributors are Bella Distribution and Ingram.